CLASSROOM OF THE ELITE

NOVEL 1

HORIKITA SUZUNE

Judging by looks alone, she is certainly a beauty. However, her refusal to sugar-coat anything means she doesn't have any friends.

"So then, what in the world should I do?"

"Ayanokouji-kun, would you prefer to regret while you suffer or regret while you despair? Which would you like more?"

AYANOKOUJI KIYOTAKA

The protagonist. Both his entrance examination scores and his practical skills are at or below average. He's a plain, ordinary person seeking extraordinary friends.

KUSHIDA KIKYOU

A beautiful, angelic girl who easily grabs the attention of both men and women. Naturally, she's the most popular student in class.

"I want to become friends with Horikita-san!"

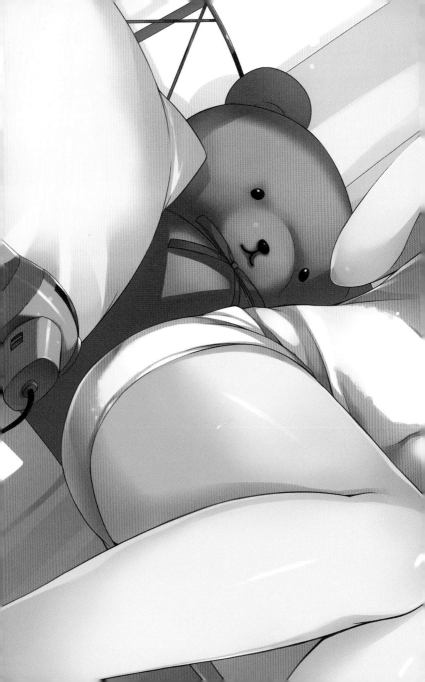

"Hello!"
As the call connected, she gave a great sigh. However, she quieted down immediately afterward.

"Teacher. May I ask you one question?"

CLASSROOM OF THE ELITE

NOVEL 1

CONTENTS

CLASSROOM OF THE ELITE

NOVEL 1

STORY BY
Syougo Kinugasa

ART BY
Tomoseshunsaku

Seven Seas Entertainment

CLASSROOM OF THE ELITE VOL. 1

© Syougo Kinugasa 2015
Art by Tomoseshunsaku

First published in Japan in 2015 by
KADOKAWA CORPORATION, Tokyo.
English translation rights arranged with
KADOKAWA CORPORATION, Tokyo.

Seven Seas press and purchase enquiries can be sent to
Marketing Manager Lianne Sentar at press@gomanga.com.
Information requiring the distribution and purchase of
digital editions is available from Digital Manager CK Russell
at digital@gomanga.com.

Follow Seven Seas Entertainment online at
sevenseasentertainment.com.

TRANSLATION: Timothy MacKenzie
ADAPTATION: Jessica Cluess
COVER DESIGN: Nicky Lim
INTERIOR LAYOUT & DESIGN: Clay Gardner
PROOFREADER: Peter Adrian Behravesh, Stephanie Cohen
LIGHT NOVEL EDITOR: Nibedita Sen
MANAGING EDITOR: Julie Davis
EDITOR-IN-CHIEF: Adam Arnold
PUBLISHER: Jason DeAngelis

ISBN: 978-1-64275-137-6
Printed in Canada
First Printing: May 2019
10 9 8 7 6 5 4 3 2 1

THE STRUCTURE OF JAPANESE SOCIETY

KNOW THIS IS KIND OF SUDDEN, but, please, it will only take a moment. I want your honest opinion.

Are people equal or not?

A proper society will constantly strive for equality. There are those who clamor for men and women to always be considered equal. As a result, we raised the employment rate for women, we made specialized subway cars only for women. Sometimes, women will even argue over the order of names in a family register. The public opinion of people with disabilities has also changed. We're now told that we should not use the term "disabled people" when referring to them, so as not to discriminate. Nowadays, children are taught that all people are created equal.

But is that true? I have my doubts. If men and women have different abilities, then their roles should also differ.

People with disabilities are still disabled, no matter what polite euphemisms you use. No matter how you try to avert your eyes, the meaning of the word does not change.

So, my answer would be, "No, we are not equal." To be human is to be unequal. Equality does not exist.

Long ago, in a bygone era, a great man said that heaven does not set one man above or below any other. However, he did not necessarily adhere to the idea that everyone is equal. Did you know that there is more to that famous passage? The rest goes like this: *Everyone is equal when they are born, so I ask, why do we see differences in position and status?* And it continues: *Do you or do you not encourage learning to create a difference?* So then, education creates an imbalance. The point's spelled out there, in the incredibly famous work *Gakumon no Sume*. Even though this is the year 2015, the modern era, nothing about these teachings has changed. The situation has only grown more complex and fraught.

In any case, we are human beings. We are living, thinking creatures.

I don't think it right to simply say that we are unequal and then live our lives based on pure instinct. In other words, though "equality" is a complete lie, we cannot accept inequality, either. Right now, I'm trying to come up with a new answer for humanity's eternal question.

Hey, you there. You, the one reading this book right now. Have you ever given serious thought to the future?

Have you ever considered the purpose of going to high school or to college? Though the future may seem hazy right now, do you think you'll find a job someday? That's what I used to think. Back when I finished my compulsory education and became a high school student, I hadn't really considered the future. I'd only felt joy at being nearly free of obligation. I didn't consider the incredible influence that school would continue to have in my life, on my future. I didn't even understand the purpose behind studying language or numbers.

CLASSROOM OF
THE ELITE

2 WELCOME TO THE SCHOOL LIFE OF YOUR DREAMS

"**A**YANOKOUJI-KUN, do you have a moment?"

She came. She was here. It was terrifying. I'd been feigning sleep during class, pondering society's true purpose while I pretended to nap, when the devil approached me. Shostakovich's Symphony No. 11 played in my head, music that captured the sense of people fleeing from pursuing demons and the desperation that comes at the end of the world. Right then, it was the perfect accompaniment.

Even though my eyes were closed, I understood. I could feel the devil's presence as she waited for her slave to awaken. So, as a slave, how exactly could I get out of this situation?

My computer-like brain instantly executed all the calculations to arrive at the answer I most needed.

Conclusion: I'd pretend not to hear her. I had dubbed

this the "Sleeping Strategy." If she were a kind girl, then she would say something like, "Aw, well, there's nothing to be done. I'd feel bad to wake you, so I'll forgive you. ★" "If you don't get up, I'll kiss you!" would also be okay.

"If you do not awaken within three seconds, I will bestow additional punishment upon you."

"What do you mean, 'punishment'?" I asked.

In an instant, I'd abandoned my "Sleeping Strategy" and yielded to her threats of force. Well, at least I offered some resistance by not meeting her gaze.

"See, you *are* awake after all, aren't you?" she said.

"I know enough that I'm afraid to make you angry."

"Glad to hear it. Well then, may I have a little of your time?"

"If I refuse?"

"Well, even though you have no right to veto such a decision, I suppose I *would* be exceptionally displeased."

She continued with, "And when I am displeased, then I will prove a major obstacle to your school life, Ayanokouji-kun. For example, I might set a great number of thumbtacks on your chair. Or, when you go to the toilet, I might splash water on you from above. Or stab you with the needle of my mathematical compass. Those kinds of obstacles, I suppose."

"That's nothing but harassment, or rather, bullying! And besides, that last one sounds strangely familiar, because you've already stabbed me before!"

I reluctantly sat up at my desk. A girl with beautiful, sharp eyes and long black hair that framed her face stared down at me. Her name was Horikita Suzune, a student of the Tokyo Metropolitan Advanced Nurturing High School, Class D, and my classmate.

"Don't worry. That was only a joke. I wouldn't splash water on you from above."

"What's more pressing are the thumbtacks and the compass needle! Look at this! There are still marks from when you stabbed me the last time! Will you take responsibility if it scars me for life?" I rolled up my right sleeve and displayed my forearm to Horikita, so she could see the scars she'd left behind.

"Evidence?" she asked.

"Huh?"

"What about the evidence? Did you decide I'm the culprit without evidence?"

She was right; there was no evidence. Even though Horikita was the only one in class close enough to stab me with a needle, I'd be hard-pressed to call that definitive proof...

Well, I needed to confirm something first anyway.

"So, I'm required to help you? I've thought on it again, and, after all, I—"

"Ayanokouji-kun. Would you prefer to regret while you suffer or regret while you despair? Which would you like more? Because if you refuse me and force my hand, it will be your responsibility."

I was stuck with Horikita's two completely absurd choices. It appeared she would not accept any delays. Though it was a mistake to make a deal with this devil, I gave up and obeyed.

"All right, then. What am I supposed to do?" I asked, filled with trepidation. Her requests no longer surprised me. I certainly didn't like how this situation had turned out, but... I thought back to when I'd met this girl two months ago, on the day of the entrance ceremony.

2.1

APRIL. The school entrance ceremony. I rode the bus to school, bobbing and shaking in my seat. While I looked idly out my window, watching the city's scenery change, the bus picked up more and more passengers.

Most of them were young people wearing high school uniforms.

There was also a frustrated salary worker, who looked like the type to have once mistakenly groped someone aboard a crowded bus. An unsteady elderly lady stood in front of me, wobbling so badly I thought she was in danger of falling. Considering I'd known how packed this bus would likely be, I supposed I was simply reaping what I'd sown by getting on.

I was fortunate to have found a seat, but it was still crowded. I forgot about the unfortunate elderly woman and patiently waited to arrive at my destination, my mind clear as a passing stream. The weather was especially fine today, not a single cloud in the sky. It was so refreshing that I nearly fell asleep then and there.

However, my gentle respite was promptly obliterated.

"Excuse me, but shouldn't you offer up your seat?"

My eyes, which were about to close, snapped back open. Huh? Could this person be angry with me? But I realized that it was someone else being scolded.

A young, well-built blond man of high school age had sat down in one of the priority seats. The elderly woman stood right next to him, and another woman stood beside her. This second, younger lady appeared to be an office worker.

"Hey, you there. Can't you see that this elderly woman is having trouble?" the office lady said.

She seemed to want the young man to offer up his seat.

Her voice carried quite well throughout the quiet bus, attracting several people's attention.

"That's a really crazy question, lady," the boy said.

I wondered whether the boy was angry, unobservant, or just painfully honest. In any case, he grinned broadly and crossed his legs. "Why should I offer up my seat? There's no reason for me to do so."

"You're sitting in a priority seat. It's natural to offer up those seats to the elderly."

"I don't understand. Priority seats are just that: priority seats. I have no legal obligation to move. Since I'm currently occupying this seat, I should be the one who determines whether or not I move. Am I supposed to give up my seat just because I'm young? Ha! That reasoning is nonsense."

He didn't speak like a normal high school student. His hair was dyed blond, which made him stand out.

"I'm a healthy young person who certainly wouldn't find standing inconvenient. However, I'd obviously expend more energy by standing than I would by sitting. I have no intention of doing such a pointless thing. Or are you suggesting I should act a bit livelier, I wonder?"

"Wh-what kind of attitude is that to take with your superiors?" she demanded.

"Superiors? Well, it's obvious that both you and the old woman there been alive longer than I have. There can be no doubt about that. However, the word 'superior' implies that you're referring to someone of a higher position. In addition, we have another problem. Even though our ages are different, wouldn't you agree that you have an impertinent attitude and are being extremely rude?"

"Wha— You're a high schooler, aren't you?! You should be quiet and listen to what adults tell you!"

"It's f-fine, whatever..." the elderly woman mumbled.

She apparently didn't want any further commotion and tried to calm the office lady. But after being insulted by the high school student, the younger woman still seemed very upset.

"Apparently, this elderly woman is more perceptive than you, which is nice. Also, I haven't given up on Japanese society yet. Please enjoy your remaining years."

After flashing a pointlessly vigorous smile, the boy slid his earphones in and began listening to rather cacophonous music. The office lady now clenched her teeth in frustration. Though she tried needling the boy by arguing further, his smug, self-important attitude remained fixed.

At any rate, I had to at least partly agree with the boy.

If you ignored the question of a moral imperative, it was true that he wasn't legally obligated to give up his seat.

"I'm sorry..." Desperately fighting back her tears, the office lady apologized to the elderly woman.

Well, it was all just a minor incident on the bus. I was relieved that I hadn't been caught up in the situation. Honestly, I couldn't care less about giving up my seat for an elderly person.

Clearly, the egotistical boy had won. At least, everyone secretly thought so.

"Um... I think that the lady is right."

The woman received unexpected support from some-one standing alongside her. The helper, a girl wearing my high school's uniform, gave her brave and frank opinion to the boy.

"And the new challenger is a pretty girl, eh? It would seem that I'm rather lucky with the fairer sex," the boy said.

"This poor woman appears to have been suffering for quite some time now. Won't you offer up your seat? While you might consider such courtesy unnecessary, I think it would contribute greatly to society."

Crack! The boy snapped his fingers.

"A contribution to society, you say? Well, that *is* a rather interesting opinion. It's certainly true that offer-ing up one's seat to the elderly could be viewed in such a positive light. Unfortunately, I have no interest in con-tributing to society. I care only for my own satisfaction. Oh, and one more thing. You're asking me, the one in the priority seat, to give up his spot, but couldn't you simply ask one of the other people seated on this crowded bus? If you truly cared for the elderly, then something like pri-ority seating would be a rather trivial concern, wouldn't you agree?"

The boy's haughty attitude remained unchanged. Both the office lady and the elderly woman simply wore bitter smiles in response. However, the girl didn't back down.

"Everyone, please listen to me for just a moment. Won't someone give up their seat for this woman? It doesn't matter who. Please."

How could someone pour so much courage, determination, and compassion into so few words? That was no simple feat. The girl might have seemed like a nuisance to those around her, but she appealed to the other passengers earnestly and without fear.

Though not in a priority seat, I was near the elderly woman. I imagined if I raised my hand and offered my spot, then the matter would be settled.

However, like everyone else, I didn't move. None of us had thought it necessary to move. The boy's attitude and remarks aside, everyone on the bus had, for the most part, agreed with him.

Now, of course, the elderly have undeniable worth to Japan. But we, the youth, will continue to support Japan into the future. Also, considering that our society ages more and more every year, you could say that our youthful value only increases. So, if you were to examine both the elderly and the young and ask yourself which group is more valuable, the answer should be obvious. That's really the perfect argument, wouldn't you say?

But still, I wondered what the others would do. As I looked around, I saw two kinds of people: those who had pretended not to have heard anything and those who looked hesitant.

However, the girl sitting next to me was different. She alone wasn't swept up by the confusion. Her face remained expressionless.

While I unintentionally stared at her, our eyes met for an instant. Even without speaking a word, I could tell that we shared the same opinion. Neither of us considered it necessary to give up our seat.

"E-excuse me. You can have mine." Shortly after the girl's appeal, a working woman stood, unable to bear the guilt any longer, and offered up her seat.

"Thank you very much!" the elderly woman said.

The working woman smiled, lowered her head, and guided the elderly woman to the now-vacant seat.

The elderly woman expressed her gratitude repeatedly, and slowly sat. Watching the scene unfold from my peripheral vision, I crossed my arms and closed my eyes. Soon, we arrived at our destination, and all the high school students began to disembark.

As I got off the bus, I saw a gate formed from natural rock waiting just ahead. All the young boys and girls dressed in school uniforms were passing through this gate.

The Japanese government had created the Tokyo Metropolitan Advanced Nurturing High School with the express purpose of developing future leaders. This would be my school from now on.

Okay, stop for a moment. Take a deep breath. All right, here we go!

"Wait!"

The instant I tried to take my first courageous step, someone called out to me. It was the girl who'd sat next to me on the bus.

"You were looking at me. Why?" she asked.

She narrowed her eyes while we spoke.

"Sorry. I guess I was just interested, is all. I mean, you didn't think about giving up your seat to the old woman, did you?"

"That's right. I didn't consider giving it up. Is there something wrong with that?"

"Oh, no, not at all. I didn't intend to give up my seat, either. In fact, I firmly abide by the philosophy of letting sleeping dogs lie. I dislike trouble."

"You dislike trouble? Then I don't think you and I are anything alike. I didn't give up my seat because I thought it would be pointless. That's all."

"But doesn't that seem worse than just not liking trouble?"

"Perhaps. I'm simply acting according to my own beliefs. That's different from someone who just dislikes trouble, like you. I don't want to spend any time around people like you."

"I feel the same way," I muttered.

I had only wanted to share my opinion, but I wasn't too keen on going back and forth with her like this. We both sighed and proceeded to walk in the same direction.

2.2

I DISLIKED THE ENTRANCE CEREMONY and imagined that many first-year students probably felt the same. The principal and the students exchanged excessive words of gratitude, there was far too much time spent standing in lines, and, with so many irritating things to deal with, it all felt like a huge pain in the butt. But those weren't my only complaints. The entrance ceremonies for elementary school, junior high, and high school all mean the same thing: the start of another major trial for children. In order for students to enjoy their time at school, they must make friends, and there are only a few key days after the entrance ceremony to properly do that. Failure to do so signals the beginning of a rather tragic three years.

As someone who dislikes trouble, I decided I'd like to establish proper relationships. Unfamiliar with the notion, I'd spent the day before in preparation, running through different scenarios.

For instance, should I burst into the classroom and actively start talking to people? Should I secretly pass around a slip of paper with my email address, so as to better befriend someone? Someone like me needed to practice, because this environment was so different from what I'd experienced thus far. I was completely isolated. I had ventured alone into a battlefield, and it was do or die.

Looking around the classroom, I walked toward the seat that bore my nameplate. It was at the back of the room, near the window. A good place to sit, generally. As I looked around, I saw that the room was already halfway filled with students. The others were either immersed in their class materials or already talking with other people. Perhaps they'd all been friends beforehand or had only recently gotten acquainted. Well then, what should I do? Take action during this free time and try to meet someone? In front of me, a rather rotund boy sat at his desk, hunching over. Perhaps it was my imagination, but he appeared lonely.

The boy exuded an aura that seemed to shout, "Please, someone be my friend!" However, if you just went up to someone and start talking, you might be bothering them. Should you wait for the right time? But then you might wait too long and be left friendless. I just had to... No, no, wait, I couldn't be hasty. If I started a thoughtless conversation with someone I didn't know, I ran the risk of making a serious social gaffe.

Not good. I was trapped in a downward spiral.

In the end, I couldn't talk to anyone at all. At the rate things were going, I'd be completely alone. Had I heard someone say, "Is he still all alone?" Had I heard chuckling? Perhaps it was all in my head. What on earth are "friends," anyway? Where do friends come from? Do people become friends after sharing a meal together? Can you become friends with someone after you walk to the bathroom together for the first time? The more I thought about it, the more I wondered: What is friendship? Is it something deep and meaningful? I tried to piece it together.

Trying to make friends is incredibly bothersome. Besides, don't human relationships tend to form naturally? My thoughts were in utter disarray, as though a raucously loud festival was being staged inside my head. While I sat lost in a haze, the classroom quickly filled. Fine. Whatever. Nothing ventured, nothing gained, right? After a long period of conflict, I finally began to rise from my seat. However...

Before I knew it, the rotund, bespectacled boy in front of me had started to talk with another classmate.

Wearing a bitter smile, I realized that there was no new friendship to be cultivated there. *I'm happy for you, Glasses-kun. It looks like you made your first friend.*

"I got beaten to the punch!"

I was at my wit's end, stuck in useless navel-gazing. Reflexively, I let out a deep sigh. My high school experience seemed poised to be exceptionally dour. Then, someone sat down beside me.

"That's quite a heavy sigh, considering the school year has only begun. Meeting you again makes *me* want to sigh."

It was the girl who'd fought with me at the bus stop and then walked off.

"So, we were placed in the same class, huh?" I mumbled.

Well, there were only four classes for all of the first-year students, after all. Statistically, it wasn't impossible for us to be together.

"Nice to meet you. I'm Ayanokouji Kiyotaka."

"You just went ahead and introduced yourself?" she said.

"Well, this is the second time that we've spoken. Isn't it fine for me to do so?"

I had wanted to introduce myself to someone anyway, so it wasn't as though I could just keep quiet. Besides, in order to become familiar with my class, I had to at least know my neighbor's name...even if she was this audacious girl.

"Do you mind if I refuse?" she asked.

"I don't think sitting next to someone for an entire year without knowing their name would be comfortable."

"I disagree."

Shooting me a glance, she placed her bag on her desk. Apparently, she wasn't going to tell me her name. Lacking any interest in the classroom, the girl simply sat upright in her chair like a model student.

"Do you have a friend in another class? Or did you enroll here all on your lonesome?" I asked.

"You're a curious one, aren't you? You won't find talking to me very interesting, though."

"If I'm bothering you, you can just tell me to be quiet."

I wouldn't introduce myself if it made her angry. I thought that the conversation was over, but then the girl sighed. Apparently, she'd changed her mind. She turned her gaze on me and introduced herself.

"I'm Horikita Suzune."

For the first time, I got a good look at her face.

Wow. She was cute. Or rather, she was beautiful. Even though we were in the same grade, I'd have believed it if you told me she was a year or two older.

Such a calm, cool beauty.

"Let me tell you about myself," I said. "I have no particular hobbies, but I'm interested in just about anything.

I don't need many friends, but I think it would be nice to have at least a few. And, well, that's about it."

"Spoken just like someone who avoids trouble. I don't think I could ever like such a person," she said.

"Jeez, I feel like you trashed my entire existence in one second," I muttered.

"I pray this will be my only upset."

"I sympathize, but, unfortunately, I don't think your prayers will be answered." I pointed to the classroom entrance. Standing there was—

"This seems like a rather well-equipped classroom. It would appear to live up to people's expectations, hmm?" Yes. The boy who'd quarreled with those women on the bus.

"I see. This certainly is bad luck," she said.

This troublemaker had been placed in Class D with us. Without seeming to notice our presence at all, he went over to the seat labeled "Kouenji" and sat. I wondered if such a person had ever considered even the idea of friendship. I tried observing him for a little bit. Kouenji put his feet on top of the desk, took a nail file from his bag, and hummed while he treated his fingernails. He acted as though he were completely alone.

Apparently, the rude comments he'd made on the bus had been an accurate reflection of his opinions. Within

ten seconds, more than half the class had begun drawing away from Kouenji. His imposing nature dominated
the space. Looking over, I saw that Horikita's gaze had
lowered, and she seemed to be reading one of her own
books. Oh, shoot. I'd forgotten that conversational back-
and-forth was one of the basics of maintaining interest.
I'd squashed one of my chances to become friends with
Horikita. Leaning down, I glanced at the title of her
book: *Crime and Punishment*. Now that was interesting.
A story that debated whether it was right to kill someone,
so long as it was done for the sake of justice.

So sad. Perhaps Horikita's taste in books was reflected
in her personality. Well, at any rate, we'd introduced ourselves, so perhaps we could at least become neighborly.
After a few minutes, the first bell rang. At that precise
moment, a woman entered the classroom. When I first
saw her, my initial impression was that she firmly believed in discipline. If I had to guess, I would have placed
her age at thirty. She wore a suit and had delicate features.
Her hair seemed long, and she'd tied it into a ponytail.

"Ahem. Good morning to you, students. I'm the instructor for Class D. My name is Chabashira Sae. I usually teach Japanese history. However, at this school, we
do not change classrooms for each grade. For the next
three years, I will be acting as your homeroom teacher,

so I hope to get to know all of you. It's a pleasure to meet you. The entrance ceremony will be in the gymnasium one hour from now, but first, I will distribute written materials with information about this school's special rules. I will also hand out the admissions guide."

The students in the front seats passed back the familiar documents I'd received after being accepted.

This school differed from the multitude of other Japanese high schools in a few key ways. Here, all students were required to live in dormitories located on school premises. Also, except for special cases, such as studying abroad, students were forbidden to contact anyone outside the school. Even contact with your immediate family was forbidden without authorization. Naturally, leaving school grounds without permission was also strictly forbidden.

However, the campus also came equipped with many excellent facilities. With its own karaoke spot, theater, café, boutique, and more, you could easily compare this school to a small city. The campus spread over more than 600,000 square meters.

This school boasted another unique feature: the S System.

"I will now hand out your student ID cards. By using your card, you can access any of the facilities on campus, purchase goods from the store, and so on. It acts like a credit card. However, it is imperative that you pay attention to the points that you spend. At this school, you can use your points to buy anything. Anything located on the school premises is available for purchase."

Our points, loaded onto our student ID cards, acted as a kind of currency. The lack of paper money would prevent many students' financial troubles. However, students needed to keep a watchful eye on their spending habits. At any rate, the school provided these points free of charge.

"Your student cards can be used simply by swiping them through the machine scanner. The method is simple, so you shouldn't get confused. Points are automatically deposited into your account on the first of every month. You should all have received 100,000 points already. Keep in mind that one point is worth one yen. No further explanation should be necessary."

The classroom erupted.

In other words, we had received a 100,000-yen monthly allowance from the school upon admission. I'd expect nothing less from a massive institution run by the Japanese government. 100,000 yen is a rather large sum of money for a high schooler.

"Shocked by the amount of points you've been given?

This school evaluates its students' talents. Everyone here has passed the entrance examination, which itself speaks to your value and potential. The amount you've received reflects the evaluation of your worth. You can use your points without restraint. After graduation, however, all of your points return to the school. Because it's impossible to exchange your points for cash, there's no advantage to saving them. Once points have been deposited into your account, it's up to you how to spend them. Do as you like. In the event that you don't want to spend your points, you may transfer them to someone else. However, extorting money from your peers is not allowed. This school monitors bullying very carefully."

As bewilderment spread among the students, Chabashira-sensei looked over the room.

"Well, it appears no one has any questions. I hope that you enjoy your time here as students."

Many of my classmates could not hide their surprise at the large amount of points.

"This school doesn't seem as strict as I thought," I muttered.

I thought I was talking to myself, but Horikita looked in my direction. She must have imagined I was speaking to her.

"This school is extremely lenient, isn't it?"

Despite all of the restrictions, like being forced to live in the dormitories, being forbidden to leave the campus, and being prohibited from contacting anyone on the outside, no one here seemed to have any complaints. In fact, you might even say that we'd been given such preferential treatment that it was like we'd been transported to paradise. Of course, the Advanced Nurturing High School's most impressive statistic was its near 100 percent placement rate for students advancing into higher education or entering the workforce.

This government-sponsored school's thorough guidance of its students hoped to ensure a better future. In fact, the school heavily advertised this. Many of its alumni went on to achieve fame. Typically, no matter how famous or impressive a school might be, the areas of specialization are limited. For example, one school might specialize in sports or in music. Another might focus on something related to computers. However, at this school, any student could hope to succeed, regardless of their field.

Only this school had that kind of name-brand value. I'd assumed that the atmosphere would be cutthroat, but the majority of students looked like typical kids.

No, that wasn't quite right. After all, we'd been capable enough to pass the entrance exam. If we could reach graduation day peacefully, without incident, then we would have achieved our goal... Was such a thing really possible, though?

"This is almost *too* much preferential treatment. It's frightening."

As Horikita spoke, I realized I felt the same way. We hardly knew anything about this school. It was as if a veil of mystery shrouded everything. Because a school like this could make any wishes a reality, I'd thought some kind of risk would have to be involved.

"Hey, hey! Do you want to check out a store with me on our way back? Let's do some shopping!" one girl cried.

"Sure. With this much, we can buy anything. I'm so glad I got into this school!" another said.

Once the teacher was gone, the newly rich students began to grow restless.

"Everyone, can you please listen to me for a moment?"

A student with the air of an upstanding young man quickly raised his hand. His hair wasn't dyed. He looked like an honors student. Based on his appearance, I got the impression he wasn't a delinquent.

"Starting today, we're all going to be classmates. Therefore, I think it'd be good for us to introduce ourselves and become friends as soon as possible. We still have some time until the entrance ceremony. What do you say?"

He'd just done something incredible. The majority of students were lost in thought, unable to speak up.

"Agreed! After all, we still don't know a thing about each other, not even our names," someone shouted.

After the ice had broken, the previously hesitant students began to speak.

"My name's Hirata Yousuke. Back in junior high, lots of people called me Yousuke. Feel free to use my first name! I guess my hobby is sports in general, but I especially like soccer. I'm planning on playing soccer here, too. Nice to meet you!"

Hirata had effortlessly introduced himself to the class. He seemed exceptionally brave. And he'd talked about his love for soccer, too! His level of popularity must've increased two, no, maybe four times. Why, the girl seated next to Hirata had hearts in her eyes! If someone like Hirata became our class's linchpin, I wondered if he'd keep everyone honest and motivated until graduation.

Someone like him would probably end up dating the cutest girl in class. That was how these things typically went.

"Well then, I'd like everyone to introduce themselves, starting from the front. Is that okay?"

Although the girl at the head of the class looked a little bewildered, she quickly made up her mind and stood.

Or rather, she'd been pressured, in response to Hirata's words.

"M-my name is...Inogashira Ko-Ko..."

The girl, last name Inogashira, seemed to freeze during her introduction. Was she drawing a blank, or had she not considered what she was going to say beforehand? As her words halted, she paled. It was rare to see someone get so incredibly nervous.

"Do your best!"

"Don't panic! It's okay!"

Kind words poured out of our classmates. But it seemed to have the opposite effect on the girl; the words stuck in the back of her throat. The silence continued for five seconds. Ten seconds. You could've cut the tension with a knife. Some of the girls started giggling. Inogashira was paralyzed with fear. She couldn't move a muscle. Another girl spoke up.

"It's okay to go slowly. Don't rush."

Although it might seem kind, saying, "Do your best!" and, "It's okay!" it actually conveys a completely different meaning. To someone who is extremely nervous, "Do your best!" and, "It's okay!" can actually seem forceful, as if indicating she needs to match her classmates. On the other hand, saying, "Just take things slowly. Don't rush," allows her to take things at her own pace.

After that, the girl calmed down and regained her composure. She took a few small breaths and tried again.

"My name is Inogashira...Kokoro. Um, my hobby is sewing. I'm pretty good at knitting. I-It's nice to meet you all."

She was able to finish without stopping. Looking alternately relieved, delighted, and embarrassed, Inogashira sat down. Other introductions followed hers.

"I'm Yamauchi Haruki. I competed in table tennis during elementary school, and in junior high I was the ace player on our baseball team. I was number four. I got hurt during the inter-high school championships, though, and I'm undergoing rehab now. Nice to meet you."

I didn't think that the number of his baseball uniform was essential information...

Besides, I'd thought the inter-high championship was a national sports competition for high school students. Junior high school kids were supposed to be ineligible.

Was he trying to crack a joke? He seemed like a talkative guy who got carried away pretty easily.

"Well then, I'm next, aren't I?"

The cheerful girl who stood up was the same one who'd told Inogashira to go slowly and calm down. She was also the same girl who'd helped out the elderly woman on the bus that morning.

"My name is Kushida Kikyou. None of my friends from junior high made it to this school, so I'm alone here. I'd like to get to know all of your names and faces right away and become friends as soon as possible!"

While most of the students had only said a few words of introduction, Kushida continued to talk.

"My first goal is to become friends with everyone. So, after we're finished with introductions, I'd love for you to share your contact information with me!"

She wasn't just saying that. I could tell right away that this girl was the type to open up her heart to anyone.

Her encouraging words to Inogashira hadn't been platitudes, but a genuine reflection of her feelings.

"So, after school or during vacations, I want to make all sorts of memories with lots of people. Please feel free to invite me to lots and lots of events! Anyway, I've talked for a long time, so I'll end my introduction here."

She said it as though she knew I'd been critiquing everyone's introductions. I felt strangely uncomfortable, and I wasn't sure why.

What should I say when my turn came? Should I make a joke? Should I go into it with really high energy in order to get some laughs? No, that wouldn't work. Going out of control would just ruin the atmosphere. Besides, that didn't really fit my personality anyway.

The introductions continued while I wrestled with my anxiety.

"Well then, next up is..."

As Hirata looked encouragingly toward the next student, that student glared back. His hair was dyed a fiery red. He both looked and sounded like a delinquent.

"What, are we a bunch of little kids or something? I don't need to introduce myself. People who want to do that can go ahead. Just leave me out of it."

The red-haired guy scowled at Hirata. He had quite a presence, his attitude intense and overpowering.

"I can't force you to introduce yourself, of course. However, I don't think that getting along with your classmates is a bad thing. If I've made you uncomfortable, I apologize."

When Hirata bowed his head, some of the girls glared at the guy with red hair.

"Isn't it fine to introduce yourself?" one of them snapped.

"Yeah, yeah!"

As I'd expected, the pretty-boy soccer star had captured most of the girls' hearts in the blink of an eye. However, half of the male students started to look angry, probably out of jealousy.

"Shut it. I don't care. I didn't come here to make friends."

The guy with red hair got up from his seat. It seemed he had no intention of getting to know anyone. Several other students followed suit and left the classroom together. Horikita got up and briefly glanced my way. When she realized I wasn't moving, she started to walk out the door. Hirata looked a little lonely when he saw Horikita head out.

"They're not a bad bunch. It's my fault. I was being selfish and made people do this."

"No way. You didn't do anything wrong, Hirata-kun. Let's just leave those guys be, okay?"

Although some people had rebelled at the idea of introductions, the students who remained were happy to continue. In the end, things wrapped up in a rather ordinary fashion.

"I'm Ike Kanji. I love girls, and I hate pretty boys. I'm currently in the market for a new girlfriend. It's nice to meet you! All the better if you're a cutie or a beauty!"

It was difficult to tell if he was joking or not. At the very least, the girls looked at him with revulsion.

"Wow. You are *so* cool, Ike-kun," one girl said, in a completely emotionless voice. Of course, her statement was 1000 percent false.

"Seriously? Seriously? Oh, man. I mean, I thought that I wasn't bad or anything, but...heh heh."

Apparently, Ike thought that she was being serious. He blushed. Instantly, the girls started to laugh.

"Oh, wow. He's *cute*, huh, everyone? He's looking for a girlfriend!"

Dude, they're making fun of you. Ike continued to jovially go along with the teasing. He didn't seem like a bad guy, though.

Next up was the combative boy from the bus, Kouenji. While inspecting his bangs in a hand mirror, he combed his hair.

"Excuse me, can you introduce yourself?" Hirata asked.

"Hmph. Fine."

He smirked like an aristocrat, displaying his impudent attitude. As he shifted in his seat, I thought he might leave, but Kouenji placed both of his legs on his desk and introduced himself.

"My name is Kouenji Rokusuke. As the sole male heir to the Kouenji conglomerate group, I will soon be tasked with carrying Japan into the future. I sincerely look forward to making your acquaintance, ladies."

He aimed his introduction solely at the opposite sex, rather than the entire class. After hearing that he was rich, some of the girls looked at him with sparkling eyes, while others regarded Kouenji as if he were nothing more than a weirdo. That was only natural.

"Starting today, I will mercilessly punish anyone who makes me uncomfortable. Please exercise proper precaution so that you may avoid that."

"Um, Kouenji-kun. What exactly do you mean when you say, 'anyone who makes me uncomfortable'?" asked Hirata, who looked uneasy at the word "punish."

"I meant exactly what I said. If asked to give an example, well... I would say I hate ugly things, for instance. So, if I saw something ugly, I would do just as I said."

Fwish! He flipped his long, flowing bangs.

"Ah, thank you. I will be careful then."

There was the guy with red hair, Horikita, Kouenji, Yamauchi, and Ike. Apparently, this class was full of people with bizarre idiosyncrasies.

I, too, was especially peculiar, in that there was nothing peculiar about me. I had wanted to be free, free as a bird, but prior to this I'd languished in a cage. I had wanted to fly into the expansive open skies. If you looked out the window, you could watch birds gracefully soaring... Well, not right now, but in general. Anyway, that's the kind of guy I was.

"Well then, time for the next person. Can you please introduce yourself?"

"Huh?"

Oh, shoot. My turn had come while I'd been daydreaming. Students turned, waiting for my introduction.

Hey, hey! Don't look at me with so much anticipation. Oh well, I might as well try my best.

Clack! The chair rattled as I stood.

"Um. Well, my name is Ayanokouji Kiyotaka. And, uh, I don't really have any special skills or anything. I'll do my best to get along with all of you. It's, uh, nice to meet you."

Well? Was *that* my introduction?

I'd failed!

I instinctively buried my head in my hands. I hadn't had time to construct a proper introduction because I'd been too busy daydreaming. It was the worst possible intro. It didn't attract attention, and absolutely no one would remember it.

"It's nice to meet you, Ayanokouji-kun. I always want to be friends with everyone, just like you. Let's both do our best, okay?" Hirata responded with a refreshing smile.

Everyone clapped. Their applause felt somewhat like pity, which strangely pained me. Despite that, however, I felt kind of glad.

2.3

EVEN THOUGH PEOPLE said this place was tough, the entrance ceremony was the same as any other school's. Some important people offered words of thanks, and the ceremony concluded without incident. Then, it was noon. After we received some general information about the campus, the crowd dispersed.

70–80 percent of the students headed toward the dormitories. The remaining students quickly formed into groups. Some made their way to cafés, while the louder ones went out for karaoke. The hustle and bustle quickly died down. On a whim, I decided to swing by the convenience store on my way back to the dormitory. Of course, I went alone. I didn't have a chaperone, or acquaintance, or anyone like that.

"My, what an unpleasant coincidence."

Entering the convenience store, I ran into Horikita once again.

"Come on, there's no need to be so hostile. Anyway, did you need to buy something?" I asked.

"Yes, just a few things. I came to get some necessities."

There was no shortage of things you needed when starting life in a dorm, especially if you were a girl. Horikita took various necessities like shampoo off the shelves and promptly threw them into the basket she was carrying. I'd thought she would choose higher quality items, but she only took the cheapest options.

"I thought girls usually made a fuss over what kind of shampoo they bought."

"Well, that depends on the person, doesn't it? I'm the sort who doesn't know when you might need money," she replied.

She shot me an icy glare that seemed to say, *Could you please not inspect other people's purchases without their permission?*

"At any rate, I was terribly surprised that you stayed for introductions," she said. "You didn't look like the type to hang out with a circle of classmates."

"I decided to participate precisely because I don't like trouble. Why didn't you introduce yourself to them, Horikita? You could have gotten to know several other students, and it would have been a chance to make friends."

Quite a few of the students had exchanged cell numbers, too. If Horikita had participated, she would probably have become quite popular. What a waste.

"There are several reasons why I objected, but I suppose it might be better if I simply explain, hmm? My introduction might have sown discord, depending on how things went. Thus, doing nothing avoided creating more problems. Am I wrong?"

"But, statistically speaking, there was a high probability that you could have hit it off with everyone after introducing yourself," I said.

"How did you arrive at that conclusion? Actually, if I argue this with you now, we'll just end up in an endless debate. Let's say that the probability of making friends was high, like you said. So, how many people did you get to know?"

"Ugh..."

She gazed at me.

That was a rather splendid argument. The fact that I hadn't yet exchanged contact information with anyone worked in Horikita's favor. It proved there was no guarantee that introductions led to friendship. I instinctively averted my eyes.

"In other words, you have no evidence to support your claim that self-introductions lead to making friends, do you?" she asked. "Besides, I never intended to make friends in the first place. If I have no need to introduce myself, then I also have no reason to listen to anyone else's introductions. Have I convinced you?"

That reminded me of the disastrous first time I'd tried to introduce myself to Horikita. Come to think of it, it might have been a miracle that I'd managed to get her name.

When I asked her if I shouldn't have introduced myself to her, she shook her head. People tended to have hidden depths, no doubt about it. Horikita might have been a more solitary, more aloof person than I'd imagined.

We roamed around the convenience store without looking at each other. Even though she was somewhat uptight, being with her didn't feel uncomfortable.

"Whoa! There's even an amazing selection of noodle cups here! This school is super convenient!"

Two rather noisy male students stood before the instant foods. They tossed a veritable mountain of noodle cups into their basket and made their way to the cash register. Besides noodles, they'd stocked up on snacks and juice. Hey, it'd be nearly impossible to go through all your points; better to spend them.

"Noodle cups. They have so many kinds."

These were definitely one reason I'd come to the convenience store.

"So, do boys really like this kind of stuff? I can't imagine that it's healthy," Horikita said.

"I like them just fine, I guess."

I picked up a noodle cup and examined the price tag. It said 156 yen, but I couldn't tell whether that was expensive or cheap. Even though the school referred to its credit system as points, the prices were all listed in yen.

"Hey, what do you think? Is this price high or low?"

"Hmm. I'm not sure. Why, is there something curious about it?"

"No, I was just wondering."

The store's prices seemed reasonable. One point appeared to really equal one yen. Given that the average freshman's allowance was around 5,000 yen, the amount of money we'd received seemed impossibly large. Horikita, noting my odd behavior, gave me a quizzical look. I grabbed a noodle cup to avoid suspicion.

"Wow, this is enormous. It's a G Cup, huh?"

Apparently, that stood for "Giga Cup." Just looking at it made me feel full. On an unrelated note, Horikita's breasts were neither small nor huge. They exquisitely straddled the line between the two. The perfect size.

"Ayanokouji-kun. Were you thinking about something stupid just now?" she asked.

"Er. No?"

"I felt like you were acting strangely."

She could sense my inappropriate thoughts just by looking at me. She was a sharp one.

"I was just wondering whether or not I should buy this. What do you think?"

"Oh. Well, I suppose that's fine. Anyway, do *you* really think you should buy that? This school offers far healthier food options. Don't you think it's better to avoid eating junk?"

Like Horikita said, I had no reason to eat junk. However, since I had an irresistible urge, I took one package of regular-sized instant noodles with "FOO Yakisoba" written on it and tossed it into my cart. Her attention wandering, Horikita moved away from the food and began hunting for daily essentials. I planned to use witty jokes to score more points with her next.

"If you're looking for something *a cut above the rest*, how about this razor with five blades? I bet it'd do the job."

"Why in the world would I want to shave with *that*?"

I grinned smugly and pretended to shave an imaginary beard, but she didn't laugh. Far from it. Instead, she looked at me like I was dirt.

"Look at me," she said. "I don't have anything to shave. Not on my chin, not under my armpits, and not down *there*."

I mumbled hesitantly, my spirit crushed. It looked like my jokes failed colossally with women.

"I have to say, I'm a little envious of your ability to babble inanely to someone you've only just met."

"Well, I feel like you've been saying stupid crap, too, and you only just met *me*."

"Is that so? I've merely stated facts. Unlike you." She calmly tossed my words back at me, shutting me up. To be fair, I *had* said some random nonsense. The smooth, eloquent Horikita, on the other hand, was always well-spoken, no matter how you sliced it.

Horikita chose the cheapest face wash. I would have thought girls cared more about that kind of thing, too.

"Don't you think that this one is better?" I took an expensive cream off the shelf and showed it to her.

"Unnecessary." She refused it.

"Well, but—"

"I already said it was unnecessary, didn't I?" she snapped.

"Yes..."

I gently returned the face wash as she glared at me. I thought I could carry on a conversation without making her angry, but I'd failed.

"You don't seem adept at socializing. You're terrible at conversation."

"Well, if it's coming from you, then it's definitely true," I grumbled.

"That's right. I consider myself, at the very least, to have a good eye for people. Normally, I wouldn't want to hear you talk anymore, but I will put in a painful level of effort to listen to you."

I'd said that I wanted to be her friend, but, apparently, she didn't feel the same. With that, our conversation abruptly stopped. Two new girls entered the convenience store. It was a little strange, but I became aware of something crucial: Horikita really was cute.

"Hey. What's up with this?"

While looking around the store, desperate for a new topic, I'd found something strange. Some toiletries and food had been tucked away in the corner of the convenience store. At first glance, they appeared to be the same as the other items, but there was one big difference.

"Free?"

Horikita apparently also thought it strange, so she picked up one of the items. Daily necessities like toothbrushes and bandages had been stuffed into a clearance bin and labeled "Free." The bin was also marked with the proviso "three items per month." These were obviously different from the store's other goods.

"They must be emergency relief supplies for students who use up their points. This school is so incredibly lenient," I said.

I had to wonder how far their leniency extended, though.

"Hey, shut it! Just wait a sec! I'm looking for it right now!"

A sudden, loud voice drowned out the store's peaceful background music.

"Come on, hurry up. You have a line of people waiting on you!"

"Oh, yeah? Well, if they have any complaints, they can take it up with me!"

Apparently, trouble was brewing by the register. A dispute had broken out between two young men who were glaring at each other. I recognized the one with the thoroughly ill-tempered look on his face. It was the student from my class, the guy with the red hair. He had his hands full of noodle cups.

"What's going on here?" I asked.

"Huh? Who are *you*?"

I had meant to appear amicable, but the guy with red hair scowled at me. Apparently, he was under the mistaken impression that I was an enemy.

"My name's Ayanokouji. I'm from your class. I just asked because it sounded like there was trouble."

At my explanation, the red-haired guy looked somewhat mollified and lowered his voice a little. "Oh. Yeah, I remember you. I forgot my student ID card. Forgot that it pretty much acts as our money from now on, too."

I looked at his empty hands. He'd put the noodle cups away. He started to leave, probably heading back to the dorms, where he'd likely forgotten his card. To be honest, the fact that the student ID was necessary for payment hadn't yet sunk in for me, either.

"I can pay for you. I mean, it'd be annoying if you had to head all the way back to the dorms. I don't mind."

"That's true. You're right, it'd be absolutely annoying. Thanks."

The store wasn't particularly far from the dorms, but by the time he got back there would be a long line of students buying lunch.

"My name's Sudou," he said. "Thanks for helping me out. I owe you."

"Nice to meet you, Sudou."

Sudou handed me his noodle cup, and I walked over to the hot water dispenser. After watching our short exchange, Horikita sighed, aghast.

"You're acting like a pushover right from the start. Do

you intend to become his servant? Or are you doing this to make friends?" she asked.

"I didn't care about making friends. I just wanted to help. No big deal."

"You don't seem to be afraid."

"Afraid? Why? Because he looks like a delinquent?" I asked.

"A normal person would try to keep someone like him at a distance."

"I guess, but he doesn't seem like a bad person to me. And you don't appear to be scared either, Horikita."

"It's mostly defenseless people who stay away from those types. If he acted violently, I could rebuff him. That's why I don't withdraw."

Horikita's words were always a little difficult to understand. To begin with, what did she mean by "rebuff"? Did she carry pepper spray to keep off perverts or something?

"Let's finish our shopping. We'll be a bother to the other students if we dawdle," she said.

Wrapping things up, we presented our student ID cards to the machine by the register. Since we didn't have to deal with small change, our transaction was speedy.

"You really can use it like money..." I said.

My receipt showed the price of each item and the remaining amount of points. The payment had gone through without any problems. I poured hot water into my noodle cup while waiting for Horikita. I'd thought it might be tricky, but opening the lid and pouring hot water up to the line was simple enough.

Anyway, this school was eerie.

What merit could every student possibly have that would warrant such a massive allowance? Considering that there were about 160 people enrolled in my grade, simple calculation suggested that there were 480 people total in this school. That alone would mean 48 million yen each month. Annually, that would equal 560 million yen. Even for a government-supported school, that seemed like overkill.

"How does the school benefit from giving us this much money?"

"I wonder. The campus has more than enough facilities for the number of students, and I wouldn't think it necessary to hand out so much. Students who should be studying might slack off."

Perhaps it was some kind of reward for working hard and passing a test or something. Indeed, student motivation might increase if offered an incentive. However, the school had just handed out 100,000 yen to everyone, with no strings attached.

"I won't tell you what to do, but I think it would be

best to avoid wasting your money. It's difficult to fix friv- olous spending habits. Once a person gets used to an easy life, they find they need more and more. When you lose it, the shock can be great," Horikita said.

"I'll keep that in mind."

I didn't really intend to waste money on miscella- neous junk, but she had a point. After paying and exiting the store, I found Sudou seated outside, waiting for me. When I saw him, he gently waved me over. I waved in return, feeling somewhat embarrassed, yet happy.

"Are you really going to eat here?" I asked him.

"Of course. It's just common sense."

Sudou perplexed me with his matter-of-fact reply. Horikita sighed in exasperation.

"I'm going back. I'll be stripped of my dignity if I spend more time here," she said.

"What do you mean, 'dignity'? We're just high school students. We're ordinary. Or, what, are you the high-born daughter of some noble family or something?"

Horikita didn't flinch at Sudou's harsh tone. Seemingly irritated, Sudou set his noodle cup on the ground and stood.

"Huh? Hey, listen to people when they're talking to you! Hey!" he said.

"What's his problem? He just suddenly got angry."

Horikita said this to me, ignoring Sudou. This was apparently too much for Sudou, who started to shout.

"Hey, get over here! I'll smack that smug look off your face!" he yelled.

"Look, I'll admit that Horikita has a bad attitude, but you're taking this too far."

It was apparent that Sudou's patience had run out. "Huh? What was that? She has a bratty, obnoxious attitude. That's bad, especially for a girl!"

"For a girl? That's rather outdated thinking. Ayanokouji, I would advise you not to become his friend," Horikita said. With that, she turned her back on Sudou.

"Hey, wait! You shitty girl!"

"Calm down." I held Sudou back as he actually tried to grab Horikita. She made her way in the direction of the dorms without stopping or glancing back.

"What the hell is her deal? Goddamn it!" he shouted.

"There are many different types of people, you know."

"Shut it. I hate those stuffy, too-serious types."

He continued to glare at me. Sudou grabbed his noodle cup once again, ripped off the cover, and began eating. Just a little while ago, he'd fought in front of the register, too. He probably had a short fuse.

"Hey, you guys first years? This is our spot."

As Sudou slurped his ramen, three boys called out to

us. They seemed to have come out of the same store and were carrying the same brand of noodle cups.

"Who are *you*? I was already here. You're in the way. Get lost," Sudou barked.

"You hear this guy? 'Get lost,' he says. What a cocky little first-year punk."

The three laughed in Sudou's face. Sudou shot up, slamming his noodle cup against the ground. The broth and noodles splashed everywhere.

"'First-year punk,' huh? You tryin' to make fun of me, huh?!"

Sudou had an *extremely* short fuse. If I had to judge, he seemed like the type to immediately threaten anyone or anything that crossed him.

"You're awfully mouthy, considering we're second-year students. We already put our bags here, see?"

Plop! With those words, the second-year upperclassmen students put down their bags and guffawed loudly.

"See, our stuff's here. Now, beat it," one of them said.

"You got a lot of guts, asshole."

Sudou didn't back down, unfazed by being outnumbered. It looked like fists were going to fly at any moment. I, of course, didn't want any part of it myself.

"Oh, wow, scary. What class are you in? Wait, never mind. I think I know. You're in Class D, aren't you?"

"Yeah, so what?" Sudou snapped.

The upperclassmen students exchanged glances and burst into laughter.

"You hear that? He's in Class D! I knew it! It was a dead giveaway!"

"Huh? What's that supposed to mean? Hey!"

As Sudou barked at them, the boys grinned and stepped backwards.

"Aw, you poor things. Since you're 'defective,' we'll let you off the hook, just for today. Let's get going, guys."

"Hey, don't run away! Hey!" Sudou shouted.

"Yeah, yeah, keep on yapping. You guys'll be in hell soon enough anyway."

Be in hell?

They appeared calm and composed. I wondered what they'd meant. Previously, I'd been certain this school would be filled with upper-class young men and women, but there seemed to be plenty of rowdy, combative people like Sudou or those upperclassmen.

"Ah, damn it! If those had been nice second-year students, or cute girls, that would've been great. Instead, we had to deal with those annoying morons."

Sudou didn't bother to clean up his mess. He thrust his hands into his pockets before heading back. I looked at the wall outside the convenience store, discovering two surveillance cameras.

"This might lead to problems later," I muttered.

Reluctantly, I bent down, picked up the cup, and started cleaning up the mess. Come to think of it, as soon as those second-year students found out Sudou was in Class D, their attitudes had changed. Although it ate at me, I couldn't explain it.

2.4

∙ ∙

AROUND ONE PM, I made my way back to the dormitory, my home from that day onward. At the reception desk, I received a keycard for Room 401 and a handbook containing information about the dorm's rules, then boarded the elevator. I quickly flipped through the handbook, which only detailed the most basic things that we needed for our daily routines. The dates and times for garbage disposal were listed, as well as a notice about avoiding excessive noise. I also saw notes about not wasting water or electricity, and so on.

"So, they don't place restrictions on electricity or gas usage?"

I'd assumed that the school would deduct the cost from our points. This school really went to great lengths to have a perfect system for its students. However, I was a little surprised that they'd implemented co-ed dormitories. After all, this was a high school, so the rules stated that unsuitable romantic relationships were frowned upon. In short, sex was strictly forbidden...obviously. I mean, a member of the clergy wouldn't say that engaging in illicit sexual activity was okay.

While I privately doubted that such pampered students could develop into fine, upstanding adults, it would be wise to make the best of the situation for now. My room was about eight tatami mats wide. Also, though this was a dorm, it was the first time I'd lived alone. I refused to have any contact with the outside world until graduation. Considering my situation, I unintentionally cracked a smile.

This school boasted a high employment rate upon graduation, and its facilities and student services were unmatched throughout the country, making it the preeminent high school in Japan. I found such things trivial, however. I'd chosen this school for one fundamental reason.

At this high school, people were not allowed to contact students without permission, even if they were friends or immediate family. I greatly appreciated that. I was free. In English, they would call it, "freedom." In French, they would call it, "liberté."

Isn't freedom simply the best? When I wanted to eat something, I could eat it. I almost didn't want to graduate. Before being accepted, I'd honestly thought I would be been fine either way, that the difference between passing and failing would have been trivial. But my true feelings finally welled up. I was glad to have been admitted here.

No one else's eyes or words would ever reach me. I could start ag—no. I could begin anew entirely. A new life. I resolved to enjoy my time here to the fullest, but without drawing attention to myself. Still in my uniform, I dived into my already-made bed. I felt far from tired, however. I was so incredibly excited about my new life that I was unable to calm down. My eyes remained wide open.

ON OUR SECOND DAY of school—well, I suppose technically it was the first day of class—we spent most of our time running over the course objectives. Apparently, many of the students were quite surprised, if not a little disappointed, by how genuinely warm and friendly the teachers at this school looked. Sudou had already made a spectacle of himself by spending most of the class asleep. I thought that the teachers would notice, but they showed no signs of doing so. After all, it was up to every individual student whether or not he or she wanted to listen in class. I wondered if this was how teachers typically interacted with students once they left compulsory education.

I took in the relaxed atmosphere, and soon it was lunchtime. Students stood up and left with their new acquaintances, disappearing from my view. I couldn't help but feel slightly envious as I watched them. Unfortunately, I still hadn't managed to befriend a single one of my new classmates.

"How pathetic."

Only one person had noticed how I felt, and she met my pain with derisive laughter.

"What? What's pathetic?" I asked.

"'I want someone to invite me along. I want to eat with someone!' Your thoughts are like an open book," Horikita said.

"But you're alone, too, aren't you? Haven't you thought the same thing? Or do you intend to spend three years here without making a single friend?"

"That's right. I prefer to be alone," she replied quickly, without hesitation. It sounded like she was being honest. "Why don't you stop worrying about me and instead think about yourself?"

"Well, I..."

I certainly wasn't proclaiming my intention to be social. Honestly, at the rate things were going I might be unable to make any friends, spelling trouble for my future. I'd likely end up alone again, and that would make me stand out. It could make me a target for bullying.

Less than a minute after the end-of-class bell rang,

about half of the students had disappeared. Those who remained either secretly wanted to go, like me, were unconscious of their surroundings, or preferred being alone, like Horikita.

"Well, I was thinking of heading to the cafeteria. Anyone want to come with me?" announced Hirata as he stood. He was clearly one of those all-around good guys. I had to take my hat off to him. In my heart of hearts, I'd been waiting for a savior to bestow a chance like this upon me. *Yes, Hirata, I will go with you.* I slowly tried to raise my hand, and...

"I'll go, too!"

"Me, too! Me too!"

Girls gathered around Hirata one after another, and I lowered my hand. Why did those girls have to take his offer? This could've been my chance to make friends with Hirata! *You don't need to jump all over him for lunch just because he's kind of handsome!*

"How tragic."

Horikita's derisive laugh morphed into scorn.

"Don't just assume you know what I'm thinking," I said.

"Does anyone else want to come?"

Hirata looked around the room, possibly feeling a bit lonely because no other boys had joined him. Hirata scanned the classroom, and his eyes met mine. *Over here!*

Notice me, Hirata! There's someone here who wants an invitation! Hirata didn't avert his eyes, just as I would expect from someone with a handle on his life who cared about the people in his class! He understood my appeal!

"Hey, Ayano—"

Hirata began to call my name, but in that instant—

"Come on. Hurry up, Hirata-kun!"

A fashionista-type girl latched onto Hirata's arm. Ah... The girls stole Hirata's attention. They left the classroom together, all looking rather happy. I remained alone with my arm outstretched. Somewhat embarrassed, I tried to play it off by pretending to scratch my head.

"Well then." Horikita shot me another pitying look before departing the classroom, leaving me alone.

"That was pointless."

Reluctantly, I got up and decided to head toward the cafeteria by myself. If I didn't feel like I could eat alone in there, I'd just score some supplies from the convenience store.

"You're Ayanokouji-kun, right?"

On my way out, a beautiful girl suddenly called my name. It was Kushida, one of my classmates. This was the first time I'd actually taken a good look at her, and it caused my heart to start pounding in my chest like a jackhammer. She had short, straight, dyed-brown hair that almost brushed the tops of her shoulders. While it certainly wasn't crude, the school had recently approved rather short skirt lengths. I had a strong feeling that this was one of the more recent uniforms.

She was holding something in her hand. I couldn't tell if it was a pouch with a lot of key holders or what.

"I'm Kushida, from your class. Do you remember me?" she asked.

"Yeah, kinda. Do you need something?"

"To tell you the truth, there's something I wanted to ask you. It's just one little question. Ayanokouji-kun, are you on good terms with Horikita-san?"

"I wouldn't really say we're on good terms. Just casual acquaintances, I guess. Did she do something?"

It looked like her business was with Horikita rather than me, which was a little disappointing.

"Oh, no. Well, do you remember when I said I wanted to get along with everyone in class? That's why I wanted everyone's contact info. But…Horikita turned me down."

Ugh. Horikita was so oblivious. *If such a positive, outgoing girl asked for your info, it would've been nice for you to throw me a bone and give me* her *contact info while you were at it. I could probably have gotten to know everyone in the class in almost no time at all.*

"Weren't you two talking outside the school on the day of the entrance ceremony?"

Considering we'd all ridden the bus together, it was no wonder that she'd seen my meeting with Horikita.

"I was just wondering what kind of person Horikita-san is," Kushida continued. "Is she the type who'll talk a lot when she's with a friend?"

She seemed to want information on Horikita, but I couldn't give her any answers.

"I don't think she's very good at interacting with others. Why are you asking about Horikita, anyway?"

"Well, during our introductions, Horikita-san walked out of the classroom, right? It seems like she hasn't talked to anybody yet, so I'm a little worried about her."

Kushida had said that she wanted to get along with everyone when she introduced herself.

"I understand what you're saying, but I only just met her yesterday. I can't really help you."

"Hmm. I see. I thought that you two must have been old friends before starting school here. I'm sorry to have asked you such a strange question."

"Oh, no, it's all right. Anyway, how did you know my name?"

"How? You introduced yourself the other day, didn't you? I remembered."

Kushida had listened to my hopelessly lame self-introduction. Somehow, that made me really happy.

"Well, it's nice to meet you again, Ayanokouji-kun," she said.

Although I was a little bewildered by her outstretched hand, I wiped my palms on my pants and shook hands with her.

"Yeah, nice to meet you," I said.

Today was probably my lucky day. Even though there'd been some low points, some things had gone well. Since humans were creatures of convenience, the positives quickly overrode the bad memories.

3.1

AFTER TAKING A QUICK PEEK into the cafeteria, I opted instead to go to the convenience store, buy some bread, and return to class. About ten people had remained in the room. Some had pushed their desks together so they could all eat as a group, while other, more solitary students quietly ate their lunches alone. Everyone here had brought a lunch box from the cafeteria or convenience store.

I was going to eat by myself, but then Horikita returned and sat down beside me. On Horikita's desk sat a delicious-looking sandwich. Her aura seemed to say, "Don't talk to me," so I returned to my seat without speaking. Just as I was about to sink my teeth into a sweet bun, music played through the speakers.

"At five PM Japan Standard Time today, we will be

holding a student club fair in Gymnasium No. 1. Students interested in joining a club, please gather in Gymnasium No. 1. I repeat, at—"

A girl with a sweet voice continued the announcement. Club activities, huh? Come to think of it, I'd never joined a club before.

"Hey, Horikita—"

"I'm not interested in joining a club."

"I didn't even ask you anything yet."

"Well, what is it?"

"Are you interested in joining a club?"

"Ayanokouji-kun, do you have dementia, or are you just an idiot? Didn't I just tell you that I'm not interested?"

"That doesn't mean you won't join, though," I replied.

"Now you're just splitting hairs. Don't argue for the sake of arguing."

"Okay then."

So, Horikita had no interest in making friends *or* joining clubs. She seemed annoyed whenever I tried to talk to her. I wondered if she'd come to the school only to advance into higher education or get a job. If she wanted to advance to higher education, I wouldn't have found that too surprising, but I did consider it a bit of a waste.

"You don't really have any friends, do you?" she asked.

"Sorry. But, hey, I can at least talk to *you* pretty well now."

"Listen, don't count me as one of your friends."

"O-oh…"

"Well, since you apparently want to go find out about the clubs, do you intend to join one?" she asked.

"Oh, I'm not sure, I guess. I'm still thinking about it. Probably not, though."

"You don't plan to join a club, but you want to go to the club fair? How odd. Do you plan to use this as a pretext for talking to people and making friends?"

How could she possibly be so sharp? No, I was probably just easy to read.

"Since I failed to make any friends on my first day, I thought that clubs would be my last chance."

"Can't you invite anyone other than me?" she asked.

"It's precisely because I don't have anyone else to invite that I'm having such a hard time!"

"True. However, I don't think you seriously mean what you're saying, Ayanokouji-kun. If you seriously want to make a friend, you should be more insistent."

"I can't, though. I've devoted myself to walking a lonely road."

Horikita took up her sandwich and quietly resumed eating. "I have trouble comprehending your contradictory way of thinking."

I wanted to make friends, but I couldn't. Horikita apparently found that incomprehensible.

"Have you ever joined any clubs, Horikita?" I asked.

"No, I've never been in one."

"Then, do you have any experience? You know, doing this or that?"

"What exactly do you mean by 'that'? I can't help but feel like that's a mean-spirited question."

"Mean-spirited? Why? What did I say wrong?"

In one quick motion, Horikita karate-chopped me in the side. I coughed after being struck, unable to believe that a girl could hit so hard.

"Wh-what was that for?!" I cried.

"Ayanokouji-kun. I've warned you thoroughly, but it would appear that you haven't been listening. I think I may have to dole out rather merciless punishment to you later."

"Absolutely not! Violence doesn't solve anything!"

"Oh, really? Violence has existed since the dawn of time. Violence has historically proven to be the human race's most effective means of achieving resolution. Violence is the most reliable method to make others listen, or safely deny their demands. Not to mention that, in many countries, the police who enforce the law use handguns and batons, wielding violence as a tool to make arrests."

"You sure are rambling..."

She gave a grand speech, insisting that hitting me had not been wrong. She also stated that her unreasonable behavior was reasonable. If I tried to argue, she would viciously tear me down.

"I think that I will employ violence to rehabilitate you, Ayanokouji-kun, and purge you of those impure thoughts. How does that sound?"

"Okay then, what if I said the same thing to *you*, Horikita? What about that?"

At best, men who raised their hand against women were called "lowlifes" and "cowards."

"I wouldn't particularly mind, because I don't think you'll get the chance. Besides, if I never say anything wrong, then you'll never be able to reproach me."

Her answer was totally unexpected. She really seemed to believe that she was always right. Even though she looked and spoke with the civility befitting an honors student, on the inside, she was a cruel beast.

"Okay, I get it, I get it. I'll be careful from now on."

I gave up on Horikita and looked out the window. Ah, the weather today was so nice.

"Club activities, hmm. I see..."

Horikita mumbled to herself as she pondered something.

"Well, if it's only for a little while after school, I'll go with you," she said.

"What do you mean 'a little while'?"

"You asked me earlier, didn't you? You said you wanted to go to the club fair."

"Oh, yeah. I never planned to stick around. I was just looking for a chance to go. Is that okay?"

"If it's just for a little while. All right, we'll go after class."

After our conversation ended, we resumed eating our lunches. I had said that she was unpleasant earlier, but maybe things had turned around. Perhaps Horikita was actually a good person.

"Watching you flail about as you fail to make friends sounds somewhat interesting."

Nope. She was unpleasant.

3.2

• •

"THERE ARE MORE PEOPLE here than I expected."

After class had ended for the day, Horikita and I went to the gymnasium. Nearly all of the students assembled there were freshmen. There were about a hundred people waiting around. We stood near the back of the room and waited for the fair to begin. While waiting, we glanced over the pamphlet that students received upon entering the gymnasium. The pamphlet contained detailed information about club activities.

"I wonder if this school has famous clubs. For example, something like karate."

"Every club seems to operate on a high level. It looks like many athletes and club members here are famous throughout the nation."

Even though this school didn't seem like a top-tier

institution for activities like baseball and ballet, the clubs here certainly looked great.

"These facilities are significantly more substantial than ordinary schools. Look, they even have O_2 chambers. The equipment here is so luxurious, it puts the professionals' stuff to shame. Oh, but it looks like they *don't* have a karate club after all."

"I see."

"What? Were you interested in karate or something?" I asked.

"No, not particularly."

"It seems like it'll be hard for newcomers to get into the athletic clubs," I said. "Even if a first year managed to break in, they still might just be a benchwarmer forever. I can't think that would be much fun."

Everything around here seemed far too orderly.

"Wouldn't that depend on one's efforts, though? Surely by training for one or two years, anyone could get in and play."

Training, huh? I didn't think I'd be able to put in that amount of effort, no matter how desperate I was.

"I didn't realize that the concept of training even existed for someone who always avoided trouble, like you."

"What exactly does me not liking trouble have to do with that?" I asked.

"Would you agree that someone who avoids trouble also avoids unnecessary manual labor? You said it first. You should keep to your word, I think."

"I didn't really think about it that deeply."

"If you keep acting so non-committal, you're never going to be able to make any friends," she said.

"You wound me, Horikita."

"Thank you all for waiting, first-year students. We will now begin the club fair. A representative from each club will explain their function. My name is Tachibana, the student council secretary and the club fair's organizer. It's nice to meet you all."

After Tachibana delivered the opening remarks, representatives from each club quickly lined up on a stage. It was quite a diverse crowd. The club representatives included everything from burly athletes in judo uniforms to students dressed in beautiful kimonos.

"Hey, if you want to get a fresh start, why not try joining an athletic club? The judo club looks good, doesn't it? That upperclassman looks kind, and I'm sure he'd encourage you."

"What do you mean 'kind'?! He looks like a gorilla! He'll kill me for sure!" I snapped.

"He'll probably talk passionately about how easy judo is."

"Cut it out!"

Sheesh. I'd thought that we were having a decent conversation, but she'd done nothing but stick it to me.

"Even if I wanted to join, the athletic clubs all look really intimidating. I get the impression they don't accept beginners."

"Beginners should be welcomed. The more members a club has, the more money they receive from the school. That's how they're able to get better training equipment."

"Sounds like they're using the beginners for the money..."

"It would be ideal to gather many new members as a budgetary increase, and then simply to bench them the rest of the time, like phantom members. If you were skilled at manipulation, that is."

"What an unpleasant world... You have a pretty strange way of thinking," I muttered.

A girl dressed in archery gear stepped onto the stage. "Hello, my name is Hashigaki, the captain of the archery club. Many students may be under the impression that archery is an old-fashioned, simple activity, but it is actually a fun and rewarding sport. We welcome beginners with open arms. If you're interested, please consider joining."

"Hey, look, they seem to be welcoming newcomers. Why don't you try joining? In order to increase their budget, that is," I said.

"I hate the idea of joining a club solely for that reason! Besides, athletic clubs are just gatherings of people with nothing better to do. Also, I probably wouldn't have fun if I didn't know anyone there. I'd end up quitting in the blink of an eye."

"Isn't that simply your twisted personality talking?"

"Yeah, you're absolutely right. But athletic clubs are a no-go."

I thought about joining a nice, calm, quiet club.

"Tch!"

As the seniors introduced their respective clubs one after the other, I saw Horikita suddenly tense. She looked at the stage, her face pale.

"What's the matter?"

She didn't even seem to notice me anymore. I followed her line of sight to the stage, but I didn't find anything of note there. Just the representative of the school baseball team, dressed in uniform, giving his introduction. Had she fallen in love with him at first sight? No, I doubted it. Surprise? Disgust? Or maybe she was overjoyed? To be honest, Horikita's expression was complex and hard to read.

"Horikita, what's the matter?"

"............"

It was like she couldn't hear my voice. She kept staring

intently at the stage. I decided that I'd stop talking to her and simply wait for an explanation. The baseball team's introduction wasn't any more compelling than the others. All things considered, the greeting was rather stock, no matter their schedule, appeal, or how welcoming they were to newcomers.

It wasn't just the baseball club. Nearly every club's introduction was similarly ordinary. If anything surprised me about the fair, it was the substantial number of minor liberal arts-related clubs and organizations, such as the tea ceremony club or the calligraphy club. Also, I was surprised that you only needed a minimum of three people in order to form a new club.

Every time one club finished and the next sprang up, the first-year students talked among themselves about what they thought. I noticed that the gymnasium's atmosphere was rather lively. Each club's representatives, including their supervising instructors, continued to explain their organizations to the unruly first-year students without a hint of displeasure. Perhaps they were just that desperate for more members, even if their ranks only increased by one.

As the upperclassmen finished their introductions, they walked off the stage and headed toward an area where some plain tables had been set up. Probably a reception area designed to accept new members. Eventually, everyone walked off until only one person remained. Everyone focused their attention upon him, and I realized that Horikita had been staring at that specific person this whole time.

He appeared to be about 170 centimeters in height, so he wasn't very tall. He was slender, with sleek black hair. He wore sharp glasses and had a piercing, calculating gaze. Standing in front of the microphone, he calmly looked around at the first-year students. What was his club, and what in the world was he going to say? My interest had been piqued.

Unfortunately, my expectations were dashed immediately. He didn't say a single word. Maybe he was drawing a blank? Or perhaps he was so nervous that he couldn't speak?

"Do your best!"

"Did you forget to bring your notecards?"

"Ha ha ha ha ha!"

The first-year students hurled comments at him. However, the upperclassman stood on the stage calmly, without trembling. The laughter and comments didn't seem to faze him. When the laughter had reached a crescendo, it suddenly died. He wore an apathetic expression.

"What's with this guy?" remarked an astonished student. The gymnasium buzzed with people talking, yet the boy on the stage still did not move. He simply stood there, quiet and motionless, staring fixedly at the crowd. Horikita stared back at the student with an intense gaze, not breaking her line of sight even for a second.

The relaxed atmosphere gradually changed, and things took an unexpected turn. It was as if some chemical reaction had taken place. An unbelievably tense, quiet mood gripped the entire gymnasium. Even though no orders had been given, the silence was so terrible that it seemed to have gagged everyone. Not a single student looked able to open his or her mouth. The silence continued for about thirty seconds or so...

Then, the student started his speech, slowly scanning the crowd.

"I'm the student council president. My name is Horikita Manabu," he said.

Horikita? I glanced at the Horikita next to me. Perhaps they just happened to have the same surname. Or, maybe...

"The student council is looking to recruit potential candidates among the first-year students to replace the graduating third years. Although no special qualifications are required for candidacy, we humbly ask that those considering application not be involved in other club activities. We generally do not accept students involved elsewhere."

He spoke in a soft tone, but the tension around us was so thick it felt like you could cut it with a knife. He had managed to silence over a hundred new students in that spacious gymnasium. Of course, it wasn't his position as student council president that granted him this deference. That was simply Horikita Manabu's power. His presence dominated everyone around him.

"Furthermore, we in the student council do not wish to appoint anyone who possesses a naive outlook. Not only would such a person not be elected, he or she would sully the sanctity of this school. It is the student council's right and duty to enforce and amend the rules, but the school expects more than that. We gladly welcome those of you who understand this."

He didn't pause even once during his eloquent speech. Immediately after finishing, he hopped off the stage and left the gymnasium. None of the first-year students could utter a single word as we watched him go. We didn't know what would've happened if we'd tried to talk. Everyone in the room shared the same thought, apparently.

"Thank you all for coming. The club fair has ended. We will now open the reception area to anyone interested in signing up. Also, registration will be open until the end of April, so if any student wishes to join at a later date, we ask that you please bring the application form directly to the club you wish to join."

Thanks to the laid-back organizer, the tension in the air dissipated. Afterward, the third-year students who'd introduced their respective clubs started taking applications.

"............"

Horikita remained still as a statue, giving no sign she would budge.

"Hey, what's wrong?" I asked.

Horikita didn't answer. It was like my words didn't even reach her ears.

"Yo, Ayanokouji. You came, huh?"

As I was lost in thought, someone called out to me. Sudou. Our classmates Ike and Yamauchi were also with him.

"Oh, hey, you three. Looks like you guys are getting along well, huh?" I responded, feeling a bit envious of Sudou.

"So, you joined a club, too?"

"Oh, no, I just came to check things out. Wait, 'too'? Did *you* join a club, Sudou?"

"Yeah. I've been playing basketball ever since elementary school. I thought I'd join the team here."

I had thought he was athletic, judging from his physique. Basketball was clearly his game.

"What about you two?"

"We just came because we felt it might be fun, you know? Besides, we thought we might have a fateful encounter afterward," Ike said.

"What do you mean, 'fateful encounter'?"

I wanted Ike to explain his rather odd-sounding goal. He crossed his arms and responded proudly, "I want to get my first girlfriend in Class D. That's my goal. That's why I'm keeping my eyes open for an encounter."

Apparently, Ike considered having a girlfriend to be of the utmost priority.

"Also, I have to say, that student council president was something else. He was so imposing. I got the feeling he ruled the place, you know?" he said.

"I know, right? He made everyone shut up without saying a word. That kinda stuff is impossible," I replied.

"Yeah. Oh, by the way, I made a group chat for the guys yesterday." Ike took out his phone. "Do you want to join in, too? It's pretty handy."

"Huh? Me? Is that okay?" I asked.

"Of course it's okay. We're all in Class D together, after all."

That was a rather unexpected proposal. I was happy to be invited to the group chat. Finally, I'd found the perfect chance to make friends! However, when I took out

my cell phone to exchange contact information, Horikita disappeared into the crowd. Worried about her, I stopped what I was doing.

"What's wrong?" Ike asked.

"Oh, nothing. You ready?"

I returned to my phone and exchanged contact information with Ike and the other guys. Horikita was free to do whatever she wanted, and I didn't have the right to stop her. For a moment, I'd felt like following her, but in the end I decided not to.

4 LADIES AND GENTLEMEN, THANK YOU FOR WAITING

"**G**OOD MORNING, Yamauchi!"

"Good morning, Ike!"

Arriving to class, Ike wore a broad grin as he called out to Yamauchi. It was rather unusual for them to get here so early. It'd been one week since the entrance ceremony, and Ike and Yamauchi would always make it to class right before the bell rang.

"Whew, man! I was looking forward to today so much that I barely slept last night!"

"Ah ha ha! This school is just the best! I can't believe that it's almost time for swimming! And when I say swimming, I mean girls. And when I say girls, I mean girls in school swimsuits!"

It was true that the swimming classes were co-ed. In other words, that meant that Horikita, Kushida, and all of the other girls would be...showing off a lot of skin. The girls backed away from Ike and Yamauchi's rabid excitement. I, on the other hand, sat in my chair, isolated and alone. I couldn't do so forever. I had to proactively work at joining a group of friends.

Fortunately, their conversation had ended, so I stood up. However, just then...

"Hey, Professor! Come here for a sec!"

"Uh, you called?"

A chubby boy, apparently nicknamed "The Professor," approached them slowly. If I remembered correctly, his name was Sotomura or something like that.

"Professor, can you record the girls wearing their swimsuits for us?" Ike asked.

"Leave it to me. I'll pretend to be sick so that I can skip class and observe."

"*Record?* What are you planning?" I asked.

"The Professor is going to rank the girls' breast sizes for us. If we're lucky, he'll get some pictures with his phone."

"Hey, hey." Sudou visibly drew back in response to Ike's plan. If the girls found out about it, the consequences would be severe. However, despite the content of the conversation, I was jealous of their easy banter. Having friends had to be nice. I wanted friends, too.

"Pathetic," a familiar voice said.

"So, you're here, too, huh, Horikita?"

"I just arrived while you were looking at those boys over there. You didn't notice me. If you want to be their friend, why not try just talking to them?" she asked.

"Shut up and leave me alone already. If I could just do it, I wouldn't be agonizing over it."

"From what I've seen, you don't seem to be unsociable or lacking in communication skills, though."

"There are a lot of reasons why I can't do it. So far, you're the only person I've been able to talk to, Horikita."

Even though I'd exchanged contact information with Ike and the others, I still hadn't been able to actually hold a conversation with them yet.

"Wait just a minute. I already warned you not to, but you wouldn't be thinking of me as your friend, would you?" said Horikita. She took a few steps away from me, as if in disgust.

"It's fine. No matter how low I sink, I'd never dream of being your friend," I replied.

"I see. I feel a little relieved."

I wondered just how much she hated having friends.

"Hey, Ayanokouji!" Ike called my name. When I looked up, I saw him beaming at me.

"Wh-what is it?" I asked.

I stood, stuttering as I did so. Horikita no longer

showed any interest in me. A chance to enter into a new group of friends had suddenly fallen into my lap.

"To tell you the truth, we're taking bets on the girls' chest sizes."

"We've come up with some probabilities."

The Professor took out a tablet and opened a spreadsheet. The names of all the girls in our class were displayed. There were numbers listed as well. I honestly had no interest in gambling, but I couldn't let this opportunity go to waste.

"Umm. So, is it okay if I join you?" I asked.

"Yeah! Come on, do it. Do it!"

As of right now, Hasebe was the likeliest contender for the biggest breasts in the class. The odds sat at one to eight I hadn't heard most of the names before. I couldn't even remember my classmates' names. This was too awful.

"This is way more elaborate than I would have thought. Aren't you observing them a little too closely?"

"Come on. We're men, aren't we? Men have only two things constantly on their minds: tits and ass!"

Even if that were true, he really had no filter whatsoever. By the way, Horikita was ranked lowest. If you managed to win the bet, that was over thirty times your wager back. Well, in terms of breast size, it was obvious who would win and who would lose. Horikita had no chance.

"So, what's your wager? It's 1000 points to join."

"I see..."

I clearly lacked information. Scanning the list, I realized that not only did I not know the breast sizes of half the people here, I didn't even know the names and faces of most the girls. Actually, aside from Horikita and Kushida, I couldn't recall hearing about anyone else. Kushida seemed to have fairly large breasts, but not large enough to take first place.

"Come on, play with us. It's no fun if there're only a few people betting, you know?"

"I'll do it!"

"Me too, me too!"

"I have experience scouting girls and checking out their tits!"

While I considered the offer, boys crawled out of the woodwork around me, getting blatantly excited over the size of the girls' breasts. The girls in the classroom looked at us like we were dirt.

"I'll join, too. By the way, my money's on Sakura," Yamauchi chimed in. Sakura was a somewhat plain girl who wore glasses, but because I'd barely talked to anyone, I honestly didn't know that much about her. While it looked like he was pondering something, Yamauchi tapped the Professor and Ike on the shoulders and whispered something to them.

"I'm only telling you guys about this. The truth is, I actually confessed to Sakura."

"What?! S-seriously?!" Ike was the most surprised and flustered by this. Had his goal to become the first guy in class to snag a girlfriend fallen through?

"Yeah, seriously. But keep this on the down low. It's just between us, okay? I mean, I thought she was really plain at first, but then I saw her wearing regular clothes. She was *huge*, man."

"You doofus. If she's not cute, you shouldn't ask her out, even if she's got huge tits. I wouldn't date anyone unless they were in the same league as Kushida or Hasebe. I'm not interested in such a Plain Jane."

He spoke harshly because no one else was around. I wondered how much I believed Yamauchi when he said that he'd asked Sakura out. I had my doubts. In the end, I decided to place my bet on the girl with the highest odds.

4.1

"ALL RIGHT! The pool!"

After lunch had ended, it was finally time for swim class. Finally, the moment Ike and the others had so desperately been waiting for. Without even trying to hide his excitement, Ike leapt up and headed with the others toward the indoor pool. I followed behind them in what I thought was a stealthy manner.

"Come on, let's go together, Ayanokouji!"

"Huh? O-okay."

I'd hesitated somewhat upon receiving Ike's invitation, but I hurried to join and followed them to the locker room. Sudou promptly removed his uniform and started to change, showing off his physique. He'd built up his body through his years of basketball playing. Even in comparison with the other students, he was clearly in incredible shape. While the others wrapped themselves in bath towels, Sudou unabashedly wore only his underwear. He stood there, semi-nude, and took his swimsuit out of his bag. I couldn't keep myself from blurting something out.

"Sudou, you're pretty bold. Aren't you nervous being around other people?"

"In sports, you can't get flustered every time you have to change. If you act all shifty, it'll have the opposite effect. You become the center of attention."

He could say that again. In these sorts of places, sneaky guys got mocked.

"All right, I'm going on ahead."

A moment later, Sudou left the locker room. I quickly finished changing as well.

Upon seeing the fifty-meter pool, Ike cried out, "Whoa, this school is something else! It's even better than the city pool, don't you think?" The water was clear and beautiful, and because it was indoors, we didn't have to worry about the weather. The perfect environment.

"What about the girls? Aren't they here yet?"

Ike looked around, sniffing the air like a dog.

"They take a while to change, so they're probably not ready," I said.

"Hey, I wonder would what happen if I just suddenly jumped into the girls' locker room?" Ike said.

"They'd gang up on you, beat the crap out of you, and then file charges, probably."

"Don't give me such a realistic, deadpan answer and ruin my fun!" Ike began to tremble with fright as he played that scenario in his head.

"If the girls sense you staring at them in their swimsuits, they'll probably hate you."

"Come on, like there's a guy out there who *wouldn't* stare! Agh. What am I gonna do if I get a boner?"

If that happened, they'd probably hate Ike from that moment all the way until the day of our graduation. Wait a second, what was happening? Had I started talking naturally to Ike and the others? Even though until this morning I hadn't been able to join their group, I suddenly had my foot in the door, so to speak. This was the moment for a new friendship to be born.

"Wow! It's so spacious! It's so much bigger than the pool at my junior high school."

A few minutes after the boys had arrived, a girl's voice could be heard.

"A-are they here?!"

Ike looked ready to strike. If you were that obvious about it, the girls were bound to hate you. Even so, I was curious, too. I mostly wondered about Hasebe and Kushida, but a little about Horikita as well. I was particularly interested in Hasebe, the girl rumored to have the biggest tits in class. I didn't think there'd be any harm in taking a little peek. However, it turned out that all of the boys' wishes were dashed by an unexpected turn of events.

"Hasebe isn't here! Wh-what's going on, Professor?!" Ike cried.

The Professor, who had been watching the class, was now in a panic. Standing on the second-floor observation deck, he scanned the room. Ike and the others also looked around. At this height, the Professor's beady, bespectacled eyes should have spotted his prey instantly. However...

He couldn't find the girls anywhere. He looked to his right and left, as if in disbelief. Could they still be changing? Or could...

"B-behind you, Professor!"

"What?!"

Ike pointed and shouted. The situation had become clear. Hasebe stood behind the Professor on the observation deck. One by one, the rest of the girls appeared, until they'd all emerged onto the second floor. Sakura was among them.

"Wh-what's going on? How did this happen?"

Ike slumped to the ground and buried his face in his

hands, shaken by this unbelievable turn of events. Hasebe seemed to be self-conscious about being considered a beautiful girl. Furthermore, she seemed to dislike getting curious looks from the boys. She was not amused at their attempts to ogle.

"Aw, but I thought I'd get to see big tits! Big tits! I thought this was my chance!"

Ike appeared to be contemplating suicide. His wails of agony reached Hasebe.

"Gross," the girls muttered among themselves. Ike was being far too obvious, so it wasn't surprising that the girls hated him...

"Ike, don't be sad! Come on, there are still tons of girls out there for us!" Yamauchi said.

"Y-yeah, that's right. You got a point. I can't get down in the dumps now!" Ike cried.

"Bro!" Yamauchi and Ike reaffirmed their manly bond of friendship, clasping their hands together.

"What are you two doing? That looks like fun."

"K-K-Kushida-chan?!"

Kushida showed up between the two of them. She was clad in her school-issued swimwear, which nicely showed off her voluptuous figure. In an instant, nearly all of the boys' eyes were glued to Kushida's body. She must have been a D or E cup. I didn't know for sure, but

I estimated. She was a lot bigger than I'd thought. Her butt and thighs were also more voluptuous than I had pictured, which was strangely captivating. However, all of us boys quickly averted our gaze.

Ah, the weather was so nice today... World peace truly was wonderful.

Once the inevitable physiological reaction kicked in, it was quite a terrible shock.

"Why the pained expression?" Horikita examined my face closely, with a suspicious look.

"I'm currently in the midst of an internal battle," I replied.

Horikita was in a school swimsuit. How to put it? Yeah. She looked good. Not bad at all. But if I stared, it was likely that something bad would result. I thought it best to grin and bear it until I calmed down.

"............"

For some reason, Horikita was checking me out all over.

"Ayanokouji-kun, do you exercise?" she asked.

"Huh? No, not really. I'm not particularly proud of this, but in middle school I was the kid who never had any after-school plans."

"Well, you say that, but...judging from the development of your forearms and your back muscles, you seem above average."

"I guess my parents blessed me with good genes?"

"I don't think that's the only reason."

"Jeez, what's with you? Do you have a muscle fetish or something? Is that it?"

"I suppose if you deny it that much, I have to believe you..."

She appeared somewhat dissatisfied. I guessed that Horikita had a rather discerning eye and enjoyed using it.

"Are you a good swimmer, Horikita-san?"

Although Horikita gave a slightly puzzled look in response to Kushida's question, she quietly answered. "I wouldn't say I'm particularly good or bad at it."

"I was really bad at swimming when I was in junior high. But I gave it my all and practiced really hard, and now I think I've gotten better," Kushida said.

"I see." Horikita gave a disinterested response and backed away slightly, clearly signaling that she didn't want to continue the conversation further.

"All right, everyone, line up!"

A macho-looking middle-aged man, the kind of guy who apparently devoted himself to sports, gathered everyone together and started the class. He looked like a PE teacher, but also seemed like the kind of guy who was attractive to men and women alike.

"There are sixteen of you, huh? I thought there would've been more, but this is all right."

Clearly, some of the students in that count had ditched class, but it didn't appear to frustrate him.

"After you warm up, I want to see what you can really do. Swim for me," the coach said.

"Excuse me, sir. I can't really swim, though..."

A lone boy sheepishly raised his hand and spoke up.

"Since you have me as your teacher, you'll be swimming by summertime. Don't worry about a thing."

"Well, we don't really need to force ourselves to swim, do we? It's not like we're going to the beach or anything."

"No way. I don't mind at all if you're bad at swimming now, but I'll make sure you guys are winners in the end. Besides, being able to swim will definitely come in handy later in life. Definitely."

Swimming would definitely come in handy? Well, I suppose knowing how to swim would be convenient. However, hearing a teacher say something like that made me feel uncomfortable. Though, he probably just wanted to keep the students from sinking like rocks.

Everyone started their warm-up exercises. Ike kept peeking at the girls. The teacher asked us to swim for about fifty meters. Students who could not swim were allowed to touch the bottom of the pool with their feet. I hadn't been in a pool since last summer. The water must have been temperature-controlled, because I didn't feel chilled when I entered and adjusted right away. After getting in, I started to swim lightly.

After fifty meters, I waited for everyone else to finish.

"He he he, that was an easy win for me. Did you all see my super swimming skills?" Ike crowed.

He'd swum expertly, and now got out of the pool with a smug, self-satisfied grin. *No, Ike, your performance wasn't really that different from anyone else's.*

"Well, it looks like everyone can swim, for the most part."

"Of course, sir. Back in junior high, people called me 'the flying fish,' you know."

"I see. In that case, I'll have you start competing against each other. We'll separate groups by gender. Fifty-meter freestyle."

"C-compete?! Are you serious?" Ike cried.

"I'll give out a special bonus to the first-place winner: 5000 points. The student who comes in last place, however, will have to take supplementary lessons. Get ready."

The skilled swimmers cheered with joy, while the less confident students groaned.

"Because we don't have very many girls, I'll split you into two groups of five people, and the student with the fastest overall time will be the winner. As for the boys, I'll look at the top five finishing times and then move on to a final round."

I'd never imagined that the school would award points as a prize. Perhaps this was a way to light a fire under the students. Rather well thought out, I had to say. Excluding the observers and the one student who couldn't swim, there were sixteen boys and ten girls competing. The girls started first, while the boys sat on the sidelines, filled with excitement as they cheered... no, as they *assessed* the girls.

"Kushida-chan, Kushida-chan, Kushida-chan, Kushida-chan, Kushida-chan. Haaaaaaa..."

It looked like Kushida had completely entranced Ike.

"You're scaring everyone, Ike, settle down," I mumbled.

"B-but, Kushida-chan is so goddamn cute, isn't she? And her breasts are pretty big, too!"

Kushida immediately dominated the boys' attention. Would any of the other girls catch up to her? If you focused on her face alone, Horikita could definitely have been in the top tier, but because she loathed social interaction so much, her popularity had dipped. Despite that, many of the boys thought she looked great, so she got plenty of cheers at the starting line.

"Everyone, burn these images into your mind! Remember the fap material you see here today!" Ike cried.

"Yeah!" everyone shouted.

Somehow, swimming had strengthened the boys' bond. The only exception was Hirata, who seemed to avoid looking at the girls. The whistle blew, and five of the girls dove into the water. Horikita was in the second lane. She took the lead at the beginning of the race and kept her distance from the others, maintaining her position at the front of the pack. She swam confidently, effortlessly covering the fifty meters.

"Wow! Awesome, Horikita!"

Her time was approximately twenty-eight seconds. She was pretty fast. Horikita slowly got out of the pool and went to the side, not even appearing out of breath. To the boys, results were of secondary importance. Their eyes were glued to the girls' jiggling butts. I stared at Horikita, too. Was it because we were getting along? Well, she *was* a girl. There was something there, I thought. Yeah.

After that came the second race. Kushida, the most popular girl, was in the fourth lane. The boys cheered for her, smiling and waving.

"Whoo!"

Wow, those guys were really riled up. Some even tried to sneakily cover their crotches. During our introductions, Kushida had announced that she wanted to make friends with everyone in class. It looked like her wish had already pretty much come true. It wasn't just the boys, either; girls were around her constantly, too, chatting away happily. Kushida had an air that attracted other people.

The second race began. The contest ended up being rather one-sided. A girl named Onodera, who had been on swim teams before, won by a mile. She finished with a time of about twenty-six seconds, netting her the win. Kushida finished at about thirty-one seconds, which was a fairly good time, but only resulted in her getting fourth place. I went over to the side of the pool to talk with Horikita.

"You were so close. Second place, I mean. I guess that those guys on the swim team were really tough, huh?"

"I don't mind whether I win or lose. Enough about me. Are you feeling confident in yourself?" she asked.

"Oh, definitely. I just can't come in last."

"That's not really something to take pride in. I thought boys were supposed to be fixated on winning and losing."

"I don't like competing against people. I just like avoiding trouble, after all," I said.

I'd given up on trying to get first place from the very beginning. All I wanted was to avoid taking those supplementary lessons. I was assigned my spot and placed in the second lane, while Sudou was in the first, right next to me. It was impossible to even hope to match Sudou's pace, so I didn't plan to try. I aimed to come in somewhere in the middle, just not last. With that in mind, the race started, and we dove in.

Sudou finished the fifty-meter race with incredible speed. The boys and girls cheered in admiration.

"Wow, you're amazing, Sudou. You finished the race in twenty-five seconds!" they cried.

I, on the other hand, finished in thirty-six seconds. It looked like I got tenth place. All right, no supplementary lessons for me.

"Sudou, won't you consider joining the swim team? If you practice, you could probably win at competitions!"

"Basketball is my only sport. Swimming's just for fun." Sudou, who hadn't even broken a sweat, calmly got out of the pool.

"Oh, wow, he has absolutely outstanding motor skills."

Ike, feeling envious, elbowed Sudou.

"Kya!"

A girl let out a joyful scream as Hirata took his starting position. Whereas Sudou's body had attracted the boys' admiration, Hirata's body attracted the girls. He was slender, but also well built. You could say he was a macho pretty boy. After hearing the girls' delighted squeals for Hirata, Ike spat in response. Sudou didn't seem very amused either, and shot Hirata a glare.

"I'm going to blow you out of the water. I'll use all of my power," he growled.

Didn't he say that he swam just for *fun*?

After the teacher blew the whistle, Hirata dove into the pool with beautiful form. Every time Hirata's arms cut through the water, the girls cheered by the side of the pool. His form was effortlessly cool.

"He's surprisingly fast," Sudou commented. It was certainly true that Hirata swam fast. There was no doubt that he'd shot ahead of the four other boys who were competing with him. This, of course, prompted more shrieks from the girls. Hirata didn't fail to live up to our expectations: He came in first place. Deafening cheers reverberated throughout the room.

"Sensei, what was his time?" asked Ike, impatiently.

"Hirata's time was...26.13 seconds."

"All right. You can do it, Sudou. You can definitely win against him! Bring down the hammer of justice!"

"Leave it to me. I'll demolish him and his popularity..."

Ike's encouragement had Sudou all fired up, but even if Hirata lost, it wasn't likely that his popularity would drop.

"Hirata-kun, you were so cool! You're not just good at soccer, you're really good at swimming!" one girl cried.

"You think so? Thank you!" he said.

"Hey, why are you ogling Hirata-kun like that?" another girl said.

"Huh? *I'm* 'ogling'?!"

There was an indignant squeal.

Hirata's immense popularity was unbelievably frustrating.

"Come on, girls, knock it off. Please don't fight over me. I belong to everyone. I want to be everyone's friend. Besides, what if someone who's better at swimming comes along?"

Kouenji mistakenly seemed to assume that the cheers were for him. He put on a refreshing smile and then planted his feet by the starting line.

"Hey. Uh, why is Kouenji wearing a speedo?"

"Wh-what?"

Although the school allowed such tight swimwear, Kouenji was the only one in our class wearing it. The briefs drew attention to his crotch, and the girls all looked away. However, in the third race, all eyes were on Kouenji. The stance he took at the starting line was just like an athlete's. His posture wasn't the only impressive thing, either. He looked to be in even better physical shape than Sudou. Sudou and all of the other boys in class held their breath as they attentively focused on Kouenji.

"I'm not particularly interested in winning or losing... but I don't like losing," said Sudou, to no one in particular.

As the whistle blew, Kouenji dove into the pool with textbook form.

"Whoa! Wow!"

Sudou gave a surprised shout in response to Kouenji's unexpectedly aggressive swimming. Hirata also stared in apparent amazement. Kouenji splashed fiercely as he swam, but it didn't slow his incredible speed. He was unquestionably faster than Sudou. After checking the time, the teacher reflexively looked at his stopwatch twice.

"23.22 seconds."

"My abdominal muscles, back muscles, and psoas major muscle seem to be in good shape, as usual. Not a bad performance," Kouenji said.

After getting out of the pool, he smirked and swept his hair up. He wasn't short of breath at all. It was as if he hadn't even swum in the first place.

"I'm fired up!" Sudou didn't want to lose, so his competitive spirit flared. To be honest, Sudou was the only one who had any chance of winning against Kouenji. The final round was more like a one-on-one match between the two of them.

"I'm really looking forward to this. Both Kouejin-kun and Sudou-kun are so fast," Kushida said.

"A-ah, yeah."

Standing beside a swimsuit-clad beauty, I'd entered a state of emergency, my heart pounding in my chest.

"Hmm? What's the matter? Your face looks red for

some reason. Are you not feeling well, by chance?" she asked.

"Oh, no, no, that's not it at all..."

"Well, even so, something seems unusual. Why do we have swimming classes in April, anyway?"

"Because we have such an incredible indoor pool. Oh, yeah, that reminds me... You were pretty fast, Kushida. I can't believe that you weren't very good at swimming in junior high."

"You're much faster than average, too, Ayanokouji-kun."

"Nah, I'm pretty average. I don't really like to exercise."

"Is that so? But you look like a really manly guy, Ayanokouji-kun. Even though you're so slim, I could say that you're even better built than Sudou, and he plays basketball."

Kushida examined my body in shock and awe, as if she were thinking "*Really? Really?*" I was ten times more nervous now than when Horikita had stared at me.

"I was just born naturally muscular. There's no special reason behind it. To tell you the truth, I'm not in any clubs."

The conversation revolved around good health. I felt somewhat nervous, but strangely satisfied as well. We continued in this way for a while; I'd wanted to talk with Kushida alone.

"Wow, Kouenji is amazing. I thought that Sudou would have won in a landslide... What the heck is going on, Ayanokouji?" Ike asked.

It looked like Kouenji had beaten Sudou by about a five-meter lead in the final round. After he'd finished observing the race, Ike zeroed in on me, his face like a demon's.

"Uh, nothing really. I didn't do anything," I replied.

"That's not what I'm talking about!"

He wrapped his arms around my shoulders and whispered in my ear.

"I'm aiming for Kushida-chan. Don't get in the way!"

I didn't exactly plan to get in the way, but his goal was slightly unrealistic. I didn't think Kushida was the type who'd stoop to being with someone like Ike. Of course, I didn't think she'd get with me, either.

CLASSROOM OF
THE ELITE

5 ▸ FRIENDS

"**K**IKYOU-CHAN, do you want to stop by a café on our way back today?"

"Sure, let's go! Oh, but wait just a minute, okay? I want to invite one more person."

Kushida headed toward Horikita, who was putting her textbook into her bag. "Horikita-san, would you like to come with us to a café today?" She asked.

"Not interested." Horikita threw Kushida's invitation back in her face, with no room for ambiguity. *Couldn't you just lie and say you were planning to go shopping, or that you were waiting for a friend?* Despite the harsh rejection, Kushida kept smiling.

This wasn't a particularly unusual scene. Ever since the entrance ceremony, Kushida had regularly tried to invite Horikita to do fun things with her. I thought it would be nice for Horikita to accept an invitation at least once in a while, but perhaps that was just a bystander's selfish interpretation. No one had ever met with anything but rejection when they'd tried to invite Horikita.

"I see. Well then, I'll try inviting you again another time."

"Wait, Kushida-san." Surprisingly, Horikita called out to Kushida. Had she finally given in? "Don't invite me again. It's a bother," said Horikita coldly.

However, Kushida didn't appear saddened. Instead, she smiled as she answered, "I'll invite you again."

Kushida then ran back to join her friends, and they left the hall.

"Kikyou-chan, just stop inviting Horikita-san. I hate her—"

Just before the door closed, I faintly heard one of the other girl's words. Horikita, who was right next to me, must have heard as well, but she gave no indication that she cared.

"You won't try to invite me places, will you?" she asked.

"Nope. I understand your personality well enough. It's pointless to even try."

"I'm relieved to hear that."

After Horikita finished getting ready, she walked out of the classroom by herself. I absentmindedly stuck around for a little while, but soon grew bored and got up. *Time to go home*, I thought.

"Ayanokouji-kun, do you have a moment?"

Hirata, who was still hanging around, called out to me when I passed by. Unbothered, I responded to him softly. It was unusual for Hirata to notice me.

"It's about Horikita-san, actually. I was wondering if something was wrong. Some of the girls were talking about it earlier. Horikita always seems to be alone."

Maybe it wasn't Kushida especially. Perhaps Horikita was just the kind of person who strongly disliked company.

"Could you possibly tell her to try to get along with people a little?"

"Well, that's up to the individual, isn't it? Besides, Horikita isn't really making trouble for anyone else," I replied.

"You're right, of course. However, many people have voiced their concerns about it. I absolutely do not want any bullying in our class."

Bullying? Such talk seemed premature, but perhaps there were signs of it. Was he warning me, then? Hirata looked at me with the purest of intentions.

"Well, I think it'd be better for you to tell her directly rather than talk to me, Hirata," I said.

"You have a point. Sorry for bringing it up."

Horikita was always alone, day after day. If this continued, within a month she'd be like a tumor in our class.
However, this was Horikita's personal problem and something I probably shouldn't involve myself with.

5.1

AFTER LEAVING CLASS, I went straight toward the dormitory. Kushida, who was supposed to have left with a friend earlier, appeared to be waiting for someone while leaning up against the wall. Noticing me, she smiled like always.

"I'm so glad! I was waiting for you, Ayanokouji-kun. There's something I wanted to talk to you about. Do you have a minute?" she asked.

"Yeah, sure..."

She couldn't be confessing her feelings for me, could she? Nah, there was about a 1 percent chance of something like that.

"I'll just ask you outright. Ayanokouji-kun, have you seen Horikita-san smile even once?"

"Huh? No, not that I can remember."

Apparently, Kushida had come to talk about Horikita again. Thinking back, I didn't recall ever seeing Horikita smile once. Kushida took my hand in hers, closing the distance between us. Did she smell of flowers? I breathed in an extremely pleasant scent.

"You know, I...I want to become friends with Horikita-san," she said.

"I think she guesses your feelings. At first, a lot of people tried reaching out to her, but now you're the only one."

"You seem to know Horikita-san pretty well, Ayanokouji-kun."

"It's not like I'm watching her or anything, it's just that you tend to learn a lot about the person who sits next to you."

Girls were girls, after all, and they'd been really eager to form groups since the first day of school. They were also more aware of cliques and social circles than guys, and in this class of about twenty people, four held the most influence. You could claim they put up a façade, that they weren't genuinely being themselves.

However, Kushida was the exception. She definitely held favor within each group, but more than that, she was tremendously popular with everyone. She was persistently warm and gentle toward Horikita, as part of her continued efforts to become her friend. That wasn't something an ordinary student could do. That was probably why everyone adored her.

Plus, she was really cute.

Cuteness makes everything better.

"Didn't Horikita already warn you not to try again? I don't know what you can say to her next time," I said.

I knew that Horikita wasn't the type to mince words. If approached, she would probably respond harshly. To be honest, I didn't want to see Kushida hurt.

"Won't you...help me?" she asked.

"Uh..."

I didn't answer right away. Normally, I would immediately agree to such a cute girl's demands. However, since I was the type to avoid trouble, I couldn't answer her. I didn't want to see Horikita hurt Kushida by saying something merciless. I thought I'd turn her down to avoid any later heartbreak.

"I understand how you feel, Kushida, but..."

"So that means...you can't?"

Cute + Pleading + Upturned Eyes = Lethal.

"Well, I guess I don't have a choice. Just this once, okay?"

"Really?! Oh, thank you, Ayanokouji-kun!" she cried. Kushida's face lit up.

She was cute. Even though I'd agreed to help her, I was

still the kind of person who preferred to remain in the background. I shouldn't do anything reckless.

"So, what exactly are we going to do? Even if you say you want to be friends with her, it's not that simple."

Personally, I wasn't equipped to know how to make friends.

"You're probably right... Well, first I think we should try to make Horikita-san smile," Kushida said.

"Make her smile, huh?"

Smiling means letting your guard down in front of another person, even if just a little. Such a relationship could most likely be referred to as friendship. Kushida seemed to understand people well, especially when it came to making them smile.

"Do you have an idea how?" I asked.

"Well, I thought *you* could help me think of something, Ayanokouji-kun." She giggled sheepishly and lightly smacked her own head. If she were an ugly girl, I would have been totally turned off, but Kushida made it charming.

"Smile, huh?" So, because Kushida had asked, I was going to help her make Horikita smile. Was such a thing possible? I wondered. I doubted it.

"Well, anyway, after class, I'm going to try inviting Horikita out again. If we wind up back at the dorms, though, I'll have no idea what to do. Is there any place that she wants to go to?"

"Ah. Well then, how about Palate? I've gone to Palate often, and Horikita might have overheard us talking about it before."

Palate was one of the most popular cafés on campus. I had heard about Kushida and the other girls going there often after class. And if I'd heard about it, then Horikita must have also been aware.

"How about if you two went to Palate and ordered, and then 'bumped' into me by chance? Would that work?"

"Probably not. I think that might be expecting a little too much. What if your friends helped out, Kushida?"

The instant Horikita noticed Kushida's presence, she would probably get up and leave. I thought it'd be better to create a situation that would make leaving difficult. I told Kushida my idea.

"Ooh! That certainly sounds like it would work! You're so smart, Ayanokouji-kun!" she cried. Kushida nodded in agreement while she hung on my every word, eyes sparkling.

"Oh, no, I don't think my plan has anything to do with being smart. Anyway, that's what I was going for."

"I understand. I'm excited for the result!"

No, don't expect too much. That'll be trouble.

"If you try inviting her, Kushida, she'll probably refuse you outright. So, how about I invite Horikita?"

"Okay. I think that Horikita-san trusts you, Ayanokouji-kun," she said.

"Why do you think that? What proof do you have?"

"Well, I guess it just looks that way to me. She seems to trust you more than anyone else in the class, at the very least."

That doesn't mean I'm best suited for this task, though.

"That's only because I was able to talk to her, but that was a coincidence."

I'd just happened to be seated next to her on the bus. If that hadn't happened, then I probably wouldn't have talked to her.

"But don't you meet almost *every* person for the first time by chance? And then they can become your friend, or your best friend...or even your boyfriend or girlfriend, or your family."

"That's true."

I supposed that was one way to look at it. Coincidence had allowed me to talk with Kushida like this. Therefore, it was possible that Kushida and I might eventually become lovers.

5.2

CLASSES HAD ENDED. The other students left for their various after-school activities, talking to one another about where they would go. Meanwhile, Kushida and I exchanged looks, signaling each other to go ahead with the plan.

"Hey, Horikita. Do you have some free time after class today?" I asked.

"I don't have any time to waste. I have to go back to the dormitory and prepare for tomorrow."

Prepare for tomorrow? I was pretty sure all she did was study.

"I wanted you to go somewhere with me for a little bit."

"What are you after?"

"Do you think that by inviting you out, I'm after something?"

"Well, when you invite me so suddenly, I naturally have my doubts. However, if there is a specific matter that you wish to discuss, I wouldn't mind listening."

I didn't have anything to talk about, of course.

"Well, you know that café on campus? The one with a ton of girls? I don't have the guts to go there all by myself. I kind of get the feeling that guys are banned from entering there or something. Don't you?"

"I certainly can't argue that most of their customers seem to be women, but aren't men also allowed to patronize the café?"

"Well, yeah, but no guy goes there alone. Only if they're with friends who are girls, or if they're someone's boyfriend."

Horikita tried to recall what Palate was like, seemingly lost in thought for a moment.

"You may very well be right. It's unusual for you to express such a well-reasoned opinion, Ayanokouji-kun."

"But I'm still interested in it. So I wanted to invite you to come along with me."

"I suppose that's natural, since you supposedly have... no one else to invite, correct?" she asked.

"That makes it sound like I'm imposing on you, but yeah. Basically."

"And if I refuse?"

"Well, that would be that. I'd have no choice but to accept. I can't force you to give up your private time, after all."

"I understand. Your issue with the café is certainly accurate. I can't stay there for too long, though. Is that all right?"

"Sure. We'll be quick."

In my mind, I added the word "probably" to that last thought. If she knew that Kushida was involved in this, Horikita would probably have some strong words for me. I'd begun to think that, since I was able to talk to Kushida, I might be able to make friends with Horikita myself. Besides, whether it was a café or a lecture hall, Horikita always came with me, even as she complained about it. For someone like me, who had difficulty making friends, this was probably a miracle.

The two of us left the classroom and made our way to Palate on the first floor. Girls began to congregate there, one after another, enjoying their time after class.

"There are so many people here," Horikita said.

"Is this your first time doing anything social, Horikita? Oh, yeah, I suppose it would be. You're always alone."

"Was that supposed to be sarcastic? How childish."

I'd meant to engage in some playful ribbing, but apparently that was impossible for Horikita. After we placed our order, we both got our drinks. I ordered the single serving of pancakes.

"Do you like sweets?" she asked.

"I just wanted to have pancakes."

I didn't particularly like or dislike cakes and stuff, but I needed a believable reason.

"There aren't any open seats, though."

"I guess we'll just have to wait a bit. Oh, never mind. There are some open seats over there."

I noticed that two girls quickly got up from their table, and I hurriedly went to secure our spot. Horikita passed around the table. I set my bag down on the floor, took my seat, and looked about casually.

"Hey, I just thought of something. If the people around here see us like this, they'll probably think we're a couple..."

Horikita remained expressionless, or rather, cold. Being in such crowded surroundings was making me anxious. As I considered what was about to happen, my stomach started to hurt.

I thought I heard the two girls sitting next to me say, "Let's go," before grabbing their drinks and leaving. Another patron sat down immediately. It was Kushida.

"Ah, Horikita-san. What a coincidence! And Ayanokouji-kun too!" she said.

"Hey."

Kushida had given us a simple greeting, maintaining the ruse that this was a coincidence. Horikita regarded Kushida with narrowed eyes, then slowly turned her gaze toward me. Of course, this was something that Kushida and I had planned out in advance. Kushida's friends had already secured four seats for us ahead of time. When I arrived at Palate, I sent them a signal so that they could make two seats available. After some time, the other girls next to me left, giving Kushida a chance to come and sit down. As a result, our meeting looked like it'd come about via coincidence.

"Did you come here together, Ayanokouji-kun? Horikita-san?" Kushida asked.

"Yeah, we just happened to. Did you come by yourself?" I asked.

"Yeah. Today, I—"

"I'm leaving," Horikita said.

"H-hey, we just got here, though."

"You don't need me now that Kushida-san is here, though. Right?"

"Hold on, that's not a problem. Kushida and I are just classmates."

"You and I are just classmates, too. Besides..." She gave Kushida and me an icy look. "I don't like this. What are you plotting?" She'd seen through our plan and was trying to get me to admit it.

"N-no, it was just a coincidence," Kushida said.

Kushida shouldn't have said such a thing. Asking, "What do you mean?" and acting ignorant of Horikita's prodding would've been the better response.

"When we sat down earlier, I saw the two girls seated here were from Class D, along with the two girls seated next to us as well. Was that just a coincidence, too?"

"Oh, wow, really? I didn't notice at all," Kushida said.

"Also, we came straight here after classes ended. No matter how much those girls rushed, they could only have been here for about one to two minutes at the most. It was far too early for them to get up and leave. Am I wrong?"

Horikita was even more incredibly observant than I'd thought. Not only did she remember our classmates' faces, but she'd quickly grasped the situation.

"Um, well..." A bewildered Kushida signaled for me to save her somehow. Horikita noticed. Any further deception on our part would just make it worse.

"Sorry, Horikita. We planned this."

"I thought as much. I thought this whole thing was a little suspicious right from the start."

"Horikita-san. Please be my friend!" Kushida just

came out and asked her directly, no longer trying to hide anything.

"I've already said this many times. I want you to leave me alone. I have no intention of becoming friends with anyone in class. Can you not understand that?" Horikita said.

"Always being alone is a very sad way to spend your life. I just want to get along with everyone in class."

"I wouldn't deny you your wish, but it's wrong to try forcing people into something against their will. Being alone doesn't make me sad."

"B-but..."

"Besides, do you think that I would be happy if you forced me to become your friend? Do you think that feelings of trust would arise out of something forced?"

Horikita wasn't wrong. It wasn't that she couldn't make friends, but that she considered them unnecessary. Kushida wanted something, but Horikita would not reciprocate.

"It's my fault for not being clear enough with you, so I don't blame you this time. But if you try this again, please keep in mind that I will not forgive you."

As she said that, Horikita took her untouched latte and stood up.

"Horikita-san, whatever you say, I really want to be friends with you. When I saw you, I felt like it wasn't the first time we'd met. I wondered if you felt the same way," Kushida mumbled.

"This is a waste of time. I find everything you're saying unpleasant." Horikita raised her voice, cutting Kushida off without mercy. Even though I'd told Kushida I would help her, I had absolutely no intention of butting in. But...

"I kind of understand your thoughts on the matter, Horikita. I've actually often wondered if friends are really necessary," I said.

"*You're* saying that? You've been trying to make friends since day one."

"I won't deny it. However, you and I are similar. I wasn't able to make friends until I came to this school. In junior high, I never knew anyone's contact information or hung out with anyone after class. I was always alone."

Kushida was visibly surprised when she heard me say that, like she couldn't believe it.

"I think that partly explains why I was compelled to talk to you," I said.

"That's the first time I've heard something like that. However, even if you and I share some things in common, I think we took different paths to reach this point. You wanted friends but couldn't get them. I considered friends unnecessary, so I didn't make any. Saying we are similar would be incorrect. Am I wrong?"

"No. But telling Kushida that she was being unpleasant is going too far. Are you really okay with this? If you choose not to get along with anyone else, you'll be alone for the next three years. That sounds pretty painful."

"It will be my ninth year in a row of being alone, so I'll be fine. Oh, and if you include kindergarten, it would actually be slightly longer."

Had she just nonchalantly dropped a bombshell? That she'd always been alone for as long as she could remember?

"Can I go now?" Horikita asked.

She sighed deeply and looked straight into Kushida's eyes.

"Kushida-san, if you don't try to force me into anything, I won't be rude. I promise. You're not stupid, so you understand what I'm telling you, right?"

With one final simple "*Well then*," Horikita left. Kushida and I remained in the noisy cafe.

"Well, that was a failure. I tried to lend a helping land, but it was pointless. I guess she's gotten too accustomed to being alone," I said.

Kushida wordlessly collapsed into her seat. However, she instantly recovered, and her usual smile returned.

"It's okay. Thank you, Ayanokouji-kun. It's true that I wasn't able to become her friend, but...I was able to learn something important. That's enough for me. I'm sorry, though. I feel like Horikita-san might hate you now because you helped me."

"Don't worry about it. I just wanted Horikita to consider the benefits of friendship." Thinking it'd be inconsiderate for the two us to hold up table space for four people, I moved to sit next to Kushida.

"Even so, I was shocked when you said that you didn't have any friends, Ayanokouji-kun. Is that true? I didn't think you were like that at all. Why were you all alone?"

"Hmm? Oh, yeah, it's true. Sudou and Ike are the first friends I've ever made. I still don't really know if that's my fault or the fault of the circumstances I was in."

"But when you made friends, did it make you happy? Is it fun?" Kushida asked.

"Yeah. There are times when I find it annoying, but sometimes I feel like I'm happier than I was before."

Kushida's eyes sparkled as she smiled at me, nodding her head in agreement.

"Horikita has her own way of thinking. There's probably nothing that we can do about that."

"Do you really think so? Is it not possible to make friends with her?" she asked.

"Why are you desperate to be her friend? Kushida, don't you already have more friends than everyone else? There's no reason to focus on Horikita."

Even if it meant that she wouldn't be friends with everyone in class, she didn't need to try so desperately.

"I wanted to be friends with everyone. Not just the people in Class D, but the students from other classes, too. But if I can't become friends with one girl in my class, then that means I'll never achieve my goal..."

"Just think of Horikita as a special case. Your only option is to wait for a real coincidence to come along."

Not something forced, but a natural event that would connect the two of them. When that time came, they might possibly become friends.

CLASSROOM OF THE ELITE

6 THE END OF EVERYDAY LIFE

"HA HA HA HA! God, you're so dumb. You're hilarious, man!"

Ike chatted loudly with Yamauchi during second-period math. It'd been three weeks since the entrance ceremony. In that time, Ike and Yamauchi, along with Sudou, had collectively come to be known as "The Idiot Trio."

"Hey, hey, do you want to go do karaoke?"

"Yeah, let's go!"

A group of girls nearby were making plans for after class.

"I was really worried for a while, but it looks like everyone's opened up to each other quickly."

"Ayanokouji-kun, haven't you made quite a few friends?" asked Horikita, copying what was written on the blackboard into her notebook.

"Somewhat, I suppose."

Although I was anxious at first, I'd gotten to know Sudou from our encounter at the convenience store, and I'd bonded with Ike and Yamauchi through the incident at the pool. Sometimes we ate lunch together. Even though I was far from having a best friend, before I knew it, I could say that I had *some* friends. Human relationships are rather mysterious, so I couldn't pinpoint the precise moment we became friends.

"Sup?" Halfway through class, Sudou crashed through the door and barged into the classroom. He slumped in his seat with a yawn, clearly not caring how late he was.

"Oh, hey, Sudou. Wanna get lunch later?" Ike called out to Sudou from across the room.

The math teacher continued the lesson without even really paying attention. Normally, the teacher would have flicked a piece of chalk at him, but perhaps out of some feeling of *laissez faire*, all of the teachers tolerated that kind of behavior. Even when it came to poor language, being late to class, or dozing off, no one cared. While at first our class had acted more reserved, now everyone was far too flippant. Of course, there were a few students like Horikita who studied diligently.

My cell phone vibrated in my pocket, indicating that I'd received a message. It was from the guys' group chat that I was a part of. It looked like they'd decided to eat lunch in the dining hall.

"Hey, Horikita. Do you want to have lunch with me?" I asked.

"I will have to decline. Your group is rather unrefined, anyway."

"I can't deny that."

When guys were alone, all they talked about were girls and dirty jokes. Who's cute, who's going out with who, how far they've gone, etc. Adding a girl into the group would probably have been a bad idea.

"Whoa. Seriously, he has a girlfriend? Awesome."

Based on Ike's conversation, it sounded like Hirata was dating Karuizawa. Watching Karuizawa from afar, I saw that she was gazing lovingly at him from across the room. As for my own impression of Karuizawa, well, she was certainly cute. But she had this atmosphere around her that it made difficult for uncertain people to approach her. In other words, she seemed like one of those intensely "girly"-type girls. In junior high, she'd probably pounced on pretty boys like Hirata. These were my own uncharitable assumptions, but I probably wasn't far off.

Oops. I had pretty mean-spirited opinions about her, although, not really to the extent that it would be considered defamation. I apologized to Karuizawa in my head.

"I hate that look on your face."

Horikita glared icily at me. She must have read my sleazy inner thoughts. How fast did you need to move to become a couple right after starting school? I was agonizing over just making friends. If I'd gone up to Horikita and asked, "Would you go out with me?" she definitely would've smacked me. At any rate, if I were to get a girlfriend, I'd prefer a kinder, more ladylike girl.

6.1

For third period, we had history class with Chabashira-sensei. When the bell rang, Chabashira-sensei walked into the noisy classroom. Her entrance didn't alter the students' behavior.

"Quiet down a little, please. Today's lesson will be a bit serious."

"What do you mean, Sae-chan-sensei?"

They already had a pet name for the teacher.

"It's the end of the month, so we're going to have a short test. Please pass these to the back."

She handed out the papers to the students in the front row. Eventually, the single-sheet test reached my desk. It contained questions in the five main subjects. With only a few questions per subject, it really was short.

"Huh? I wasn't listening, though. This is so unfair!" a student cried.

"Don't say that. This test is just for future reference. It won't be reflected in your report cards. There is no risk involved, so don't worry. Of course, cheating is prohibited."

Her phrasing struck me as odd. Normally, only general grades were reflected in your report card. But the way Chabashira-sensei said they wouldn't be reflected in our report cards made me think that the grade could be reflected in some other way. Well...perhaps I was worrying too much. If this had no effect on our report card, then there was no need to be so cautious.

As soon as the pop quiz began, I scanned the questions. There were four questions per subject, for a total of twenty. Each question was worth five points, for a total of one hundred points. Most of the questions were extraordinarily easy, to the point where it was almost a letdown. In fact, the questions seemed to be about two levels less difficult than the ones on the entrance examination. It appeared far too easy.

However, just as I thought that, I reached the end of the test. The final three questions were an order of magnitude higher in terms of difficulty. The final math problem couldn't be solved without complex formulae.

"No way. These questions are seriously way too hard..."

These questions couldn't be geared toward a first-year high school student. The final three questions were clearly of a different quality than the others, so it was possible they'd been put on the test by mistake. Even though the results wouldn't be reflected in our grades, what in the hell were they evaluating with this?

Well, I guess I'll just solve these problems the same way I did on the entrance exam.

Chabashira-sensei monitored us. As she slowly patrolled the classroom, she kept a watchful eye to dissuade us from cheating. I quickly glanced at Horikita, who would never even think of cheating. Her pen danced across the paper as she filled in all of the answers. It looked like she was easily going to get a perfect score.

I continued staring intently at my test until the bell rang.

6.2

"IF YOU JUST COME RIGHT OUT and tell me straight, I'll forgive you, okay?"

"Tell you *what* straight?"

After we'd finished lunch, I was chatting with Sudou and the other guys next to the vending machine in the hall. All of a sudden, Ike sidled up next to me.

"We're friends, right? Comrades that stick together through thick and thin?"

"Uh, yeah. I guess so."

"So then, naturally...you would tell us if you got yourself a girlfriend, right?" he asked.

"Huh? A girlfriend? Well, sure. If that happens, I will."

Ike put his arm over my shoulder.

"Come on. You're going out with Horikita, aren't you? I'm not gonna forgive you if you get ahead of us!"

"Huh?"

I noticed Yamauchi and Sudou both eyeing me suspiciously.

"You idiot. We're not dating. Absolutely not. Seriously."

"Okay, but what were you guys talking about all sneaky-like during class today? I guess it's not a story for us, huh? Were you talking about dates or making plans for dates, huh?! Ah, I could kill you, I'm so jealous!"

"It's nothing. Besides, Horikita isn't the dating type."

"I don't know about that. We never really talked to her before. If Kushida hadn't brought it up, we probably wouldn't even know her name. She disappears into the background, like a shadow."

Was that true? I couldn't recall Horikita really talking to anyone except for Kushida or me.

"You wouldn't even know her name? That's awful."

"So, do *you* know all your classmate's names, Ayanokouji?"

I could remember about half of their names. I got the point.

"She does have a really cute face though, doesn't she? That's why we noticed her."

Yamauchi and the guys nodded in agreement.

"She has such an uptight personality, though. I don't like girls like her," remarked Sudou, drinking his coffee.

"Yeah, I know. It's like she's really snippy, yeah? I'd rather go out with a cheerful girl who I can have an easy conversation with. She has to be cute, of course. Just like Kushida-chan." Of course. Kushida was still Ike's favorite.

"Ahh. To go out with Kushida-chan...or rather, do naughty stuff with her!" cried Yamauchi.

"You moron! Like hell you can date Kushida-chan! And you're forbidden from fantasizing about her, too!" Ike cried.

"Come on, you think *you* can date her, Ike? Besides, I've dreamt of sleeping next to Kushida-chan!"

"What?! Well, *I've* dreamt of her doing super sexy poses while in cosplay!"

The two of them went back and forth over their wild Kushida fantasies. *Come on, guys. High school students are free to fantasize, but that's just being plain rude to Kushida.*

"Who do you have your eye on, Sudou? Seen any cute girls in basketball?" Ike asked.

"Huh? Oh, no one. Not yet, anyway. We don't really have room for any girls on the team right now."

"Really? If you *do* have a girlfriend, though, you better not be hiding it! You have to tell us! You have to!"

"Yeah, sure," Sudou said. Despite how disgusted he seemed by the conversation, he nodded.

The subject of girlfriends made me remember Hirata.

"Oh, yeah, isn't Hirata dating Karuizawa now?" I asked.

"Yeah, you're right. Hondou saw them holding hands just the other day!"

"Yeah, they're dating. No mistake about it. They were walking together, shoulder to shoulder."

"They were, huh? I wonder if they've already done naughty stuff together."

"Of course they have! Ah, I'm so jealous! I'm *too* jealous!"

It felt kind of unbelievable that a first-year high school student would already have had sex. But I supposed it was true.

Unintentionally, I'd started thinking like these guys.

"Listen to me. I've got the most experience with sex and stuff," said Yamauchi, sprawled out on the hallway floor.

"I think it'd be better to ask Hirata," Ike said.

"Do you honestly think that Hirata would give us the details? Like, if we asked about her breasts, or if she were a virgin, or things like that? Do you really think he'd tell us? Come on," I said.

What kind of experiences were they planning to ask about?

I walked over to the nearby vending machine to buy something to drink.

"Get me some cocoa!" Yamauchi called.

"If you want something, buy it yourself."

"Can't. I've already almost used up all of my points. I have about 2,000 left."

"How could you possibly have used more than 90,000 points in just three weeks?" I asked.

"I bought stuff I wanted. Here, check it out. It's awesome!" said Yamauchi, taking out a handheld gaming device.

"I bought this with Ike. It's a PS Viva! A PS VIVA! It's amazing that a school sells this kind of stuff."

"How much did it cost?"

"About 20,000. With the optional stuff included, it came to about 25,000."

Dude, don't spend all of your points right away.

"I don't usually play games all that much, but now that I'm living in a dorm, I figured I could play with friends. Oh, you know that Miyamoto guy in our class? He's really good at video games."

Miyamoto was the rather plump boy. I'd never spoken to him directly, but I got the impression he was the type who'd talk about things like games and anime all the time.

"You should buy one too and join in. Sudou said that he'd get one with next month's allowance."

They were already ganging up on me. Yamauchi handed over his game system so I could give it a try. It was a lot lighter than I expected. The screen displayed a warrior, huge sword strapped to his back, petting a pig. What kind of world was this?

"Honestly, I'm not really that interested. What...*is* this, anyway? Some kind of fighting game?"

"You've heard about *Hunter Watch*, right? It's sold more than 4.8 million copies worldwide, man! I've had an incredible knack for games ever since I was a little kid. Overseas professionals constantly scouted me. I always turned them down, though."

You can proclaim something a worldwide phenomenon, but whether or not it's actually good is another matter. There were about seven billion people in the world. The people who'd purchased this game accounted for less than 0.1 percent of the global population.

"Anyway, how in the world can such a delicate girl wear such heavy equipment? Is her armor plastic or something? If it were iron, even someone with Sudou's physique would struggle with it."

"Ayanokouji, you really want an element of realism in your games? What, are you a foreigner? People who say that kind of stuff are usually okay with games where you can automatically regenerate your life. Are you one of those? Do you want some Western-developed game where you shoot guys then hide somewhere and get all of your health back? Because, if you ask me, *those* games are unrealistic!"

I couldn't understand Yamauchi at all.

"Well, you know what they say: 'seeing is believing,' right? Just try it. When you start playing, we'll help you farm for materials. Collecting honey is hard work, you know? So you can buy me some cocoa, then."

"For crying out loud..."

I didn't exactly need the honey, but I bought the cocoa to avoid any further hassle.

"Ah, friendship is such a blessing! Thank you!" Yamauchi said.

I didn't want that kind of friendship. I tossed the cocoa to Yamauchi, who caught it against his stomach. Now, what did I want to drink? Hesitating, I noticed a button on the machine.

"Oh, so they have this, too."

There was a button for mineral water, which was free of charge.

"What's wrong?"

"Oh, nothing. Just was wondering if the cafeteria offers anything for free."

"Oh, you mean like the vegetable meal set? Ugh, there's no way I'd want to go through school with only vegetables and water."

Yamauchi cackled as he drank his cocoa. If you used up all of your points, then you'd have no choice but to take the free stuff, like vegetables and water. However, it was easy to avoid that situation. As long as you didn't spend all of your points like Yamauchi, that is.

"There are quite a few people who eat the vegetables, actually," I said.

Since I went to the cafeteria often, I recalled seeing many students eating the free meal sets.

"It's not because they like it. It's probably because it's the end of the month."

"Well, that might be so." While I felt a little uneasy about it, I pressed the button for milk and took the bottle after it came tumbling down.

"Ah, why can't next month come any faster? I want my dream life back again!" Yamauchi and the other guys laughed as they lamented.

6.3

HEY, we're going to go hang out with Kushida-chan and some other people after class. You want to come?

I received that text message in the middle of my afternoon class while absentmindedly jotting down notes. Ah, weren't these supposed to be the halcyon days of our youth? This was the first time that friends had invited me to hang out after class. I had no reason to refuse their invitation, but I thought I'd ask who was going.

I mean, I didn't want to be surrounded by a bunch of people I didn't know. That would be awkward.

I quickly received a reply. I saw Ike and Yamauchi's names, as well as Kushida's. Including me, that made five people. Didn't seem like anyone whom I didn't already know was included. Well, that sounded fine. I confirmed that I'd go, and a response quickly followed.

Kushida-chan is my target, so don't you dare get in my way! –Ike-sama

No, no, Kushida-chan is mine. You stay out of the way! –Yamauchi

Huh? You say you're after Kushida-chan, too?! What, are you trying to pick a fight?

It'd be nice if we all got along, but the two of them started fighting over Kushida via text. I'd been looking forward to hanging out with everyone, but now I thought it might be a hassle. When class ended, I left with Ike and Yamauchi. Even though I'd been here a while, the school grounds were so expansive that I still didn't know the area very well.

"We couldn't leave with Kushida even though we're in the same class, huh?" I said.

"She said she had to talk to a friend from another class. Kushida-chan is quite popular."

"Do you think maybe she's talking to a boy?" Ike mumbled.

"Relax, Ike. I've already confirmed it. She's talking to a girl," Yamauchi said.

"All right, all right."

"Are you guys seriously going after Kushida?" I asked.

"Of course. She's my dream girl."

Yamauchi must have shared this opinion, considering the fact he kept nodding in agreement.

"You're interested in Horikita, aren't you? She's definitely beautiful, I gotta say."

"No, I'm not. Really."

"Really? Didn't you guys sneakily exchange looks and nonchalantly touch fingertips? You know, something bittersweet and yet kind of irritating?"

While Ike relentlessly pressed me, one of the very girls we were talking about ran over.

"Sorry for being late, but thanks for waiting!" Kushida cried.

"Oh, no worries, Kushida-chan! Hey, wait a second, why are *they* here?!" Ike had been jumping up and down excitedly, but now he tumbled over and sprawled across the ground. What an energetic guy.

"Oh, I just happened to run into them on the way, so I thought I'd invite them along. Was that not okay?"

Kushida had brought Hirata and his girlfriend (at least, I was pretty sure she was his girlfriend), Karuizawa. There were also two other girls, Matsushita and Mori, who always hung around Karuizawa.

"Hey, don't we have some way of making Hirata go away?!" Ike whispered, putting his arm around my shoulder.

"I don't think there's really any reason to make him leave," I replied.

"That pretty boy will completely overshadow us! What are you going to do if Kushida-chan ends up liking Hirata, huh?! We can't let that pretty boy end up with a cutie like Kushida!"

"Well, I don't know about... Hey, wait, isn't Hirata dating Karuizawa? I wouldn't worry."

"Hey, just because you say he has a girlfriend is no guarantee. I can't relax. Besides, anyone in his right mind would choose a pretty angel like Kushida-chan over a sloppy, easy gal like Karuizawa!"

Ike furiously prattled on, his spit spraying my ear, which grossed me out. Not just the spit, either; his vile words were pretty disgusting, too. It was true that Karuizawa certainly was one of those *gyaru* types with tanned skin and everything, but she was plenty cute.

"Hey, Ike, you do know that there's no guarantee that Kushida-chan is a virgin, right?" Yamauchi joined our conversation, his anxious voice a strained whisper.

"W-well... Yeah, you might be... N-no, Kushida has to be a virgin!" Ike said.

They continued to discuss their wild, delusional fantasies, though I thought it was more misogyny than anything. If at all possible, I would've rather not been involved.

"Um, if we're a bother, perhaps we can just go

separately?" said Hirata in a reserved tone. He seemed to have noticed our secret conversation.

"W-we don't really mind at all, do we? Right, Yamauchi?"

"Y-yeah. Let's all go together. The more the merrier, you know. Right, Ike?"

Moments ago, those two had shouted that others would "be in the way" and that they needed to get rid of Hirata. But if they did such a thing, then Kushida might like them less. Whether or not there was any chance she'd like them in the first place was another matter.

"Well, obviously, that was the idea. Why are you three whispering about us?" Karuizawa's words were certainly understandable, but I was shocked to be lumped together with Ike and Yamauchi.

"Well, here's my thought. If we include Hirata and Karuizawa, then we'll have the same number of boys and girls. So that means it'd be a triple date. Ayanokouji, this could be your chance, you know?"

"So, you're good with Matsushita, Yamauchi? I'm gonna talk to Kushida-chan," Ike said.

"Hey, don't screw with me! I'm the one after Kushida-chan! We're going to get married under an old cherry blossom tree, exchanging vows like a sweet promise between childhood friends! It's fate!"

"You're full of crap! I've thought about doing that for a while now. You're a total liar!"

"Huh? It's all true, all of it!"

If you were to believe everything Yamauchi Haruki said, then he had been a skilled gamer since childhood, scouted by professionals from overseas, and a national ping pong competitor. Then, in junior high, he'd been his baseball team's ace player and a promising future star. What an incredibly gifted man.

Though there was no confirmation that any of that was the truth.

I didn't know where we were headed, so I quietly hung to the back of the group. While Ike and Yamauchi daydreamed about Kushida, they flanked Hirata on both sides.

"I'm just going to ask you, Hirata. Are you going out with Karuizawa?" Ike asked point-blank to determine whether or not Hirata was his enemy.

"Uh...where did you hear that?" Hirata asked. As expected, he looked a little surprised, or even panicked, by that question. "Oh, guess you figured it out, huh? Yeah, we're dating."

Karuizawa latched onto Hirata's arm before he could say anything. Hirata just lightly scratched his cheek, as if signaling resignation.

"Seriously?! I'm so jealous that you're dating such a cute girl like Karuizawa!" said Yamauchi, feigning envy. You'd think that lying while being unaware that you're lying would be easy, but it was surprisingly difficult.

"Kushida-chan, do you have a boyfriend?" Ike managed to shift attention over to Kushida without missing a beat. Pretty clever, huh?

"Me? Oh, no, unfortunately," she said.

Both Ike and Yamauchi clearly rejoiced, breaking out in massive grins. Their joy leaked out for everyone to see. Although it was possible that Kushida was hiding the fact that she had a boyfriend, she'd basically confirmed that she was available. I was a little glad to hear that, too.

"Oh, no, I'm crying..."

"Don't cry, Yamauchi! We're finally almost at the summit!"

Their destination no longer waited at the peak of an insurmountable mountain, but instead at the end of a precipitous path...

Hirata, Karuizawa, Ike, and Yamauchi all surrounded Kushida as they walked. The rather uninteresting pair of Matsushita and Mori followed behind the main group, while I walked farther behind them, alone.

"Hey, Ike. Where are we going?" someone asked.

"It hasn't been that long since the entrance ceremony,

remember? Just wanted to check out the campus facilities," Ike answered, seemingly irritated.

So, there was no clear destination, which meant that
this somewhat awkward experience would go on for a
while...

My unpleasant expectations unexpectedly changed.

"Hey, Matsushita-san, Mori-san. What do you two
want to go see?"

While Ike and Yamauchi happily chatted with each
other, Kushida fell back to talk to the other two girls.

"Huh? Oh, um, well...I've wanted to see the movie theater at least once."

"Yeah. Since school's done for the day, I wanted to go,
too."

"Oh, yeah! I've wanted to go as well, but haven't gotten
around to it yet. Karuizawa-san, have you gone to any
special places on dates?"

Kushida started to organize us into three groups, just
as I'd expect of her. No matter how hard I tried, I could
never have done something like that. Also, as a nice bonus, she occasionally turned and smiled sweetly at me. I
didn't expect that.

I tried not to talk unnecessarily, as I felt that would
just be a hassle. I tried to look at Kushida in a way that
showed I wasn't ignoring her. If Kushida couldn't read

the room, and merely liked being the constant center of attention, then the message probably wouldn't reach her.

However, there are people who will lash out and say something like, "Why can't you read the situation?" to a friend after he refuses to do karaoke, even though they *know* that friend said he didn't want to sing. There are, after all, self-absorbed, simple-minded people who assume that because karaoke is fun for them, that means everyone will love it. They simply cannot comprehend that some people dislike singing.

While I'd been mulling over this venomous topic, my surroundings had changed. Apparently, we'd stopped at a clothing store on campus. More precisely, it was a boutique. Everyone seemed to have come to this store a few times already, so we entered without hesitation. Generally, I wore my uniform on weekdays, and since I usually stayed in my dorm on my days off, I hadn't bought any clothes for going out.

There were many students inside, though few upper-classmen. The majority appeared to be first-year students. Perhaps it was because of my newness, but I felt really inexperienced and anxious in this atmosphere. We checked out many different items on the racks and, afterward, went to a nearby café. Hirata carried the clothes that Karuizawa had purchased, which cost about 30,000 points.

"Have you all gotten used to this school yet?"

"At first, I was really perplexed, but now I've settled in perfectly. It's like living in a dream. I don't ever want to graduate!"

"Ha ha! I get the feeling Ike-kun is enjoying his time here to the fullest!"

"I just wish we had more points, you know? Maybe 200,000 or 300,000 a month? After buying cosmetics and clothes and stuff, I've already used up almost all of my points," Karuizawa said.

"Don't you think it's abnormal for a high school student to get 300,000 points as a monthly allowance?" Hirata asked.

"Well, if you put it like that, yeah. Even 100,000 is pretty outlandish. I'm a little scared, to be honest. I'm worried about what life after graduation will be like if I keep on spending my school days like this."

"Do you mean you'll lose your sense of money management? Yeah, that does sound pretty scary, actually."

Everyone felt differently about our monthly allowance. Karuizawa and Ike both wanted more points, while Hirata and Kushida were terrified of what would happen when our life of luxury ended.

"What about you, Ayanokouji-kun? Do you think that 100,000 points is a lot or not enough?"

At that point, I'd only intended to listen, but Kushida asked me my thoughts.

"Hmm, well, I don't really fully understand it yet. I'm not sure," I replied.

"What's that supposed to mean?"

"I think I understand what you're getting at, Ayanokouji-kun. This is honestly completely different from any normal school. It's hard to understand it without really knowing all the details."

"Well, there's no point worrying about it. I'm super glad that I got into this school. I can just go out and buy whatever I want. In fact, yesterday I went out and bought some new clothes." Ike lived a positive life, always forging directly ahead.

"Kushida-chan and Hirata aside, Ike, you and Karuizawa also managed to get into this place. Aren't you guys pretty dumb, though?"

"You don't strike me as being very smart either, Yamauchi."

"Huh? I'll have you know that I scored 900 points on the APEC."

"What's the APEC?"

"You don't even know? It's a super tough test for English."

"Um, don't you mean the TOEIC, not APEC?"

Kushida gently brought Yamauchi back down to earth. APEC actually stood for Asia-Pacific Economic Partnership.

"Th-they're related though, aren't they?" he asked.

They were as far apart as it's possible to get.

"Well, this school's mission is to nurture young people who will pave the way to the future, right? So, they probably don't choose people solely on their test scores. Honestly, if this school only took in people based on standardized tests, I wouldn't have taken the entrance exam."

"Yeah, yeah. Young people who will pave the way to the future. That's exactly how I'd describe myself." Ike crossed his arms and nodded.

Despite being the premier institution in Japan, with stellar rates of advancement into higher education and employment, this school didn't appear to determine the criteria for passing or failing through test scores. If that was the case, then how in the world did it select potential students? I found myself suddenly curious.

CLASSROOM OF THE ELITE

ON MAY 1, the morning bell rang for our very first day of class. Soon afterward, Chabashira-sensei strode into the room, holding a rolled-up poster. Her expression today was even more stern than usual. Had she started menopause, I wondered? If I made that joke out loud, I think she would have swung an iron bat at my face with full force.

"Hey, sensei, did you start menopause or something?"

Unbelievably, Ike actually let that joke fly. Honestly, it was more shocking that I'd thought the same thing as Ike.

"All right, your morning homeroom is about to begin. Before we get started, does anyone have any questions? If so, now is the time to speak." Chabashira-sensei completely ignored Ike's sexual harassment. She appeared totally convinced that the students had questions they wanted answered. Immediately, several students raised their hands.

"Um, I checked my point balance this morning, but I didn't see any deposits. Points are given on the first day of every month, aren't they? I couldn't buy juice this morning."

"Hondou, I already explained this before, didn't I? Points are deposited on the first day of the month. I've confirmed that points were wired this month without any issues."

"Um, but...nothing was deposited into my account, though."

Hondou and Yamauchi exchanged glances. Ike appeared too shocked to notice them looking at each other. I'd checked my point balance that morning as well, but saw that it had remained unchanged from the day before. No more points had been deposited into my account. I'd simply thought that the points would be wired later.

"Are you kids really that dumb?"

Was she angry or delighted? I was getting an ominous vibe from Chabashira-sensei.

"Dumb? What?"

As Hondou stupidly repeated her words, Chabashira-sensei looked at him sharply.

"Sit down, Hondou. I'll explain once more," she said.

"S-Sae-chan-sensei?"

Hondou, taken aback by her unusually strict tone, slumped in his seat.

"Points were deposited. That much I know for certain. There is absolutely no chance that we forgot about anyone in this class. To think so is ludicrous. Understood?"

"Well, even if I tell you that we understand, we haven't received any points..."

Hondou, still perplexed, began to look dissatisfied. Supposing that what Chabashira-sensei said was true and that points had been wired to us, then that meant...

Had there been a discrepancy, then? Did that mean that zero points had been deposited into our accounts? My vague doubts quickly grew.

"Ha ha ha! I see. So, it's like that then, teacher? I think I've solved the mystery," Kouenji boomed, laughing.

He propped his feet up on his desk and smugly pointed toward Hondou.

"It's simple. We're in Class D, so we didn't receive a single point."

"Huh? What are you talking about? They said that we'd get 100,000 points every month—"

"I don't remember hearing that, though. Do you?" Chuckling, Kouenji boldly pointed at Chabashira-sensei.

"While he certainly has an attitude problem, Kouenji is exactly right. For crying out loud, barely anyone seems to have noticed the hint I gave you. How deplorable."

In response to this sudden turn of events, the classroom exploded in an uproar.

"Sensei, may I please ask you a question? I'm afraid I still don't understand." Hirata raised his hand. He appeared to ask on behalf of his classmates rather than out of selfish concern. Just as I'd expect of the de facto class leader. Even now, he took the initiative.

"Can you please tell us why we didn't receive any points? We won't completely understand otherwise."

That was certainly true.

"A total of ninety-eight absences and late arrivals. Three hundred ninety-one incidences of talking or using a cell phone in class. That is quite a few infractions over one month. In this school, *your class's results are reflected in the points that you receive*. As a result, you wasted all of the 100,000 points that you should have received. That's what happened."

"I should have explained this all to you on the day of the entrance ceremony. This school measures its students' true abilities. This time, you were evaluated as being worth nothing. That's all."

Chabashira-sensei spoke in a robotic fashion, devoid

of any emotion. The doubts I'd had since coming to this school were finally confirmed, though, in the worst way possible. Even though we'd started with the huge advantage of 100,000 points, Class D had lost it in just a single month.

I heard a pencil moving against paper. Horikita seemed to be tallying the number of absences, tardy arrivals, and instances of talking in class down in her notebook, perhaps trying to make sense of the situation.

"Chabashira-sensei. I do not recall hearing you explain that to us before—"

"What? Are you incapable of understanding something unless it's explained in detail?"

"Of course. There was never any talk about reducing our points. Had that been explained beforehand, I'm sure we would have avoided being late or talking during class."

"That is a rather bizarre argument, Hirata. It is certainly true that I don't recall explaining the rules of point distribution. However, didn't you all learn in elementary school not to be late or talk in class? Was that not taught throughout your elementary and junior high schools?"

"Well, that's—"

"I'm sure that in nine years of compulsory education, you learned that being late and talking in class are bad things. And now you say that you can't understand this because I haven't explained it to you? I'm afraid your reasoning is flimsy. If you had simply acted properly, then your points would not have dropped all the way to zero. This comes down to you taking personal responsibility."

There was no way for anyone to refute her perfectly sound argument. Everyone knew that bad behavior didn't pay.

"Having just entered your first year of high school, did you honestly think you'd receive 100,000 points every month with no strings attached? At a school established by the Japanese government for the express purposes of training gifted people? That's unthinkable. Try using some common sense. Why would you leave it to chance?"

Although Hirata appeared to be frustrated, he looked the teacher straight in the eye. "Well then, could you at least explain in detail how points are added or deducted? We can keep that in mind for future reference."

"I cannot tell you. We cannot disclose the methods behind our student evaluation. It's the same as any other organization. When you enter a company, it is the company's choice whether or not to tell you how it evaluates its employees. However, I'm not cruel, and I'm not trying to be cold. In fact, this situation is so pathetic that I will give you one bit of guidance."

For the first time, I saw a faint sliver of a smile on Chabashira-sensei's lips.

"Let's say that you stop being late to class and have no more absences... Even though zero points will be deducted from you this month, that doesn't mean that your points will increase, either. That means next month you will still receive zero points. From another perspective, you could say no matter how times you're late or absent to class, it doesn't matter. So, you're not really at a loss, are you?"

"Tch..." Hirata's expression darkened. Her explanation was so counterproductive that it had the opposite effect; some students seemed incapable of understanding what she meant. The students who thought they could improve their situation by remedying bad behavior had their hopes dashed. That was probably Chabashira-sensei's, or rather, this school's, intention.

The bell rang, signaling the end of homeroom.

"It looks like we spent too much time yammering. I hope that you understood the gist of it. Well, it's about time that we switch to our main topic."

From the tube she carried, she removed a white rolled-up poster and spread it out. She stuck the poster to the blackboard with some magnets. The still-confused students stared blankly at the poster.

"Are these...the results for each class?" Horikita tentatively took a guess. She was probably right. Class A through Class D were listed. To the side was a row of numbers that went up to a maximum of four digits. Class D had zero. Class C had 490. Class B had 650. And at the top was Class A, with a total of 940. In this case, 1000 points would mean 100,000 yen, wouldn't it? Every class had apparently lost points.

"Isn't something about this odd?"

"Yeah. The numbers look too even."

Horikita and I had both noticed something strange.

"You've all been doing whatever you pleased this past month. The school has no intention of preventing you from doing what you want. Your actions, such as being late or talking during class, only affect the points you receive. The same goes for how you use your points. How you choose to spend is entirely up to you. We have not put any restrictions on point usage."

"This isn't fair, though! We can't enjoy our student lives like this!" shouted Ike, who'd stayed quiet until now.

Yamauchi wailed in incredible agony. He'd already used up all of his points...

"Look here, morons. Every other class got points. The amount of points we gave you for the first month should be plenty for you to live on."

"B-but, how do the other classes still have points left? That's weird..."

"I've already told you, there's nothing unfair about it. All of the classes were scored using the same rules. Despite that, they didn't lose as many as you. That's the truth."

"But...why is there such a difference in our point values?" Hirata also seemed to have noticed that the numbers were too tidy.

"Do you finally understand now? Do you see why you were placed in Class D?"

"The reason why we were placed in Class D? Weren't we simply accepted into this school?"

"Huh? But classes are *normally* divided up like this, right?"

Students exchanged glances.

"In this school, students are sorted by their level of excellence. The superior students are sorted into Class A, the least capable in Class D. It's the same system you'd find in the major cram schools. In other words, Class D is akin to the last bastion for failures. You are the worst of the worst. You're defective. This is just the result of you being defective."

Horikita's face stiffened. She appeared shocked by this line of reasoning. It certainly made sense to sort the superior students with the other superior students and the failures with the failures. If you mixed rotten oranges with good ones, the rotten would quickly spoil the good. Inevitably, the superior Horikita would find this revolting.

I, on the other hand, was glad. This meant I couldn't go any lower.

"However, I have to say, this year's Class D was the first to ever spend all of their points in a single month. I am impressed by how much you indulged yourselves. Wonderful, just wonderful."

Chabashira-sensei's false applause echoed throughout the classroom.

"So, does that mean that once we reach zero points, we'll always stay there?"

"Yes. You will remain at zero until you graduate. But don't worry, you can still have a room in the dorms and free meals. You won't die."

Although we knew that it was possible to get by with the bare minimum, a lot of students weren't comforted by that fact. After all, we'd lived a life of luxury this past month. To suddenly restrain yourself after that would prove seriously difficult.

"Won't the other classes make fun of us?"

Sudou kicked the legs of his desk with a loud *thwack*. After hearing that the classes were divided based on merit, everyone else would probably believe that Class D was full of morons. Despair wasn't unreasonable.

"What? You're still worried about your dignity, Sudou? Well then, work to make your class into the best one."

"Huh?"

"Your class's points aren't just linked to the amount of money that you receive each month. They're also indicative of your class rank."

In other words...should we get to 500 points, then Class D would be promoted to Class C. This really did sound like a company performance review.

"Now then, I have one more bit of bad news to share with you all."

She stuck another sheet of paper up on the board. It listed the names of everyone in class. A number stood next to everyone's name.

"Judging from these, I can see that we've quite a few idiots in this class." As her heels clacked against the floor, she glanced at us. "These are the results of the short test you took a while ago. Your sensei was *so happy* after your *excellent* performance. Come on, what in the world did you all study when you were in junior high?"

With the exception of a few high scores, almost everyone tested below a sixty. Even if you ignored Sudou's *wonderful* score of fourteen points, there was Ike, scoring a little above him at twenty-four points. The average score was sixty-five.

"I'm so glad. If this were an actual test, then seven of you would've had to drop out."

"D-drop out? What do you mean?"

"Oh, what, did I not explain this to you? If you fail on a midterm or final exam in this school, then you have to drop out. If we applied that rule to this test, anyone who scored below thirty-two points would be out. You guys really are stupid, aren't you?"

"Wh-what?!" wailed Ike and the other failures.

There was a red line drawn on the paper, separating the seven people in question from the rest of the class. Among those seven people, Kikuchi had scored highest, with thirty-one points. Anyone with a score equal to or lower than Kikuchi's had failed.

"Hey, don't jerk us around, Sae-chan-sensei! Don't joke about kicking us out!"

"Frankly, I'm also at a loss," the teacher said. "These are the school rules. You should prepare for the worst."

"The teacher's right. There do seem to be a lot of morons here." Kouenji wore a smug grin while he polished his nails, his legs propped on the desk.

"What the hell, Kouenji? You scored below the red line, too!"

"Pah. Where exactly are *you* looking, boy? Look again."

"Huh? Kouenji is...huh?"

Starting from the bottom of the page, Sudou scanned upward, and there he found Kouenji Rokosuke's name. Unbelievably, Kouenji had tied for the top spot, scoring ninety points. That meant he'd been able to solve one of those super difficult problems.

"I never thought that Sudou was an idiot like me!" cried Ike, a mixture of wonder and sarcasm in his voice.

"Oh, one more thing. This school, which operates under government supervision, boasts a high rate of advancement into elite education and workforce placement. That is a well-known fact. It's very likely that most of you have chosen a college or future workplace."

Well, naturally. This school boasted the highest rates of advancement in the whole country. There were rumors that it was possible to get into a highly competitive school or company just by graduating. Rumors even suggested that graduation from this school was like receiving a recommendation to Tokyo University, the most prestigious of Japan's institutes of higher learning.

"However, nothing comes easy in this world. Mediocre people such as yourselves would have to be naive to think that you could easily get into the college or workplace of your choice."

Chabashira-sensei's words carried throughout the room.

"In other words, you're saying that if we want to get into the company or college of our choice, we must, at minimum, surpass Class C?" Hirata asked.

"You're wrong. To make your dreams of a bright future come true, your only option is to overtake Class A. This school guarantees nothing for any other students."

"Th-that's...absurd! We didn't hear anything about that!"

A bespectacled student named Yukimura stood up. He'd tied with Kouenji for the top score, indicating that there were no issues with his academic abilities.

"How disgraceful. There's nothing more pitiful than men losing their cool." As if prompted by Yukimura's words, Kouenji let out a sigh.

"Don't you feel dissatisfied being in Class D, Kouenji?" Yukimura asked.

"Dissatisfied? Why would I feel dissatisfied? I don't understand."

"Because the school says we're so low that we're basically delinquents and failures. We've been told that there's no guarantee whatsoever that we'll advance into higher education or get a job!"

"Pah. Utter nonsense. That's so marvelously stupid

that I can't even find the words." Kouenji didn't even stop polishing his nails or turn to face Yukimura as he spoke. "The school simply hasn't seen my potential yet. I pride myself on being great, and I value, respect, and regard myself more highly than anyone. So, the school arbitrarily placing me into Class D means nothing. Say, for instance, that I dropped out of school—I would be perfectly fine. After all, I am 100 percent positive that the school would come crying to take me back."

That certainly sounded like something Kouenji would say. Was it being macho? Or narcissism? It's true that if you didn't care about the school's classification of students, then it really wasn't a big deal. If you considered Kouenji's impressive intellect and physical ability, it was difficult to imagine that all of the students in Class A could be better than him. Perhaps he'd been assigned to Class D because of his personality rather than his ability.

"Besides, I don't care in the slightest if the school does or doesn't assist me to higher education or the workforce. It's been decided that I will lead the Kouenji conglomerate group. Whether I'm in Class D or Class A is a trivial matter."

It was true that for a man whose future was already decided, getting into Class A was far from a necessity. Yukimura, at a loss for words, simply sat back down.

"It looks like your bubbles have been burst. If you had simply understood the harsh reality of the situation from the start, then this long homeroom period might have meant something. Your midterm exams are in three weeks. Please think things over, and be careful not to drop out. I have confidence that you can find a way to avoid getting red marks on your report cards. If at all possible, challenge yourself to act in a way befitting a skilled individual."

Chabashira-sensei exited the room, closing the door with some force for added emphasis. The students marked in red were left dejected. Even the normally proud Sudou clicked his tongue and hung his head in shame.

7.1

"IF WE DON'T get any more points, what I am gonna do?"

"I used up all of my points yesterday..."

During the break, the classroom erupted into an uproar...or rather, chaos.

"Forget about the points. What the hell about this *class*? Why was *I* put into Class D?!" Yukimura cried resentfully. A thin layer of sweat covered his forehead.

"Wait, does this mean that we can't get into college now? Why did we even go to this school? Does Sae-chan-sensei hate us or something?"

None of the other students could hide their confusion.

"I understand that you're all confused right now, but everyone needs to calm down." Hirata, sensing the classroom tipping toward crisis, stood and attempted to rein everyone in.

"How are we supposed to calm down? Aren't you frustrated that she called us a bunch of failures?!" Yukimura said.

"Even if I was, isn't it better for us to band together so we can turn things around?" Hirata asked.

"Turn things around? I don't even agree with how we were sorted in the first place!"

"I understand. However, sitting here whining won't help us right now."

"What did you say?" Yukimura quickly went to Hirata and forcefully grasped his collar.

"Calm down, you two, okay? I'm sure that the teacher talked to us harshly so we'd be inspired to do better, right?"

That was Kushida. She slipped between the two and separated them, gently taking Yukimura's balled fist. Just as anyone would expect, Yukimura didn't try to hurt her and reflexively took half a step back.

"Besides, it's only been one month since we started here, right? Like Hirata-kun said, it's better if we all do our best together. Do you think that I'm wrong about that?"

"N-no, it's... Well, I certainly wouldn't say you're *wrong*, but..."

Yukimura's anger had almost completely vanished.

Kushida looked at everyone in class, and it was almost as if her eyes reflected a sincere wish for us to work together.

"Yeah, it's better for us to band together. Right? There's no need for you to fight, Yukimura. Hirata."

"I'm sorry. I lost my cool," Yukimura said.

"It's all right. I should have chosen my words a little more carefully."

Kushida Kikyou's presence brought everyone together. I took out my cell phone and snapped a picture of the paper with the class point totals. Horikita, taking notice, looked at me with a puzzled expression.

"What are you doing?" she asked.

"I haven't been able to figure out how points are calculated yet. You've also been taking notes, haven't you?"

If I could figure out how many points were deducted by being late or talking in class, it'd be easier to come up with countermeasures.

"Wouldn't it be difficult to figure out those details at this stage? Besides, I don't think you can resolve this simply by investigating. Everyone in our class arrived late and talked too often."

As Horikita had said, it certainly was difficult to conclude anything based on the current information. Also, Horikita's usually cool, composed attitude was gone. She seemed rather impatient.

"Are you trying to get into college, too?" I wondered.

"Why do you ask?"

"Well, when we learned about the differences between A and D, you looked shocked."

"But so was almost everyone in this class, more or less. If they'd told us at the start, that would've been one thing, but to explain it at this stage? Unthinkable."

Well, she was right about that. There was probably a lot of discontented grumbling coming from Class C and B students as well. After all, the school treated every class except for A like leftovers. Trying to get to the top was probably our best option.

"I think that before we even start talking about A or D or whatever, we should secure points."

"Points are just a byproduct of our performance, though. Not having points won't hinder our lives here at school. We have free options at almost every turn, right?" Horikita said.

If you thought about it that way, it'd be a relief for the students who'd lost all of their points.

"'Won't hinder our lives here at school,' huh?"

If you wanted to simply get by, this wouldn't be a problem. However, there were many things you could only obtain with points. Entertainment, for example. If the lack of entertainment options wasn't a problem, then it'd be fine, but...

"About how many points did you spend last month, Ayanokouji-kun?"

"Hm? Oh, my points? I spent about 20,000, approximately."

This was tragic for the students who'd used up their points. Like Yamauchi, who was ranting and raving at his desk. Ike had also spent almost all of his points.

"While unfortunate, they've simply reaped what they've sown," Horikita said.

It was certainly true that indiscriminately spending all 100,000 points in a single month was a *slight* problem.

"They baited us into spending all our points over the course of this one month, and we fell for it."

One hundred thousand points per month. Even though everyone had thought it too good to be true, we'd been too happy to care.

"Attention, everyone. Before class begins, I want you to listen seriously for a moment. Especially you, Sudou-kun." The class was still in an uproar, but Hirata claimed everyone's attention when he stood at the teacher's podium.

"Tch, what is it?" Sudou grumbled.

"We didn't get any points this month. This is a serious problem, and one that will have an enormous impact on our daily lives moving forward. It's impossible for us to make it to graduation with zero points, right?"

"You're absolutely right!" shouted one of the female students, her voice full of despair.

Hirata gave a kind nod in response, sympathizing with her.

"Of course. Therefore, we must earn points next month. To do that, we all need to cooperate with each other. So, please, take care not to be late to class or to talk during the lecture. Also, the use of cell phones during class is prohibited, of course."

"Huh? And why do *you* get to tell us what to do? Besides, that's supposing our points will increase. If they don't change at all, then it's useless."

"As long as we continue talking during class and being late, our points won't increase for sure. Although we can't go below zero points, disruption will, without a doubt, count as strikes against us."

"I'm still not convinced. Besides, even if we get serious and work hard in class, our points won't necessarily go up." Sudou snorted and crossed his arms in defiance. Kushida took notice of this and commented on it.

"Well, the teacher *did* say that the being late and talking in class were obviously bad, right?"

"Yeah, I agree with Kushida-san. It's only natural to avoid doing those things."

"That's just your own selfish interpretation. Besides,

you don't know how to increase our points. Try talking to me after you figure that out."

"I don't think that there's anything particularly wrong with what you said, Sudou-kun. I apologize if I made you feel uncomfortable." Hirata bowed his head politely toward the disgruntled Sudou. "However, Sudou-kun, it's a fact that unless we all cooperate, we won't get any more points."

"Do whatever you want. It doesn't matter. Just don't involve me in it. Understand?" Sudou snapped.

As if being in the room made him feel uncomfortable, he left immediately. I had to wonder: Would he return when class started? Or did he not intend to return at all?

"Sudou-kun really can't read the room. He's the one who was late to class the most. Couldn't we still get some points even without Sudou-kun?"

"Yeah. He really is the worst. Why is he in our class?"

Hmm. Until now, everyone had been enjoying their lives of luxury to the absolute fullest. No one had previously complained about Sudou. Hirata stepped down from the podium and, strangely, stopped right in front of my desk.

"Horikita-san, Ayanokouji-kun, do you have a moment? I want to speak with you about how we can increase our points. I'd like you to join me. Can you?"

"Why do you want us?" I asked.

"I want to hear everyone's voices. However, if I ask for everyone to weigh in, I think more than half of the class probably won't take it seriously."

So, he wanted to ask us individually? I doubted I'd be able to come up with any particularly useful ideas, but I supposed it couldn't hurt to talk. Just as I was thinking that...

"I'm sorry, can you ask someone else? I'm not particularly good at discussing things with others," said Horikita.

"We wouldn't force you to speak up. If you could help think of something, that would be good. Simply being there would be enough," Hirata said.

"I'm sorry, but I have no interest in something meaningless."

"This is the first trial we're facing together as a united Class D. So then—"

"I refuse. I won't participate." Her words were stern, yet composed. While she'd considered Hirata's position, she refused him once again.

"I...I see. I'm sorry. If you change your mind, I'd love for you to join us."

Horikita had already stopped looking at Hirata, who withdrew dejectedly.

"What about you, Ayanokouji-kun?" he asked.

Honestly, I'd be glad to participate. I'd thought that most of the class would be involved. However, if Horikita was the only one absent, then she might be treated the same as Sudou.

"Ah...I'll pass. I'm sorry."

"No, I'm sorry for bothering you. If you change your mind, please let me know."

Hirata probably understood what I was thinking. I hadn't rejected him strongly. After the discussion ended, Horikita began preparing for the next class.

"Hirata's a great guy. He's able to get everyone to take action just like that. People can easily get depressed in these situations."

"That's one perspective, yes. If we could easily solve this by talking, then that'd be fine. However, if an unintelligent student tries to lead the discussion, the group will fall further into chaos, to the point where there's no hope of salvaging anything. Besides, I can't meekly accept my current situation."

"You can't accept what now? What do you mean?"

Horikita didn't answer my question. She fell completely silent.

CLASS HAD ENDED for the day. Hirata stood at the podium, using the blackboard to prepare for our big discussion. Because of Hirata's powerful charisma, almost everyone in our class had shown, with the exception of a few like Horikita and Sudou. When I looked around, I noticed that they'd already left the room. I decided to leave before the discussion got into full swing, as well.

"Ayanokouji!"

Yamauchi suddenly appeared from under my desk, his expression deathlike.

"Whoa! Wh-what? What's wrong?"

"Hey, buy this from me for 20,000 points. I can't buy anything!" he cried.

Yamauchi placed the game console he'd purchased the other day on my desk. Frankly, I didn't even want the thing.

"But if you sell that to me, who am I supposed to play with?" I asked.

"How the heck should *I* know? Come on, it's good, right? It's special, so it's a good deal."

"I'll buy it from you for 1,000 points."

"Ayanokouji! Come on, you're my only hope!"

"Why am *I* the only one? I can't afford it, anyway."

Yamauchi looked at me all teary-eyed, which grossed me out. I looked the other way. He must have realized I wasn't biting, so he immediately switched to a new target.

"Professor! Your best buddy has a favor to ask! Buy this game system for 22,000 points!"

He was trying to get the Professor to buy it and had shamelessly increased the price.

"Things must be really tough for the people who used up their points," remarked Kushida as she observed Yamauchi.

"What about you, Kushida? Do you have enough points? Girls have a lot of necessities, after all."

"I'm okay. For now, anyway. I've used up about half of my points. I kind of lost control the first month and overspent, so it'll be a little difficult to hold myself back. What about you, Ayanokouji-kun? Are you okay?"

"It's got to be hard not to spend money when you're so popular. I've barely used any of my points, to be honest. I haven't really needed to buy anything."

"Because you don't have friends?" she asked.

"Hey..."

"Ah, sorry, sorry. I didn't mean to offend," Kushida apologized with a giggle. She was too cute when she did that.

"Hey, Kushida-san, do you have a minute?" Karuizawa asked.

"What's up, Karuizawa-san?"

"Honestly, I've spent way too many points, and I'm seriously running low. Some of the other girls in class have lent me a few points, but I was wondering if you could help me out, too. We're friends, right? I only need, like, 2,000 points from you."

Karuizawa didn't seem all that earnest, laughing breezily while she hit up Kushida. In such a case, rejection should be the knee-jerk reaction.

"Okay, sure."

Sure?! I repeated silently, but it wasn't my business. This was a problem for the friends in question. Kushida had decided to help Karuizawa without even a hint of reluctance.

"Thank you! This is really what friends are for, huh? By the way, here's my number. Okay, see you later. Ah, Inogashira-san! Hey, to tell you the truth, I used up too many of my points..."

Karuizawa turned away just like that and went in pursuit of her next target.

"Are you sure? You know you probably won't get those points back, right?" I asked.

"I can't just ignore a friend in need. Karuizawa-san has a lot of friends, too, so I think it's probably hard for her not to have any points."

"I think using up 100,000 points is kind of her own fault, though."

"Wait, how do you transfer points?" Kushida asked.

"Karuizawa gave you her phone number, didn't she? You should be able to do it with your cell phone."

"This school really does take great care of its students. It even has a way to help students like Karuizawa-san."

True, transferring points was a lifesaver for Karuizawa, but was it really necessary to give her the money? If anything, it seemed a recipe for disaster.

The loudspeaker came alive with a soothing sound effect, and a robotic voice issued an announcement.

"Ayanokouji-kun, from first-year Class D. Please come see Chabashira-sensei in the faculty office."

"Looks like the teacher wants to see you."

"Yeah... Sorry, Kushida. Gotta go."

I was sure I hadn't done anything to get me called to the office. Exiting the classroom, I could feel my classmates' stares drilling a hole into the back of my head. Timid as a rabbit, I found the faculty office and entered. I looked all around, but I didn't find Chabashira-sensei anywhere. Baffled, I called out to a teacher inspecting her appearance in a mirror.

"Excuse me, is Chabashira-sensei here?"

"Hmm? Sae-chan? Oh, she was just here a moment ago."

The teacher had wavy, shoulder-length hair, which made her look mature. The way she said Chabashira-sensei's name made them sound close. They were near in age and probably friends.

"She must have stepped away for a minute. Do you want to wait here?"

"No, thank you. I'll wait in the hall."

I didn't like being in the faculty office. I hated attention, so the hall would do just as well. However, the young teacher unexpectedly followed me.

"I'm Hoshinomiya Chie, in charge of Class B. Sae and I have been best friends since high school. That's why we call each other Sae-chan and Chie-chan."

That information seemed kind of superfluous.

"Hey, why did Sae-chan call you? Huh? Huh? Why?" she asked.

"No idea."

"I don't understand. You were called to the office without a reason? Hmm? What's your name?"

An onslaught of questions. She scanned me from top to bottom, as if sizing me up.

"My name's Ayanokouji," I said.

"Ayanokouji-kun, huh? Oh, wow, that's a cool name. You're pretty popular, aren't you?"

What was *with* this overly friendly teacher? She acted more like a student. If this were an all-boy school, she would have immediately captured every student's heart.

"Hey, do you already have a girlfriend?" she asked.

"No... I'm, uh, not especially popular."

I tried to seem reluctant, but Hoshinomiya-sensei kept pushing herself onto me. She grabbed my arms with slender, delicate hands.

"Hmm? How unexpected. If we were in the same class, I'd never leave you alone. Perhaps because you're so innocent? Or do you like playing hard to get?"

She caressed my cheeks. I had no idea what to do. She'd probably stop if I licked her fingers, but I had a feeling that'd get me expelled.

"What are you doing, Hoshinomiya?"

Chabashira-sensei appeared out of nowhere. With a loud *thud*, she smacked Hoshinomiya-sensei on the head with her clipboard. Hoshinomiya-sensei crouched and gripped her skull in apparent pain.

"Ouch! What was that for?" she cried.

"For getting involved with one of my students."

"I was only keeping him company while he waited for you, Sae-chan."

"It would have been better if you just left him alone. Thanks for waiting, Ayanokouji. Let's go into the office."

"The guidance office?" I asked. "Did I do something wrong? I've been trying to keep a low profile here."

"A good answer. Come."

While I wondered what this was all about, I followed Chabashira-sensei. Hoshinomiya-sensei remained by my side, smiling widely. Chabashira-sensei noticed and turned, her face much like a demon's.

"You stay," she ordered.

"Come on, don't be so cold! It won't be the end of the world if I listen, right? Besides Sae-chan, you're definitely not the type to give one-on-one guidance. Pulling a new student like Ayanokouji-kun into the guidance room out of nowhere... Are you after something, I wonder?"

Grinning, Hoshinomiya-sensei scooted behind me and placed her hands on my shoulders. I sensed a storm brewing.

"So, Sae-chan, are you looking to be dominated by a younger man?"

Dominated by a younger man? What did *that* mean?

"Don't say such stupid things. That wouldn't be possible."

"Hee, you're certainly right. It wouldn't be possible for *you*, Sae-chan," Hoshinomiya-sensei muttered, her words laced with a double meaning.

"Why are you following us? This is a Class D matter."

"Huh? I can't go to the guidance room? That's not okay? Come on, I can give advice, too."

As Hoshinomiya-sensei continued to follow, a female student came up to us, a beautiful girl with light-pink hair. I'd never seen her before.

"Hoshinomiya-sensei, do you have a moment? The student council wishes to discuss something with you." She glanced at me, but quickly returned her attention to Hoshinomiya-sensei.

"All right, you have someone who needs you. Get to it." *Slap!* Chabashira-sensei smacked Hoshinomiya-sensei on the butt with her clipboard.

"Aw! She'll get mad at me if I hang around any longer. See you later, Ayanokouji-kun! All right, Ichinose-san. Let's go to the faculty office."

With that, she turned on her heel and left with the beautiful Ichinose.

Chabashira-sensei lightly scratched her head while

she watched Hoshinomiya-sensei leave. Soon after, we entered the guidance room, which stood beside the faculty office.

"So. Why did you call me here?" I asked.

"Well, about that... Before we begin, please come here."

She briefly glanced at a clock hanging on the wall, which gave the time as nine o'clock, and opened the door. Inside was a small office kitchenette. She placed a kettle on top of a stove.

"I'm going to make tea. Is roasted green okay?" she asked.

I picked up the container with the tea powder.

"Don't make any unnecessary moves. Shut up and get in here. Understand? Don't make a sound and stay until I tell you it's okay to come out. If you don't do as I say, you'll be expelled," she said.

"Huh? What do you mean by—"

She closed the door to the kitchenette without explanation, leaving me in there. What in the world was she scheming? I did as I was told and waited. Soon after, I heard the outer door to the guidance room open.

"Ah, come in. So, what did you want to talk to me about, Horikita?" I heard Chabashira-sensei say.

Apparently Horikita was in need of guidance.

"I will be frank. Why was I sorted into Class D?"

"That's quite frank."

"Today, you told us that the school sorted superior students into Class A. You said that Class D was filled with the leftovers, the last bastion of delinquents."

"That's true. You must consider yourself to be a superior person."

I wondered how Horikita would respond. I'd bet she'd confidently object.

"I solved nearly every problem on the entrance examination. I made no substantial mistakes on the interview, either. At the very least, I shouldn't have been sorted into Class D."

Looks like I would have won that bet. Horikita was definitely the type to think herself superior. She wasn't excessively self-conscious, either. She'd tied for first place on the test, as shown in the morning's results.

"You solved nearly all of the problems on the entrance examination, hmm? Normally I couldn't show the examination results to individual students, but I'll make an exception in this case. I just so happen to have your answer sheet here."

"You're incredibly prepared. It's...almost as if you knew I'd come here to protest."

"I'm an instructor. I understand the mind of a student, at least to some degree, Horikita Suzune. Just as you said, you did well on the entrance examination. You had the third-highest test score among the first-year students and were close to the highest- and second-highest-scoring students. You did exceedingly well. And you're right: We found no particular problems in your interview. On the contrary, we evaluated you quite highly."

"Thank you very much. So then...why?"

"Before I answer, why are you dissatisfied with Class D?"

"Who could be happy with an incorrect evaluation? Furthermore, the class rankings greatly impact our future prospects. Of course I'm dissatisfied."

"Incorrect evaluation? Perhaps your self-evaluation is far too high." Chabashira-sensei snickered, or rather, laughed outright. "I acknowledge that your academic ability is excellent. You're certainly very smart. However, who decided that smart people are categorically superior? We never said that."

"But...that's just common sense."

"Common sense? Didn't common sense create our current, flawed society? Before, Japan relied solely on test scores to separate the superior and inferior. As a result, the incompetents at the top tried desperately to kick down the truly superior students. In the end, we settled on a system of hereditary succession."

A system of hereditary succession meant that things like social standing, prestige, and employment were passed down to future generations. At those words, I groaned unintentionally. My chest hurt.

"You're a capable student. I don't deny that. However, this school's goal is to produce superior people. If you believe academics alone place you into a higher class, you are mistaken. That was the very first thing we explained to you. Besides, think rationally. Would we have admitted someone like Sudou if we decided superiority based solely on academic merit?"

"Tch..."

Despite the fact that this was one of the country's leading preparatory schools, this place allowed students to enroll for purposes other than academics.

"Furthermore, you may be too hasty in proclaiming that no one would be happy to be incorrectly evaluated. Take Class A, for instance. They are under incredible pressure from the school, and also the target of extreme envy from the lower classes. Competing every day with that kind of pressure bearing down upon you is far more difficult than you might imagine. There are some students who are happy to be incorrectly evaluated at a lower level."

"You're joking, right? I can't understand such a person."

"Is that so? I think that Class D boasts some of those people. Strange students who would happily be set at a low level."

It was almost as if she were talking to me.

"You still haven't given me an explanation. Was I honestly sorted into Class D? Did anything go wrong with the grading? Please double-check," Horikita said.

"I'm sorry, but you weren't sorted by mistake. You are definitely in Class D. You are at that level."

"Is that so? Then I will ask the school again, at another time."

Apparently, she wasn't going to give up. Horikita had merely determined that her homeroom teacher was the wrong person to ask.

"You'll get the same answer from anyone in a higher position. Besides, there's no need to be disappointed. As I told you this morning, it's possible for one class to overtake another. You could conceivably reach Class A before you graduate."

"I can't imagine it will be easy, though. Forget overtaking Class A; how in the world could those immature Class D misfits gain more points? I can't see how it's possible." Horikita spoke the truth. The difference in points was overwhelming.

"I don't know. You alone get to decide how you head

down that path. At any rate, Horikita, do you need to be in Class A for any special reason?"

"Well...I suppose that's enough for now. Excuse me. But know that I'm not yet convinced I was sorted correctly."

"Understood. I will keep that in mind."

A chair squeaked against the floor, signaling that the discussion was over.

"Oh, that reminds me. I've summoned another person to the guidance room. It's someone relevant to you."

"Relevant to me? No, you can't mean... bro—"

"Come on out, Ayanokouji," the teacher said.

This was a bad time to reveal myself. Maybe I just wouldn't go.

"If you don't come out, I'll have you expelled."

Jeez. A teacher shouldn't casually wield expulsion like a weapon.

"How long do you intend to keep me waiting?"

With a sigh, I entered the room. Naturally, Horikita appeared surprised and perplexed.

"Were you listening to our conversation?" she asked me.

"Listening? I know you guys were talking, but I didn't really hear anything. The walls are surprisingly thick."

"That's not true. Voices carry pretty well into the

kitchen." Apparently, Chabashira-sensei wanted to drag me into the action.

"Sensei, why would you do this?" Horikita noticed that this had all been planned and was clearly angry.

"Because I deemed it necessary. Now then, Ayanokouji, I'll explain why I called you here." Chabashira-sensei dismissed Horikita's concerns and shifted her attention to me.

"Well then, if you'll excuse me..." Horikita muttered.

"Wait, Horikita. It would be in your best interest to stay and listen. It may provide you with a hint on how to reach Class A."

Horikita stopped dead in her tracks and sat back down.

"Please keep it brief," she said.

Chabashira-sensei chuckled as she glanced over her clipboard. "You're an interesting student, Ayanokouji."

"Not at all. I'm certainly not as interesting as a teacher with a strange surname like Chabashira."

"Would you speak like that to every Chabashira in the nation? Hmm?"

If you looked all over the country for another person with the surname of Chabashira, you probably wouldn't find one.

"Well, when I read over the entrance exam's results, your scores piqued my interest. I was shocked."

On her clipboard, I saw a rather familiar answer sheet.

"Fifty points in Japanese. Fifty points in mathematics. Fifty points in English. Fifty points in social studies. Fifty points in science. You even scored Fifty points on the recent short test. Do you know what this means?"

A stunned Horikita looked over my test paper and then shifted her focus to me. "This is a rather frightening coincidence," she said.

"Oh? You believe that getting 50s all across the board was a coincidence? He did it intentionally."

"It's a coincidence. There's no evidence that it's not. Besides, what would I gain by manipulating my scores in the first place? If I were intelligent enough to achieve high marks, I would've tried to get perfect scores."

As I feigned innocence, Chabashira-sensei sighed in exasperation.

"You really do seem like an odious student. Listen. Only 3 percent of students solved the fifth math problem successfully. However, you solved it perfectly, and used a complex formula to do so. However, the tenth problem on the test had a completion rate of 76 percent. Did you make a mistake on it? Is that normal?"

"I don't know what normal is. It was a coincidence, I tell you. A coincidence."

"For crying out loud! I respect your frank attitude, but it'll cause problems for you in the future," the teacher said.

"I'll think about that when the time comes."

Chabashira-sensei shot Horikita a glance that seemed to say, *What do* you *think?*

"Why do you pretend not to know?" she asked.

"Like I said, it was a coincidence. It's not like I'm hiding that I'm a genius or anything."

"I wonder. He may be even more intelligent than *you*, Horikita."

Horikita flinched. *Please don't say anything unnecessary, Chabashira-sensei.*

"I don't like studying, and I don't plan to try hard. That's why I get those scores."

"A student who chose this school wouldn't say something like that. However, some students may have different reasons for getting in. You, for example, and Kouenji as well. I think you're fine with being in either D or A."

This school wasn't the only abnormal thing. The teachers were weird, too. Moments earlier, Chabashira-sensei had upset Horikita with just her words. It was almost as if the teachers knew every student's secrets.

"What other reasons do you have?" Horikita asked.

"You want me to explain it to you in detail?"

I noticed the sharp gleam in Chabashira-sensei's eyes. It was almost as if she wanted to provoke Horikita.

"No, we'd best stop here. Any more, and I might go mad and destroy all the furniture in here," I said.

"If you did that, Ayanokouji, I would demote you to E Class."

"Wait, there's an E Class?"

"Certainly. Of course, the 'E' stands for 'expelled.' As in, you'd be kicked out of school. Well, I suppose our conversation has ended. Enjoy your lives."

What incredible sarcasm.

"I'm leaving, too. It's almost time for the faculty meeting. I'm going to close the door, so please step outside."

She pushed us into the hallway. Why had Chabashira-sensei called both of us in together? She didn't seem like the type to do meaningless things.

"Well. Should we head back?" I asked.

Horikita didn't respond, and I walked away. Probably best if we weren't together right now.

"Wait." Horikita called out, but I didn't stop. If I managed to keep away from her until I got to the dorms, I'd be home free.

"Was your score...really just a coincidence?" she asked.

"I already said so, didn't I? Or do you have any proof that I got that score on purpose?"

"I don't, but...I also don't understand, Ayanokouji-kun.

You said that you like to avoid trouble, but you don't seem to be interested in Class A."

"You have an extraordinary fixation on Class A."

"Should I not? I'm simply striving to improve my future prospects."

"Oh, absolutely. You should. It's perfectly natural."

"When I entered this school, I thought graduation was my only goal. But the reality is different. I'm not even at the starting line."

Horikita sped up and started walking next to me.

"So, why are you aiming for Class A?"

"First, I want to ascertain this school's true motives. Why was *I* put into Class D? Chabashira-sensei said I'd been deemed a Class D student, but why? When I discover the answer, I'll aim for A. No, I will definitely make it to A."

"That's going to be difficult. You'll have to rehabilitate the problem children. You have Sudou's continued tardiness and class cutting, everyone else talking in class, and, of course, the test scores. Even if you manage all of that, you're still at zero points."

"I know that. I still think the school made a mistake with my placement."

Anxiety had replaced Horikita's previously overflowing confidence. Did she really know that was the case?

The only conclusion I could draw from today was that "despair" was a two-syllable word. If you followed the fundamental school rules, you could avoid losing points. However, it was still unclear how to turn those losses into gains. Class A had had only had a small number of points subtracted.

Even if we somehow found an efficient way to increase our points, the other classes might also find a way to do the same. Since we'd started out with such a substantial difference in points, we'd have to compete hard against the other classes in a limited amount of time.

"I can understand your thoughts, but I don't think the school will continue supervising us so carefully. If they did, there'd be no meaning in competition," Horikita said.

"I see. I suppose you could think that. So, you'll try to take care of this situation by yourself?" I asked.

"Yes."

"Don't act so proud."

A hand chopped my side. Horikita ignored my pained expression.

"Ow. Look, I understand how you feel, but you can't solve this by yourself. Think about Sudou. Even if you improve, the rest of the class will drag you down."

"No. You're right that no lone individual can solve this

problem. We won't even make it to the starting line without everyone's help."

"Well, it sounds like we've got a huge problem on our hands."

"We have three major, immediate issues. Tardiness and talking during class are the first two. Third, we must make sure no one fails the midterm exam."

"I think we'll manage those first two issues, but the midterms..."

The short test we'd taken had contained a few difficult questions, but overall it had been pretty easy. Even at that level, some students had failed. Honestly, their chances of passing the midterm exam were slim.

"I need your help, Ayanokouji-kun."

"Help?"

Horikita glared at me.

"What if I refuse? Like how you refused Hirata this morning."

"Do you want to refuse?" she asked.

"What if I said I'd gladly help?"

"I never would've thought you'd do it gladly, but I doubt you'd refuse. If you *did* refuse to work with me, then that would be the end of it. No matter what I said about our future, I'd be powerless if you refused. So, will you help me or not?"

I wanted to say what she'd said before, when she'd silenced Hirata... What was it, again? Well, it wasn't as though I would just bluntly refuse someone who asked for my help. Then again, if I told her I *would* help, she'd probably run me into the ground until graduation. I needed the heart of a demon.

"I refuse," I said.

"I always knew you'd help, Ayanokouji-kun. I'm grateful."

"I didn't say that! I turned you down!"

"No, I heard the voice inside your head. You said you'd help."

Terrifying! It was like she could read my thoughts.

"I don't even know how I could help you, though." Besides being an exemplary student, Horikita was incredibly quick-witted. She probably didn't need my skills.

"Don't worry. I don't require your brain power, Ayanokouji-kun. Leave the planning to me, and act as I tell you."

"Huh? What do you mean by act?"

"Doesn't our lack of points trouble you, Ayanokouji-kun? If you follow my instructions, I promise you we'll see a point increase. I would never lie."

"I don't know what you're cooking up, but there are other people you could count on. If you made friends, they'd cooperate with you."

"Unfortunately, no one else in Class D is nearly as easy to manipulate as you."

"No, there are several people. Hirata, for example. He's popular and smart, so he'd be perfect. Besides, he's worried that you're all alone, Horikita."

If she reached out to him, they'd probably become good friends.

"He's no good. Even if he has some talent and ability, I can't use him. To use an analogy, think about the pieces in shogi. Right now, I don't need a gold or silver general. I want a pawn."

So, you just called me a pawn? That's what you called me?

"So, if a pawn were to cooperate, he could become a gold general?"

"An interesting answer, but you don't seem like the type to make that effort, Ayanokouji-kun. Besides, haven't you been thinking, 'I've always been a pawn, I don't want to advance,' all along?"

She'd shot me down with precisely the right brand of ammunition. If I were a normal person, my feelings would've been hurt.

"Sorry, but I can't help you. I'm not suitable for this," I said.

"Well, contact me once you've given it some thought. I look forward to hearing from you."

Horikita wasn't paying attention to what I'd said in the slightest.

.

8 ▶ THE ASSOCIATION OF FAILURES

MAY 1 CAME AND WENT, and before we knew it, the
school week was over. Ike and the others had started
listening to the teacher. Only Sudou kept unashamedly
falling asleep in class, but no one tried to reprimand
him. Because we hadn't yet found a method to increase
our points, he'd apparently decided not to fix his habits.
However, many of our classmates grew to disdain him.

I was a little sleepy, myself. It was hard to stay awake
just before lunchtime. Also, I'd stayed up late last night
watching an online video. Ah, sleep would feel so nice...

"Ah?!"

Just as my head started to bob, sudden pain shot
through my right arm.

"What's the matter, Ayanokouji? You cried out. Have
you started your rebellious phase or something?"

"N-no. Sorry, Chabashira-sensei. I got some dirt in my eye."

Normally, the other students would have started whispering. But, wary of potentially losing points, they instead shot me pained glances. As I rubbed the sting on my arm, I glared at my neighbor. Horikita brandished her mathematical compass. This was insane. Why did she even have a compass ready in the first place? You didn't even really need one of those for this school. After class, I immediately went over to her.

"Certain things are off limits! It's dangerous to stab someone!"

"Are you angry with me?" she asked.

"You put a hole in my arm! A hole!"

"What? When did I stab with you a compass needle, Ayanokouji-kun?"

"You're holding a dangerous weapon right now."

"So, just because I'm holding something means I stabbed you?"

I'd spent most of the class wide-eyed, not because of the lecture, but the pain.

"Be careful. If you get caught sleeping, that would undoubtedly lead to a loss in points."

Horikita had started to take action within Class D. Her protests to the school had gone nowhere. *Ah, that hurt!* Damn it, if Horikita ever fell asleep in class, I'd return the favor. When everyone got up for lunch, Hirata spoke.

"Chabashira-sensei mentioned that the midterm is coming up soon. Remember that if you fail, you'll be expelled. Therefore, I think it would be a good idea to form a study group."

Apparently, the hero of Class D had started another project.

"If you neglect your studies, you'll get a failing grade and be expelled on the spot. I want to avoid that. However, studying won't just prevent expulsion; it may also help earn points. If we receive high marks, our class's assessment should improve as a result. I asked some of the students who scored high on the test to help prepare a study plan. So, I would like people who are anxious to come join our group. Everyone is welcome, of course."

Hirata stared directly at Sudou while making his grand speech.

"Tch."

Sudou averted his gaze, crossed his arms, and closed his eyes. Ever since Sudou had stomped all over Hirata's introduction game, their relationship had been rocky.

"Starting today at five o'clock, we will plan to study in this classroom for two hours a day until the test. If you'd like to join us, please come whenever you like. Of course, I don't mind if you need to leave partway. That's all I have to say."

Immediately after he'd finished speaking, several of the failing students got up and went over. There were three people with failing grades who didn't rush to Hirata, though: Sudou, Ike, and Yamauchi. Ike and Yamauchi seemed unsure of what to do for a moment, but in the end, they stayed in their seats. I couldn't tell whether they were afraid Sudou might lose his temper, or because they were jealous of Hirata's popularity.

8.1

"ARE YOU FREE FOR LUNCH? Do you want to eat together?"

During our break, Horikita came up and invited me out.

"It's unusual to get an invitation from you. I feel nervous."

"There's no reason to be. I can treat you to the vegetable meal set, if that's okay with you."

Wait, wasn't that the free meal?

"I'm joking. Seriously, whatever you want to eat is on me."

"Now I'm *definitely* scared. Is there some kind of catch?"

An invitation from Horikita was suspicious enough. The suddenness of the request also gave me pause.

"If people can't honestly accept kindness, then mankind will meet its end, won't it?" she asked.

"Well, I suppose so, but..."

With no other plans, I decided to follow Horikita to the cafeteria, where I chose one of the most expensive special meal sets. Together, we sat down.

"Well then, shall we eat?" she asked. Horikita started at me intently, as if she were waiting for me to begin.

"What's the matter, Ayanokouji-kun? Aren't you going to eat?"

"Oh."

There was definitely a catch, no doubt about it. Nevertheless, I couldn't just sit here and not eat. Letting the food get cold would be a waste. I hesitantly bit into my croquette.

"I know this is rather sudden, but I want to talk to you about something."

"I have a bad feeling about this..."

Just as I was preparing to flee, she grabbed my hand. "Ayanokouji-kun, I'll ask once again. Will you listen to me?"

"Ugh..."

"Ever since Chabashira-sensei's warning, fewer people have arrived late or talked in class. When I say we eliminated more than half of the reasons our class got into trouble, I'm not exaggerating."

"Yeah, that's true. It wasn't really a difficult issue to begin with, though." There was no guarantee things would continue in this vein, but at least these last few days had been considerably better than before.

"The next step is to improve our chances of scoring well on the midterm. Hirata-kun started taking action toward that end earlier."

"The study groups, huh? Well, I suppose that a study group certainly could help. Only..."

"Only what? It sounds like you're implying something. What's the problem?"

"Nothing. Don't worry about it. I have to say, it's unusual to see you so worried for others."

"I can't truly imagine failing a test. However, it's true that some students in this world can do just that."

"Sudou and the others, you mean? You're vicious as ever, I see."

"I'm just telling the truth."

Because students couldn't leave campus, contact anyone on the outside, or even attend cram schools, their only option was to help one another.

"I'm relieved that Hirata-kun set up a study group. However, Sudou-kun, Ike-kun, and Yamauchi-kun didn't join, did they? That worries me," Horikita said.

"Oh, those guys. I wouldn't say they're Hirata's enemies, but they aren't on good terms with him. They wouldn't join."

"So, in other words, there remains a high probability that those three will fail. In order to reach Class A, we need to avoid demerits and build toward a positive evaluation, correct? I think it highly likely that good test scores will help with that."

I suppose it's only natural that a student would expect their grade to reflect how much effort they put into the test.

"What if you also held a study group like Hirata's, specifically for helping Sudou and Ike?" I asked.

"Sure. I wouldn't have any objections to that. You probably find that rather surprising, though, don't you?"

"Well, everything about your behavior up until now has been surprising."

I wasn't actually surprised, though. Horikita was doing this all for her own benefit. Personally, I'd never thought that Horikita was that cold of a person.

"Well, I understand that you want to move up to Class A. However, I didn't think that you'd opt for ordinary methods like tutoring them. Typically, failing students tend not to like studying. Besides, you've kept your distance from the other students since the first day, right? I doubt someone who considers friends unnecessary would be able to bring people together easily."

"That's why I'm asking you. Fortunately, you're already friendly with these people, right?"

"Huh? Hey, wait. You couldn't mean..."

"It'll be quicker if *you* try to convince them. It shouldn't be a problem; they're happy to say that you're friends, right? Bring them to the library, and I'll tutor them."

"This is insane. Do you honestly think someone who does his best to lead an utterly harmless and inoffensive life would be able to do something that requires actual social skills?"

"It's not a matter of can or can't. Just do it," she said.

Was I her pet dog or something?

"You can aim for Class A, but don't involve me."

"You ate the food I treated you to, right? Lunch. The special set. A wonderful, delicious meal."

"I simply received the honest goodwill of another human being."

"Unfortunately, that wasn't out of goodwill. I had an ulterior motive."

"Sorry, I didn't hear a word you said. Here, have some points, my *treat*. Now we're even."

"I refuse to stoop so low as to accept handouts from others," she said.

"I think this might be the first time I'm actually angry at you..."

"So what will you do? Cooperate? Or make me your enemy?"

"It almost feels like you're holding a gun to my head."

"No, not 'almost.' I really *am* threatening you," replied Horikita.

The power of violence certainly was effective. Well... if all I did was gather them together, there wasn't anything particularly wrong with cooperating. After all, due to Horikita's stance against friendship, she wouldn't be effective at diplomacy.

Furthermore, it'd taken a lot of time and trouble to become friends with Sudou and Ike. I'd hate for them to have to drop out so quickly. Sensing my hesitation, Horikita pressed me.

"You don't think I've forgiven you for conspiring with Kushida-san and inviting me out under false pretenses, do you?" she asked.

"You said you wouldn't blame me. Bringing that up is unfair."

"I said that to Kushida-san. I don't remember saying that to *you*, Ayanokouji-kun."

"Wow. You play dirty."

"If you want my forgiveness, cooperate with me."

It looked as though I'd never had an escape route in the first place. At this juncture, the only way to avoid a hassle would be to help her.

"I can't guarantee anything. Are you okay with that?"

"I believe you'll find a way. Oh, here's my phone number and email. If something happens, contact me."

Although the circumstances were unusual, I'd gotten a girl's contact information for the first time in my high school life. It was Horikita's, though, so I wasn't particularly happy.

8.2

• •

I GLANCED AROUND THE CLASSROOM. What was I supposed to do now? If I said, "Hey, want to study with me after class?" would anyone even come?

Sudou and I were close enough that he might, but I wasn't sure about the others. Well, with nothing to lose, I decided to try.

"Hey, Sudou. Have a minute?" I called as he headed back to the classroom after lunch. He was sweating and a bit short of breath. Probably played some basketball during his lunch break.

"What are you going to do about the midterm?"

"Oh, that. I don't know. I've never really studied seriously before," he said.

"Oh, yeah? Well, I have just the thing. I wanted to form a study group to meet every day after class, starting today. Want to join?"

Sudou stared at me, his mouth slightly agape.

"You serious? If the lessons are a pain in my ass, why would studying *after* class be any better? Besides, I have club activities, so it's pointless. Plus, *you're* going to be tutoring? Your scores weren't great, either."

"Don't worry about that part. Horikita's the tutor."

"Horikita? I don't really know anything about her. Sounds fishy; I'll pass. I'll be fine cramming for the test the night before."

Sudou had refused to join, just as I'd guessed. If I persisted, it'd fall on deaf ears. Damn, was it really useless? If I tried to press him further, he might punch me. Perhaps there was no helping it. Maybe I should start with someone more manageable. I called out to Ike, who was playing on his phone.

"Hey, Ike, h—"

"Pass! I heard you talking with Sudou. Study group? No way. Not my thing."

"You do know you'll be expelled if you fail, right?"

"Well, yeah. I might have gotten failing grades before, but I'm doing much better now. I'll just cram the night before with Sudou."

Was he really fine with that? He didn't seem to grasp the danger of this situation.

"If the last test hadn't been such a surprise sucker

punch, I probably could've gotten, like, forty points."

"I know what you mean, but wouldn't it be better to stick together on this?" I asked.

"A high school student's free time is precious, you know? I don't want to waste it studying."

He waved me off, completely focused on texting with some girl. Ever since Hirata had managed to get a girlfriend, Ike was desperate to find a girl of his own. My shoulders slumped as I returned to my seat. Maybe if I told Horikita I'd tried my best, she'd forgive me.

"No good," she said.

"Uh, what do you mean by that?" I asked.

"I said 'no good.' You really didn't think it would be that simple, did you?"

Damn it. She'd completely ignored my appeal. How shameless.

"No, of course not. I still have 425 plans remaining," I grumbled.

I looked around the room. Contrary to the tension of class, lunch had a friendlier, albeit noisier, atmosphere.

I needed a method to get reluctant students to buckle down and work. Also, I needed a way to get them to study during free time, not during class. Normally I wouldn't involve myself, but they were in danger of expulsion.

I was sure that Sudou would participate if given the

chance. Now I had no choice but to find some kind of incentive. I needed him to think there'd be a juicy bonus he'd get by studying. I'd require something concrete and easy to understand. Something effective.

And then it hit me!

Blessed with a divine revelation, I turned, wide-eyed, to Horikita.

"Even though you're the tutor, getting Sudou and Ike to study is no easy feat. I'll need more of your abilities. Can you help me?" I asked.

"'More of my abilities'? What exactly am I supposed to do?"

"How about this? If they get a perfect score, you agree to be their girlfriend or something. They'll definitely jump at the chance if we offer that kind of incentive. Girls are great motivation for guys."

"Do you want to die?" she asked.

"No, I'd rather live."

"I listened because I thought you had a serious plan. I was an idiot to think so."

No, I truly believed that'd be effective. It'd be the biggest impetus to study they'd ever had in their entire lives. However, Horikita clearly didn't understand men.

"Okay, how about a kiss? If they get a perfect score, you give them a kiss."

"So, you really *do* want to die?"

"No, living would still be preferable."

Something sharp jabbed the back of my neck. Damn it. Horikita definitely didn't acknowledge the value of my methods. It would be exceptionally effective, though. Well, that meant I had to go back to the drawing board. As I considered this, I noticed someone quite conspicuous. It wasn't Hirata, but another person who might easily rally the class around her: Kushida Kikyou.

She looked great, of course, and she was bright and energetic. She was so sociable that anyone, regardless of gender, could chat with her freely. Also, Ike was madly in love with Kushida, while Sudou and the others at least had a good impression of her. On top of that, her test scores were relatively high. She was absolutely perfect.

"Hey!"

Just as I called out, I remembered that Horikita didn't want to be friends with Kushida. I stopped there.

"What is it?" Kushida asked.

"Oh, uh...it's nothing."

Horikita fundamentally disliked mingling with other people. When Kushida and I had tried to enact Operation Friendship, it had made Horikita furious. Horikita probably wouldn't approve of Kushida's involvement. I'd put my plan on hold until Horikita returned to the dorms.

8.3

BEFORE I KNEW IT, class had ended for the day. Horikita quickly departed and went straight home. The time had come to enact my plan. I needed to capture Kushida.

"Hey, do you have a minute?" I called out as she prepared to head back to the dorm. Kushida turned around.

"Oh, it's unusual for you to come talk to me, Ayanokouji-kun. Do you need something?" she asked.

"Yeah. If it's okay with you, could we talk outside?"

"Well, I was going to meet up with my friends, so I don't really have much time, but...okay."

Smiling, she followed me, not a trace of unpleasantness to be found. After we turned the hall corner, Kushida waited for me to speak. I was trembling with excitement.

"Rejoice, Kushida. You've been selected as an ambassador of goodwill. Tomorrow, your hard work begins."

"Uh, what? I'm sorry, but what do you mean?" she asked.

Etc., etc., etc. I basically explained to her that I wanted to form a study group to save Sudou and the others. Of course, I also told her that Horikita would be tutoring.

"I thought that you could use this study group as a way to get closer to Horikita. What do you think?" I asked.

"Well, I do want to get closer to her, but... well, I won't worry about that now. Besides, it's only natural to help out a friend in need."

This girl was just way too good. She seemed to truly want to prevent Ike and Sudou's expulsion.

"Are you really okay with this? If not, I won't force you to join," I said.

"Ah, I'm sorry. I didn't hesitate because I disliked the idea. I hesitated because I was happy."

Kushida leaned against the wall, gently kicking it.

"It's cruel to expel someone for getting a bad grade. Isn't it awful to have to say goodbye after you've worked to become friends with everyone? When Hirata-kun told us that he was holding a study group, I greatly admired him. But you could say that Horikita has been much more observant than I. She noticed Sudou and those other guys, after all. It's like Horikita is now starting to think of her classmates as friends. I'll do anything I can to be useful!"

Kushida took my hand and smiled. Whoa, she was seriously way too cute! There wasn't a man alive who wouldn't fall for that smile.

I couldn't afford to get carried away, though. I tried to look safe and inoffensive.

"Great! We could definitely use your help. If you're there, our chances will improve a hundred times over."

"Ah, but there's just one thing I want to ask you. I want to participate in the study group, too," Kushida said.

"Huh? Really?"

"Yes. I want to study with everyone."

My wishes had all come true. Kushida's presence would brighten our study group, which would otherwise be pretty glum. However, since she didn't get bad grades, there really wasn't a reason for her to be there.

"So then, when do we start?" she asked.

"We plan on starting tomorrow." In my mind, I added, *Horikita does, at least.*

"I see. Then I'll have to talk to everyone by the end of the day. I'll contact you later, okay?"

"Oh, do you need Sudou and the others' contact information?"

"It's okay. I already have it. The only people whose numbers I don't have are you and Horikita-san, actually..."

Well, I hadn't known that.

"This might be too forward, but are you two already dating?" Kushida asked.

"Wh-where did you hear that? Horikita and I are friends...no, just neighbors."

"It's a big rumor among the girls in our class, you know. They say that even though Horikita-san is always alone, she only seems to get along really well with you, Ayanokouji-kun. And you guys eat together, after all."

Hmm, so the girls had already started spreading rumors about us.

"That's a shame, because, unfortunately, there's nothing going on like that between me and Horikita."

"So, there's no problem swapping phone numbers, right?"

"Not at all."

And so, I got another girl's number.

8.4

. . . .

I WAS LAZING AROUND my room that night when I
received a text message from Kushida.

Yamauchi-kun and Ike-kun said okay! (•w•)b

That was fast.

Ike had waved me off when I'd tried to invite him
earlier. A girl's presence had likely played a large part in
changing his mind. Lust held unlimited power.

*I just contacted Sudou right now, but I have a good feel-
ing about it! (^w^)*

Another text message. Wow. At this rate, we'd probably get everyone together tomorrow. Because of these
speedy developments, I thought it'd be a good idea to
relay information to Horikita. I wrote a message basically saying I had Kushida's help, that Ike and Yamauchi
had agreed to come, and that Kushida would also be

participating. Then I sent the message to Horikita.

"All right. Time to take a bath, I think."

The moment I rose from my bed, Horikita called.

"Hello?" I answered.

"I don't quite understand the message you just sent me," she said.

"What do you mean you don't understand? I wrote it all out plain as day, didn't I? I said those three guys would probably come tomorrow."

"Not that part. The part about Kushida. I didn't know about that."

"I asked her a little while ago. Having someone like Kushida on our side increases the odds of getting everyone together. So I asked her, and now Sudou and Ike and Yamauchi are coming. Okay?"

"I don't remember giving you permission to do that. Her grades aren't even failing."

"Okay, look. By asking Kushida, who's spent more time networking, to help us, our chances of success have improved significantly."

"I don't like it. Shouldn't you have sought my approval first?"

"I understand that you hate outgoing people like Kushida. But isn't this just a means to an end? Or would you prefer trying to gather everyone yourself?"

"Well..."

Horikita seemed to finally understand that getting Kushida on board was a good thing. But, being prideful, she couldn't simply agree to it.

"We don't have much time until the test, either. Understand?"

Come to think of it, we really didn't have much time to make Horikita's plan work. However, Horikita was clearly stuck and unable to make a snap decision. She remained silent for a moment.

"I understand. I suppose anything worth doing requires sacrifice. However, Kushida may only help gather the students. She's not allowed to join the study group."

"But why? That was her condition for helping us. You're being ridiculous," I said.

"I will not allow her into our study group. I refuse to budge on this."

"Is this about what happened at the café? Are you just getting back at Kushida for deceiving you?"

"This has nothing to do with that. She didn't fail the test. Inviting extra people will only mean more time spent and greater confusion."

Although her argument sounded logical, I doubted that was her real reason for excluding Kushida.

"Do you openly dislike Kushida?" I asked.

"Don't *you* feel uncomfortable sitting next to someone you hate?"

"Huh?"

I didn't really understand what Horikita meant. Kushida had tried harder than anyone to befriend Horikita. I couldn't imagine why Horikita actually hated Kushida.

"Suppose the guys decide not to come if Kushida's out?"

"Sorry, reviewing these test materials is taking longer than I expected. I'm ending the call here. Goodnight."

"Hey, wait!"

She hung up on me, as expected of a misanthrope. However, if we wanted to reach Class A, compromise was necessary. I plugged my phone into my charger and lay down, thinking through everything that had happened since the entrance ceremony.

"Defective product, huh?"

That was what that second-year student had called us on our first day. In other words, we weren't just defective; we were fundamentally failing to serve our purpose. Those were the words they'd used to ridicule us. Even Horikita, who appeared flawless, probably had some defects of her own. I could kind of understand why she'd been angry today.

"What should I do?"

Should I try to force Horikita? In the worst-case scenario, she'd leave. If Horikita didn't tutor the study group, it'd waste everyone's time. With a heavy heart, I called Kushida.

"Hello?"

I heard something like a strong wind blowing into the phone. It quickly died down, though.

"Were you drying your hair or something?" I asked.

"Oh, sorry. Did you hear that? I just finished up, so don't worry."

Kushida had just gotten out of the bath... This wasn't the time to get lost in fantasies.

"Uh, this is really hard for me to tell you, but... Can we pretend that I never asked you to help get everybody together?"

She paused and then replied, "Um, why?" She sounded curious rather than angry.

"I'm sorry. I can't explain right now. Things got kind of complicated."

"Is that so? I suppose Horikita-san was opposed to me joining."

I hadn't implied that, but Kushida had managed to pick up on it. "It has nothing to do with Horikita. It's my bad."

"It's okay. I'm not particularly angry. Horikita seems to really dislike me, so I expected she'd refuse."

You could call it a woman's intuition.

"Anyway, I'm sorry. It's my bad, since I came to you for help and all."

"It's okay. You don't have to apologize, Ayanokouji-kun. But, I...don't think that Horikita-san will be able to bring Sudou-kun and the others together by herself."

I couldn't deny it.

"Hey, what did Horikita-san say, though? Was she against me gathering people, or did she not want me to join the study group?"

Kushida was so dead-on, it was like she'd been standing next to me when Horikita called.

"The latter. I'm really sorry to hurt your feelings."

"Ahh, it's okay. Really, don't apologize, Ayanokouji-kun. Horikita-san has this kind of impenetrable aura around her, like she won't let people get close to her. I expected this."

She was way too perceptive.

"Everyone agreed to join because I said I'd participate, though... Couldn't you have just lied and told me that I couldn't join? I'm worried that if they know I'm not coming now, the guys will probably get mad at Horikita-san..."

Kushida scared me a bit. Nothing escaped her.

"Could you leave things to me this time?" she asked.

"Leave it to you?"

"I'll bring everyone over tomorrow. Of course, I'll be coming along, too."

"That's—" I started.

"It'll be okay. Or can you solve all of these problems, Ayanokouji-kun? You know, gather everyone together without me?"

Unfortunately, such a thing was probably impossible.

"I understand. I'll leave it to you, then. I don't really know what's going to happen, though."

"Don't worry. You won't be responsible for anything, Ayanokouji-kun. Well then, I'll see you tomorrow."

Soon after, my call with Kushida ended. Somehow, I was even more exhausted than when I'd finished talking to Horikita. Even though Kushida said everything was fine, I had my doubts.

Horikita relentlessly opposed anyone she didn't like, regardless of who they were. It was painfully obvious that this would end in disaster. Feeling anxious, I headed into the bathroom.

I decided to stop thinking about tomorrow. No matter how much I agonized over it, tomorrow would come, and it would eventually end. Things would work out, somehow.

8.5

· ·

HORIKITA HAD BEEN sullen all morning. It would've been nice if she got adorable when she was angry. If she puffed out her reddened cheeks, she'd be cute enough to make any man would swoon. However, she remained expressionless and silent, refusing to acknowledge my existence. If I were to ignore her, though, she'd probably take out her compass. After an especially long day, we finally finished class.

"Have you gathered everyone in the study group?"

Her first words to me included "study group." She was most definitely implying something.

"Kushida's bringing them. I wonder if she'll participate," I replied.

"Kushida-san, hmm? I thought I specified that she wasn't allowed to participate..."

Satisfied, Horikita left for the library, and I followed. Kushida gave me a too-cute wink as I left. Together, Horikita and I secured a long table at the far end of the library and waited for the others.

"I've brought everyone!"

Kushida came over to where we were seated. Behind her was...

"Kushida-chan told us about this study group. I don't want to be expelled after only just starting. Thanks!"

Ike, Yamauchi, and Sudou had all shown up. However, they'd brought an unexpected visitor, a boy named Okitani.

"Huh? Okitani, you failed, too?" I asked.

"Oh, n-no. Not exactly. I was just really close to failing, so I was worried... Is it not, er, okay for me to join you? It's a little difficult to join Hirata's group..." Okitani looked up at me, puffing out his cute, slightly reddened cheeks. He was slender, with blue hair cut in a short bob. A boy attracted to anything feminine might have shouted "I'm in love!" right away. If Okitani weren't a man, it would have been dangerous.

"Is it okay if Okitani-kun joins us, too?" Kushida asked Horikita. Okitani had scored thirty-nine on the test, after all. He likely wanted to participate just to be safe.

"As long as you're worried about failing, I don't mind. But you need to be serious," Horikita said.

"Oh, okay."

Okitani sat down, seemingly happy. Kushida tried to sit next to him, which Horikita certainly noticed.

"Kushida-san, did Ayanokouji-kun not tell you? You—"

"I'm also worried about getting a bad grade," Kushida said.

"You...didn't score badly on the small test."

"Yes, but to tell you the truth, I was lucky. There were lots of multiple-choice questions, you know? So I guessed about half of them. In truth, I just barely passed."

Kushida giggled adorably, lightly scratching her cheek.

"I think that I'm about on the same level as Okitani-kun, if not slightly worse. So I want to join the study group to avoid getting a bad grade. That's okay, right?"

I couldn't hide my surprise at Kushida's unexpected scheme. She'd first confirmed that Okitani could join the study group, then turned the tables on Horikita. Now Horikita would *have* to permit her to join.

"Fine," Horikita growled.

"Thank you." Kushida smiled, bowed, and took her seat. Bringing Okitani had probably been part of her plan all along. She'd effectively used him to justify joining the group.

"Scoring lower than thirty-two means failing. Do you fail if you get exactly thirty-two points, though?" Sudou asked.

"No, you're safe if you score at least thirty-two points. Sudou, you can manage that, right?" Ike said.

Even Ike was worried about Sudou. Of course those guys would want to know the exact threshold.

"It doesn't really matter. My goal is for everyone to score fifty," Horikita said.

"Gah, isn't that going to be too tough?"

"Aiming to just skate by is dangerous. The fact that you can't easily reach that threshold troubles me."

In the face of Horikita's sound argument, the failures simply nodded reluctantly.

"I included most of what will be covered on this test. We only have about two weeks left, but I plan to thoroughly walk you through everything. If you don't understand something, please ask."

"Hey, I don't understand the first question." Sudou glared at Horikita. I tried reading the first problem as well.

"A, B, and C collectively have 2,150 yen. A has 120 yen more than B does. Also, after C gives B two-fifths of his money, B would have 220 yen more than A. How much yen did A originally start with?"

A problem with simultaneous equations, huh? The first test question should have been one that a high school student could easily solve.

"Try thinking about it. If you give up right at the beginning, you won't get anywhere."

"Look, I don't know how to study at all," Sudou said.

"Everyone got into this school."

This school didn't accept people based solely on test scores, though. Sudou had most likely been accepted because of his exceptional physical ability. If you looked at it that way, wouldn't he likely be expelled because of bad grades?

"Ugh, I don't get it either." Ike, equally bewildered, scratched his head.

"Do you understand, Okitani-kun?" Horikita asked.

"Let's see... A plus B plus C is 2,150 yen. So, A equals B plus 120. Then..." Okitani started writing out a series of equations. Kushida, seated next to him, glanced over her shoulder.

"Yeah, yeah, that looks right. Then what?"

You could certainly call Kushida bold, or even audacious. She'd claimed to have just barely avoided failing, and she was now teaching Okitani.

"Honestly, first- and second-year junior high school students could easily solve this problem. If you stumble here, it'll be impossible for you to continue," Horikita said.

"So, what, we're like elementary school kids?" Sudou growled.

"Like Horikita-san said, it'll be bad if you get tripped up here. The math problems on the short test were about this difficult, but the last problems were really tough. I didn't understand how to solve them," Okitani said.

"Listen up. This can be easily solved using a system of simultaneous equations." Without hesitation, Horikita picked up her pen and got to work. Unfortunately, it looked like only Kushida and Okitani understood.

"What even *are* simultaneous equations?" asked Ike.

"Are you seriously asking me that?" said Horikita.

Wow, these guys had really never studied at all, it seemed. Sudou threw his mechanical pencil onto the desk.

"Stop. I'm done. This isn't going to work."

Sudou had quit before we could even begin. Horikita quietly seethed at this pitiful display.

"W-wait, everyone. Let's give it a shot. If you learn how to solve *these* problems, you can apply what you learn to the questions on the test. Okay? Okay?" Kushida said.

"Well, if Kushida-chan says so, I guess I can try. But if Kushida-chan were teaching, I'd probably try even harder."

"U-um…" Kushida seemed ready to ask Horikita about that, but Horikita stayed silent. Her refusal to even answer "Yes" or "No" was troubling. However, if she remained silent much longer, the failures might abandon this study group. Kushida made up her mind and grabbed the mechanical pencil.

"Like Horikita-san said, you can solve this problem by using a system of simultaneous equations. So let's try writing them out."

Quickly, she wrote down three equations. It looked like the others were trying their best, but it still seemed hopeless. This was more like detention than a study group. They didn't seem to understand her methods in the slightest.

"So, the answer I got is 710 yen. What did you get?"

Kushida, confident in Sudou's ability to follow along, flashed him a smile.

"Um, so you used this to get the answer? How?" he asked.

"Uh…" Kushida immediately realized what had happened. None of them understood.

"I'm sorry, you're far too ignorant and incompetent," said Horikita, who'd been silent until now. "If you can't solve this problem, I seriously shiver at the thought of what the future will bring."

"Shut up. This has nothing to do with you." Sudou slammed the desk, understandably irritated by Horikita.

"You're right. This has nothing to do with me. Your suffering won't influence me at all. I just pity you. You must have spent your whole life running from anything that presented a challenge," she said.

"Say whatever you want. Academics will be useless in the future, anyway."

"Academics will be useless in the future? That's an interesting argument. How do you justify that?"

"I don't care if I can't solve this problem. Studying's useless. Aiming to become a pro basketball player will help me a lot more."

"Incorrect. Once you learn to solve these kinds of problems, your entire life will change. In other words, studying increases the possibility that you'll solve the problems you face. It's the same principle as basketball. I wonder if, so far, you've been playing basketball by your own set of rules. When you struggle in basketball, do you run away from it like you do from studying? I doubt you take basketball practice seriously. You're a natural troublemaker, someone who always causes a disruption. If I were your adviser, I wouldn't let you on the team."

"Tch!" Sudou got in close to Horikita and grabbed her by the collar.

"Sudou-kun!" Kushida grabbed Sudou's arm faster than I could move. Despite Sudou's intimidations, Horikita didn't flinch. She simply fixed Sudou with an icy glare.

"You don't interest me in the slightest, but I can tell

what kind of person you are just by looking at you. You want to play professional basketball? Do you honestly believe you can make such a childish dream come true in this world? A simpleton like you who gives up right away could never hope to go pro. Furthermore, even if you managed to become a professional player, I doubt you'd earn an annual income sufficient to live on. You're a fool to have such unreasonable aspirations."

"You!"

It was clear that Sudou was on the brink of losing control. If he raised his fist, I'd have to wrestle him down.

"So, you're just going to immediately give up on studying or on school in general? Then discard your dreams of playing basketball and spend your days toiling away at a pitiful part-time job."

"Hmph. That's just fine. I'll quit, but it's not because it's difficult. I took a day off from my club activities for this, and it ended up being a complete waste of time. Later!" Sudou said.

"What an odd thing to say. Studying *is* difficult." Horikita took a parting shot at Sudou. If Kushida weren't there, Sudou probably would have smacked Horikita. He stuffed his textbooks into his bag, not even hiding his irritation.

"Hey, are you okay?"

"I don't care. It's pointless to care about someone who lacks any motivation whatsoever. Even though he's facing expulsion, he has no will to fight."

"I thought that it was weird for someone like you, who doesn't have any friends, to put this study group together. You probably just wanted to call us stupid. If you weren't a girl, I'd smack you."

"So, you lack the courage to hit me? Don't use my gender as an excuse," Horikita said.

The newly assembled study group was already falling apart.

"I'm quitting, too. Partly 'cause I can't deal with studying, but mostly 'cause I'm annoyed. You might be smart, Horikita-san, but that doesn't mean you can act like you're better than us." Ike, clearly fed up, threw in the towel as well.

"I don't care if you get expelled. Do what you want," Horikita shot back.

"Well, I'll just pull an all-nighter."

"Interesting. Didn't you come here because you can't study?"

"Tch..." Even the typically easygoing Ike stiffened under the sting of Horikita's barbed comments. Yamauchi started putting his textbook away as well. Finally, the easily influenced Okitani got out of his seat.

"I-Is this really okay, everyone?" he stammered.

"Let's go, Okitani."

Ike left the library, trailed by the hesitant Okitani. Now only Kushida, Horikita, and I remained. Soon, even Kushida would probably reach her limit and leave.

"Horikita-san, we're not going to be able to study with anyone if things continue like this..." Kushida murmured.

"I was certainly mistaken. Even if I'd helped them avoid failure this time, we would've faced a similar dilemma soon after. We'd have to go through this irritation all over again. Eventually, they'll fail. I finally understand how unproductive this was. I don't have the time for it."

"Wait, what do you mean?"

"I mean that it's better to get rid of the dead weight."

That was Horikita's ultimate conclusion. If the failing students were expelled, then the class's average test scores would go up, and we wouldn't have to expend any extra effort.

"So, that's... H-hey, Ayanokouji-kun. Can you say something?" Kushida murmured.

"If that's Horikita's answer, then isn't it fine?"

"You think so too, Ayanokouji-kun?"

"Well, I don't want to toss them to the wolves or anything, but I'm not the tutor. There's nothing I can do about it." In the end, I felt similarly to Horikita.

"Okay. I see." Kushida grabbed her bag and stood up, her expression darkening. "I'm going to do something. Well, I'll try. I definitely don't want everything to fall apart so quickly."

"Kushida-san. Do you really feel that way?"

"Is it wrong? I don't want to abandon Sudou-kun, Ike-kun, and Yamauchi-kun."

"Even if that was how you truly felt, I wouldn't particularly care. But I don't think that you actually want to save them," Horikita said.

"What? I don't understand. Why do you say things like that, Horikita-san? Why do you try to antagonize people? That's...very sad."

Kushida hung her head briefly, then looked back up at us. She met our eyes.

"Well then. I'll see you two tomorrow," she whispered.

With that, Kushida left. Suddenly, it was just the two of us again. We sat in the complete silence of the library.

"Well, that was painful. The study group's already over," I said.

"Looks that way."

The quiet grew almost oppressive.

"I suppose you were the only one who understood me, Ayanokouji-kun. You're at least somewhat better than those worthless idiots. If there's some subject you're struggling with, I could teach you."

"I'll pass, thank you."

"Are you going back to your dorm?" she asked.

"I'm going to find Sudou and the others and have a chat with them."

"There's nothing to be gained from associating with people who'll likely be expelled soon."

"I just want to talk to my friends. Do you have a problem with that?"

"How incredibly selfish. You call them your friends, yet you simply stand by and watch as they're expelled. From my point of view, you're cruel."

Well, I certainly couldn't deny that. Horikita wasn't wrong. In the end, studying was just the test of an individual's self-motivation.

"I won't deny what you've said. I can also understand why you'd call someone like Sudou stupid. However, Horikita, shouldn't you try to understand Sudou's situation? If he only hoped to become a professional basketball player, then choosing this school in the first place makes little sense. Don't you think you'd understand him better if you considered his reasons for enrolling?"

"Not interested." Horikita dismissed me and returned to her textbook. Alone.

8.6

I LEFT THE LIBRARY and chased after Kushida. I wanted to thank for her working so hard to get the study group together, and to apologize. Besides, I wanted to do everything possible to get along with such a cute girl, you know?

Whipping out my cell phone, I pulled up Kushida's contact information. Although it was my second time calling, I felt nervous contacting her. The phone rang twice, then three times. However, she didn't pick up. Did she not notice me calling? Or was she refusing to answer it?

Kushida wasn't around campus, so I continued to search for her. When I got inside the school, I glimpsed someone who looked like Kushida from behind. It was already around six PM, so the only people here should've been involved in club activities. Well, this *was* Kushida we were talking about. She was probably waiting for one of her good friends to finish club stuff.

I decided to keep up the chase. If she were busy, I'd talk to her again later. Bearing that in mind, I pressed on. I took out a pair of indoor shoes from the cubicles in the hallway, but didn't see Kushida. Had I lost her? I thought I had, until I heard the faint clack of shoes.

I followed her up the stairs to the second floor. The sound of footsteps continued up to the third floor. The next level after that was the roof, wasn't it? Students were free to use the roof during lunchtime, but it should've been locked after class. While I thought it strange, I went up the stairs, trying to hide my presence as best I could in case she was meeting with someone. Then, I stopped partway.

Someone was up there.

I gently leaned against the handrail and peeked through a crack in the rooftop door. Through the opening, I glimpsed Kushida. No one else was with her. Was she waiting for someone?

A rendezvous at such a secluded place... Could she possibly be waiting for her boyfriend? If that were the case, I could end up cornered on all sides. While I agonized over how to sneak away, Kushida slowly set her bag down on the ground.

And then...

"Ahhh, so annoying!"

Her voice was so low that it didn't sound at all like Kushida.

"She's seriously annoying! God, how irritating. It'd be better if she just *died...*"

She grumbled to herself, as if chanting the words to some kind of spell or curse.

"Ugh, I hate stuck-up, snobby girls who think they're so cute. Why is she such a harpy? A rotten girl like her couldn't possibly tutor me."

Was Kushida annoyed with...Horikita?

"Ah, she's the worst! She's just the worst, the worst, the worst! Horikita, you're so annoying! You're so damn annoying!"

I felt like I'd glimpsed another side of this gentle girl, the most popular person in our class. She probably didn't want anyone else to see this darker side. A voice in my head whispered that it was dangerous to stay here.

However, an odd question arose. Why had she agreed to work with me if she felt such hatred toward Horikita? Kushida should have understood Horikita's personality and behavior perfectly well by now. She could have refused to help, or just left the study group to Horikita, or otherwise washed her hands of involvement.

Why force herself into the study group? Did she want

to get along with Horikita? Or did she want to become closer to another participant?

None of it made sense. I couldn't explain her reasoning.

No. She may have shown signs of this from the very beginning. I hadn't really thought about it before, but considering the state she was in right now, I had a hunch. Perhaps, Kushida and Horikita were...

At any rate, I needed to get away from there. Kushida probably didn't want anyone else to hear her diatribe. Still hiding, I quickly tried to leave.

Thump!

I'd kicked the door much louder than I'd anticipated. It'd been unexpectedly loud, really. Kushida tensed and stopped breathing. I'd instantly become her enemy. Turning, Kushida set her sights on me. I'd been seen.

After a brief silence, Kushida coldly asked, "What... are you...doing here?"

"I got a little lost. Sorry. My bad, my bad. I'll be going now."

Kushida looked straight at me, clearly seeing through my obvious lie. I'd never seen such an intense gaze before.

"Did you hear?" she asked.

"Would you believe me if I said I didn't?" I replied.

"I see..."

Kushida briskly walked down the stairs. She placed

her left forearm against the base of my throat, and pushed me up against the wall. Her tone of voice, her actions, everything about her was completely unlike the Kushida I knew. This new Kushida wore a terrifying expression, one that I could almost compare to Horikita's.

"If you tell anyone what you just heard, I won't forgive you."

Her words were ice, and I didn't think they were an idle threat.

"And if I did tell?"

"In that case, I would tell everyone that you raped me," she said.

"That's a false charge, you know."

"That's okay. It wouldn't be false."

Her words had heft and power, leaving me unable to reply. As she spoke, Kushida grabbed my right wrist and slowly opened my hand. She pushed my palm up against her soft breast.

"What are you doing?" I asked. I hurriedly tried to pull away, but she pushed on the back of my hand.

"Your fingerprints are on my clothes. That's evidence of my claim. I'm being serious. Understand?"

"I understand. I really do. So let go of my hand."

"I'm going to leave this uniform in my room without washing it. If you betray me, I'll hand it over to the police."

I glared at Kushida for a while as she kept my hand pressed against her.

"It's a promise," she said.

Kushida stepped away from me. Even though this was the first time I had felt a girl's breasts, I found I couldn't remember the sensation.

"Hey, Kushida. Which is the real you?"

"That's none of your business."

"I see. Well, I was wondering something. If you hate Horikita, then you don't need to involve yourself with her, right?"

I knew she probably wouldn't like that question, but I was curious about her motivation.

"Is it bad to want everyone to like you? Do you understand how difficult it is to accomplish that? You can't know, can you?" she asked.

"Well, I don't have that many friends, so I guess not."

Ever since the first day of school, Kushida had made an effort to exchange contact information with, invite out, and, of course, talk with the pessimistic Horikita. One could easily imagine how difficult and time-consuming that would be.

"At least on the surface, I wanted to appear to get along with Horikita."

"But the stress of that just kept building, huh?"

"Yeah. That's what I want out of life, though. That way, my existence has meaning." She answered without hesitation. Kushida had a singular way of thinking. Her own internal rules demanded she get close to Horikita.

"Let me tell you something, while I have the chance. I absolutely despise gloomy, ordinary guys like you."

The fantasy of a cute Kushida that I'd carried until now had been shattered, but I wasn't actually that shocked. Most people possessed both a public face and a private, inner self, after all. However, I felt like Kushida was both telling the truth and lying right now.

"I'm just speculating, but did you and Horikita know each other before this year? Maybe you both attended the same school in the past?"

The instant I said it, Kushida shuddered in response.

"What the... I don't know what you mean. Did Horikita-san say something about me?" she snapped.

"No, I had the impression that this was the first time you'd met. But something seemed strange."

"Strange?"

I recalled the first time Kushida had spoken to me.

"You learned my name only when I first introduced myself, right?"

"So what?" Kushida responded flatly.

"Well, where did you learn Horikita's name? Back

then, she hadn't introduced herself to anyone yet. The only person who knew was Sudou, but I doubt you'd met him by then."

In other words, Kushida wouldn't have had the chance to learn Horikita's name.

"You got close to me so you could spy on her, right?"

"Just shut up. Hearing you talk irritates me, Ayanokouji-kun. I only want to know one thing. Do you swear you'll never tell anyone what you learned here today?"

"I swear. Even if I did, it's not like anyone would believe me. Right?"

The entire class trusted and loved Kushida. The difference between us was like night and day.

"Okay. I believe you, Ayanokouji-kun." Kushida closed her eyes and slowly exhaled. "Horikita-san is rather unusual, isn't she?"

"Yes, I'd say she's really unusual."

"Other people don't influence her, or rather, she keeps her distance from everyone else. She's the complete opposite of me."

Kushida and Horikita really *were* polar opposites.

"You know, Ayanokouji-kun, you're the only one that Horikita-san opens up to."

"Wait a minute. She doesn't open up to me. Absolutely not."

"Even so, she seems to trust you more than anyone else. Out of all the people I've ever met, Horikita seems the most wary of others and yet also the most self-confident. She certainly wouldn't trust anyone worthless, even if they were unbelievably kind."

"So, you think she has good instincts for people?"

"That's why I said I believed you. Ayanokouji-kun, you're fundamentally indifferent to other people, aren't you?"

I didn't remember doing anything that would make her think so, but Kushida seemed confident in her assessment.

"It's not an out-of-place judgment. Back on the bus, you didn't show any interest in giving up your seat to the elderly woman."

Ah, so that's what she was talking about. She'd picked up on what was happening that first day. She had understood that I'd no intention of giving up my seat.

"If you believe I'm telling the truth, then you won't spread pointless rumors," I said.

"If you were really so confident, you wouldn't have felt up my breasts."

"Well, that's... I was really flustered. I panicked for a second."

Her stern expression melted into one of impatience.

"So, Kushida, would I be right to think of you as the kind of girl who lets guys touch her breasts?"

She kicked my thigh as hard she could. Panicking, I grabbed the railing.

"Hey, watch it! I could've fallen and gotten seriously hurt!"

"I kicked you because you said something stupid!" Kushida snapped, her face flushed from anger.

"Hey, wait a minute."

She still looked furious. Kushida tromped back up the stairs, grabbed her bag, then returned wearing a huge grin.

"Let's head back together," she said brightly.

"Oh. Sure."

Her attitude had drastically changed, like something out of *Dr. Jekyll & Mr. Hyde*. It was so drastic that I wondered whether I'd had a bad dream. She was her usual sunny self once more. I couldn't tell which Kushida was the real one.

8.7

● ●

I WONDERED WHAT was going to happen with Class D. Honestly, part of me felt like these were other people's problems. Back in my room, I started to watch some kind of variety show with a feeling of complete apathy. Glancing at my phone, I saw I had a message from the group chat.

The message read, *Satou's joining the group.* Satou was a particularly high-spirited girl in our class.

Hiya! Ike-kun invited me to join when we were talking earlier.

With nothing to contribute, I didn't respond and continued reading.

I heard about what happened today. Horikita is really frustrating, huh?

I was really pissed at her. Sudou was super mad. He almost lost it. I think he would've hit her.

If I see her tomorrow, I might hit her. I was really annoyed with her today.

Aha ha ha, it'll be a big problem if you hit her lol. That would be overkill!

Hey, I have an idea. Starting tomorrow, how about we completely ignore her?

Ha, I've always ignored her (lol)

I kind of want to hit her with some payback. Bully her a little and make her cry, you know? Do something like hide her shoes.

Ha ha, what are you, kids? Lol lol lol but I do kind of want to see her squirm.

Soon after Satou joined the group chat, Horikita became the main topic of discussion.

Hey, Ayanokouji-kun, you want in on bullying Horikita lol

Nah, Ayanokouji-kun is all obsessed with her, so he probably can't.

Hey, whose side are you on? Ours or Horikita's?

I supposed everyone's irritation with Horikita was inevitable. If you treated others the way Horikita did, you'd inevitably be disliked. But hitting her would be going too far, and I couldn't understand how anyone might condone ignoring her or hiding her things. That was bullying, and acting like that would leave little difference between them and Horikita.

Hey, you're reading the chat, right? Hey! Ayanokouji-kun, whose side are you on?

I'm on no one's side. If you guys want to bully her, I won't stop you.

So, you're neutral. That's the craftiest answer lol.

Think whatever you want, but you won't gain anything from this. If the school learns you're bullying her, it'll cause trouble for you. Keep that in mind.

So, you're sticking up for Horikita, huh? Ha ha.

Because we couldn't see each other face to face, it was easier for them to be jerks. If Ike and I were having this conversation in person, I doubted he'd act this way.

However, by focusing their anger on Horikita, the others were building solidarity. It would be a waste of time to continue pointlessly chatting like this. I decided to bring this conversation to a halt.

If Kushida heard about this, she'd probably hate you. Lol.

After I sent that message, I closed my phone. I received an immediate response but left it alone. Those guys probably wouldn't do anything stupid, and Satou likely wouldn't do anything without the others' cooperation.

I opened my window, listening to the insects buzzing from the nearby trees. Did the *kubikirigisu* grasshoppers make that high-pitched chirping, I wondered? The gentle night breeze rattled my window.

I'd met Horikita on the day of the entrance ceremony. We'd just so happened to be placed in the same class, and then I was assigned the seat next to hers. Before I knew it, I'd become friends with Sudou and Ike. On top of that, I'd been caught in the school's trap and knocked all the way down to rock bottom. Horikita had tried to help repair our situation, but her personality had ruined everything, further pushing her into isolation. Now, other people grew excited at the thought of bullying her.

I should've been at the center of this situation, and yet I felt like I was drifting past it.

No, drifting's the wrong word. It wasn't a pleasant situation. I felt like I was in a haze, because I didn't know the urgency of near-expulsion. This was everyone else's problem, not mine, so it just didn't register as important.

"Only a fool wouldn't use his innate abilities."

Those words stuck in my head.

"A fool, huh? I wonder if that's what I am, after all."

As I closed the window, the television's cacophonous laughter pierced my ears.

8.8

I COULDN'T GET TO SLEEP, so I got up and left. I bought some juice from the lobby's vending machine and headed back for the elevator.

"Hmm?"

I could see that the elevator had stopped on the seventh floor. Curious, I decided to check out the CCTV, which showed what was happening inside the elevator car. I saw Horikita, still dressed in her school uniform.

"Well, I don't really need to hide, but…"

Seeing her might be awkward right now, so I hid behind the vending machine. Horikita arrived at the first floor.

Looking wary of her surroundings, she exited the building. After she'd vanished into the night, I decided to follow after her. However, I instinctively hid again after I turned the corner.

Horikita stopped in her tracks. I sensed another person was with her.

"Suzune. I didn't think you'd follow me this far," he said.

Had she left in the dead of night to rendezvous with some guy?

"Hmph. I'm far different from the useless girl you once knew, niisan. I came here to catch you."

"Catch me, hmm?"

Niisan? In the dark, I couldn't see the person she was talking to. Was she meeting her older brother?

"I heard you were placed in Class D. I suppose nothing has really changed in the last three years. You've always been fixated on following me, and as a result you don't notice your own flaws. Choosing to come to this school was a mistake."

"That's... You're wrong about that. I'll show you. I'll reach Class A right away, then—"

"It's pointless. You will never reach Class A. In fact, your class will fall apart soon enough. Things at this school aren't as simple as you think."

"I will definitely, definitely reach—"

"I told you, it's pointless. You really are a disobedient little sister."

Horikita's brother stepped closer to her. From my hiding spot, I could see him plainly.

It was Student Council President Horikita. He displayed no hint of emotion. It was like he was staring at an uninteresting object. He grabbed his younger sister by the wrist—she offered no resistance—and pushed her against the wall.

"No matter how I try to avoid you, the fact remains that you're my little sister. If people around here learned the truth, I would be humiliated. Leave this school immediately."

"I-I can't do that... I will definitely reach Class A. I'll show you!"

"How incredibly stupid. Do you want to relive the pain of the past?"

"Niisan, I..."

"You possess neither the abilities nor the qualities needed to reach Class A. Get that through your head."

He moved forward, as if about to act. The situation looked fraught with danger. Resigned to facing Horikita's anger, I leapt out from my hiding space and went after her brother.

Before he knew I was there, I grabbed his right arm, which he was using to pin his sister.

"What? You..." He stared at his arm and slowly turned to me with a sharp gleam in his eye.

"A-Ayanokouji-kun?!" Horikita cried.

"You were about to throw your sister to the ground, weren't you? You do realize the floor here is concrete, right? You might be siblings, but you should know the difference between right and wrong."

"Eavesdropping is not an admirable quality," he said.

"Fine. Then let go."

"That's *my* line."

We glared at each other in complete silence.

"Stop it, Ayanokouji-kun," said Horikita, her voice strained. I'd never heard her voice like that before.

Reluctantly, I released her brother. Instantly, he tried to backhand me in the face. I instinctively took a step back to avoid it. For such a lightly built guy, he was a nasty attacker. He then aimed a sharp kick at my un-guarded spot.

"Watch it!"

He had enough power to knock me out with one blow. Looking slightly confused, he exhaled deeply, extended his right arm, and opened his hand.

If I grabbed his hand, he'd probably throw me to the ground. Instead, I slapped his hand away.

"Good reflexes. I didn't imagine you could evade all of my blows so quickly. Also, you seemed to understand quite well what I was trying to do. Have you been taught?"

After the attacks stopped, the questions began.

"Yes, I was taught piano and calligraphy. Also, when I was in elementary school, I won a national music competition," I said.

"You're in Class D, too, aren't you? What a unique boy, Suzune."

After he let go of his younger sister, he turned to face me.

"No. Unlike Horikita, I'm pretty incompetent."

"Suzune, is this boy your friend? I'm honestly surprised."

"He's...not my friend. Just my classmate." Horikita faced her brother fully, as if denying him.

"You continue to confuse independence with solitude. And you, Ayanokouji. With you around, things might get interesting."

He walked past me and disappeared into the night. So, that was the distinguished student council president. His presence explained some of Horikita's weird behavior.

"I'm going to drag myself up to Class A even if it kills me," she said.

With her brother gone, the night was silent once more. Horikita sat up against the wall, her head hanging low. Maybe I'd made things worse by getting involved. I was about to return to the dorms when Horikita called out to me.

"Did you hear everything? Or was it just a coincidence?"

"Oh. Uh, it was half coincidence, I'd say. I saw you when I bought some juice from the vending machine. I was kind of curious, so I followed you. However, I really didn't mean to meddle in your business."

Horikita fell silent once again.

"Your older brother is really strong. He doesn't lack ferocity."

"He's ranked fifth dan in karate and fourth dan in aikido."

Whew, he was *really* strong. If I hadn't pulled away, it would've ended badly for me.

"You also practice martial arts, don't you, Ayanokouji-kun? You must hold a dan rank."

"I told you, didn't I? Just piano and tea ceremony."

"You said calligraphy before."

"I...did calligraphy in addition to those, yes."

"You purposefully get lower test scores, and you say that you studied piano and calligraphy. I really don't understand you."

"My scores were a coincidence. I really did do piano, tea ceremony, and calligraphy." If there were a piano here, I could at least have performed "Für Elise."

"You saw a strange side of me."

"On the contrary, I always thought of you as a normal girl. Well, not really."

Horikita glared at me.

"Let's go back. If anyone saw us out here, they'd probably get ideas."

She was certainly right about that. Rumors about a boy and a girl hanging out alone in the dark would be bound to circulate. Not to mention the fact that our relationship seemed to be intensifying.

Horikita got up slowly and walked toward the dorm.

"Hey. Were you really okay with how the study group went?" I asked.

If I didn't broach the subject now, I'd likely never get the chance again.

"Why are you asking me? I was the one who proposed holding the study group in the first place. Besides, I got the feeling that you considered it a hassle. Am I wrong?"

"It just left a bad taste in my mouth. Look, I think things are going to get worse with the others."

"I don't care. I'm used to it. Besides, Hirata-kun picked up most of the failing students. He knows how to study, he seems to get along with others, and, unlike me, he'll be a good tutor. At the very least, they should all pass. It was pointless to try teaching the failing students myself. We would go through this same scenario for every test until graduation. It would be pointless to try making up for their failure every single time."

"Sudou and the others don't much like Hirata. I doubt they'll participate in his study group."

"That's their decision, which has nothing to do with me. Besides, if they're facing expulsion, they shouldn't grumble about trivial nonsense. If they don't get closer to Hirata-kun, then they'll be expelled. Of course, my goal is to have Class D reach Class A status. However, that's for my own sake and no one else's. I don't care about anyone else. Really, if we dump the failures on this next midterm, then the better students will be left. That's what I need, correct? In that case, attaining a higher rank will be simple. Everything will work out perfectly."

She wasn't wrong about that. Our conversation continued; Horikita was strangely talkative tonight.

"Horikita, isn't that way of thinking flawed?"

"Flawed? What's flawed? You're not going to give me some gibberish about how there's no future for someone who would abandon her classmates, are you?"

"Relax. I understand you well enough to know that you don't really understand *me*."

"Then what is it? There's no strategic advantage to helping failures."

"There are probably very few advantages, certainly. However, it does help prevent a setback."

"Demerit?"

"Do you really think that the school hasn't considered this? They've deducted points for students arriving late or playing around during class time. Let's say these students are expelled because no one helped them. How many points do you think they'll deduct from us then?"

"That's—" she began.

"Of course, we don't have any proof that's how it works. However, isn't it possible? 100 points? 1,000 points? They might even deduct 10,000 or 100,000 points. If that happens, it'll be very difficult for you to reach Class A."

"We've gone down to zero points because of our infractions. We can't go any lower. If we're currently at zero, don't you think it's best to eliminate the dead weight? That would be the same as taking no damage."

"There's no guarantee that'd be the case. There could be penalties we just don't see yet. Do you really think it's okay to take such a dangerous risk? Well. I'm sure that someone as smart as you must have thought about that already. Otherwise, you would never have suggested creating a study group in the first place. You would've just abandoned the failures from the very beginning."

I was starting to sound worked up, or perhaps I was actually *feeling* worked up. Maybe because I'd started to, rather selfishly, consider her a friend. I didn't want Horikita to come to regret her decision.

"Even if there are potential unknown negatives, it's better for the future of our class to abandon the failing students. Wouldn't you regret not abandoning them when we do finally increase our points? Right now, it's a risk that we should take."

"Do you really think so?" I asked.

"Yes. Really. I'm at a complete loss as to why you're so desperate to save them."

As Horikita was about to board the elevator, I grabbed her wrist.

"What? Do you have a rebuttal?" she said. "The problem's bigger than the two of us. In the end, the school has all the answers. All we can do is argue back and forth. I'm free to interpret the situation as I see fit, and you may do the same. That's all there is to it, right?"

"You're quite talkative. I never thought you'd be so loquacious."

"What... That's just because you were being insistent."

If she were acting like her normal self, there was no way she would have allowed me to keep talking. Normally, stopping her in this way would earn me a sharp strike. However, her refusal to hit me indicated that Horikita felt the way I did. Of course, she probably didn't even realize it herself.

"The day we met, do you remember what happened on the bus?"

"You mean when we refused to give up our seats to an elderly woman?"

"Yeah. Back then, I thought about the meaning behind giving up my seat. Should I give it up or not? Which was the correct answer?"

"I already told you my own answer. I thought it'd be meaningless, so I didn't give up my seat. No matter what reward it might bring, there was no real merit. It was a waste of time and effort."

"Merit, huh? I suppose that you think only in terms of gain and loss."

"Is that bad? People are calculating creatures, for the most part. If you sell goods, you receive money. If you do someone a favor, that debt of gratitude will be repaid. By giving up a seat, you gain the joy of contributing to society. Am I wrong?"

"No, I don't think you're wrong. I think the same thing," I replied.

"So then—"

"If you keep to that belief, you'll need to maintain a broad perspective on life. You're so angry and dissatisfied, you can't see what's in front of you."

"Who do you think you are? Do you even have the ability to find fault with me?"

"I don't know what abilities I have, but I see what you

don't. It's the one flaw of the seemingly perfect person known as Horikita Suzune."

Horikita gave an amused snort. It was as if she was saying, "If you think I have a flaw, say it."

"Your flaw is that you think of everyone else as a burden, and so you detach yourself and never let anyone come close. Isn't it possible they placed you in Class D because you consider yourself superior to everyone?"

"It's almost as if you're saying I'm the same as Sudou-kun and his group," she muttered.

"Are you saying that you aren't equal?"

"Yes. It's obvious if you look at our test scores. That's proof enough that they're mere baggage for our class to carry."

"If we're talking about studying, then Sudou and the others are certainly two or three steps behind you, Horikita. No matter how hard they worked, they likely couldn't overtake you. However, we know that this school doesn't only focus on intelligence. Suppose that the next exam was related to sports. The results would be different then. Am I wrong?"

"That's—"

"You're physically capable. From your swimming, I can tell you're one of the most capable girls in the class. Superior. However, we both know that Sudou's physical abilities far exceed yours. Ike has better communication skills than you. If the test took the form of a discussion, Ike would certainly be useful. Really, you'd most likely bring the class average down. So, does that make you incompetent? No. Every individual has his or her own strengths and weaknesses. That's what it means to be human."

Horikita tried to throw my words back at me, but she looked stuck.

"This is all pure conjecture. It's nothing more than armchair speculation," she said.

"Think back on what Chabashira-sensei said. When she called us into the guidance room, she said, 'Who exactly decided that smart people are categorically superior?' From that, we can draw the conclusion that academic ability doesn't solely determine the rankings."

Horikita looked around, as if searching for an escape so she could weasel her way out of the argument. I quickly cut her off before she could get away.

"You said you wouldn't regret abandoning the students who failed, but you would. You would feel a great deal of regret if Sudou and the others are expelled."

Horikita looked into my eyes. She still didn't seem to grasp our current situation. At least, that was the impression I got.

"You're rather talkative today, too. It's odd for someone who likes to avoid trouble to talk so much."

"You're probably right about that."

"It's frustrating, but what you said was basically correct. You've persuaded me; I have to concede that point. However, I still don't understand you. What do you want? What is this school to you? Why did you work so hard to convince me?"

"I see. So that's what you think."

"If someone lacks persuasiveness, he or she won't be able to make others believe in their cunning theories." She clearly wanted to know why I was so desperate to persuade her that Sudou and the others' expulsion was bad. "Cut the crap. I want to know the real reason. Is it for points? To rise up, even by one class level? Or is it to save your friends?"

"Because I want to know what a person with true merit looks like. What is equality?"

"Merit, equality..."

"I came to this school to find answers to those questions." The words freely spilled out of me before I could collect my thoughts.

"Could you let me go?" Horikita asked.

"Oh, sorry." I released my grip. She turned around and looked directly at me.

"There's no way that you could fool me into believing you, Ayanokouji-kun," she said.

After she said that, Horikita extended her arm.

"I'll look after Sudou-kun and the others, but for my own sake. I'll make sure that they don't get left behind, but only as a strategic means of securing an advantage for our future. Okay?"

"Don't worry. I didn't think you'd do it any differently. That's just like you, Horikita."

"We've come to an arrangement, then."

I took Horikita's hand. However, I would soon realize that I'd just made a deal with the devil.

9

THE FAILURES MOBILIZE ONCE AGAIN

THE AIR WAS RICH with the aroma of new tea. (I'm grateful for your continued patience and cooperation, dear reader.) A month and a half had already gone by since I started high school. For the most part, my days had passed without incident.

"Hey, can you hear me? Is your head okay?"

Horikita rudely smacked my forehead, then touched a hand to her own head.

"You don't seem to have a fever," she said.

"Of course I don't! I was just lost in thought, that's all." I let out a deep sigh, already regretting that I'd told Horikita I'd help her. I suppose there was no use crying over spilled milk. I'd offered to help as a means of encouragement, but, thinking back, it really struck me as being out of character.

"So, my honorable tactician. What should I do, hmm?" I asked.

"Let's see. Obviously, we'll need to persuade Sudou-kun and the others to participate once again. That means you'll need to grovel and beg for them to return."

"Why should *I* have to do that? You're the reason the group split in the first place."

"The reason we split was because they couldn't take studying seriously. Don't get that twisted."

Jeez. Did she even intend to help Sudou and the others?

"We'll never get them back without Kushida's help. You understand that, right?"

"I understand. Sacrifices are inevitable," she grumbled.

She appeared to hate the idea of Kushida's involvement. Still, she agreed despite her dissatisfaction. This was a major compromise for Horikita, who didn't want Kushida getting close to her at all.

"Okay. Can you get Kushida-san to help us immediately?" she asked.

"Me?"

"Of course. We made a deal. You agreed to be my workhorse until we reach Class A, so you have to do as I command."

I didn't remember making *that* kind of deal.

"Here, look at this written contract."

Wow, a real contract. It had my name and my seal on it and everything.

"You realize they could charge you with forging documents, right?" I asked.

I tore up the contract and tossed it away. Horikita got up and went over to Kushida, who was tidying her desk.

"Kushida-san. There is something I would like to talk to you about. Would you care to have lunch with me?" Horikita asked.

"Lunch? It's unusual to get an invitation from you, Horikita-san. Okay, I'll go." Kushida didn't waver at all. She walked with Horikita toward the school's most popular café, Palate.

That was the scene of Horikita's previous anger, when I'd invited her under false pretenses. Horikita said that she'd treat Kushida, and paid for her drink. Of course, I had to pay for myself.

"Thank you. So, what did you want to talk about?" Kushida asked.

"I'm putting together another study group for Sudou-kun and the others. Will you help me one more time?"

"What's your reason for doing this? Is it really for Sudou-kun and the others?" Kushida clearly understood that Horikita likely wasn't doing this out of altruism.

"No. This is for me."

"I see. So, you look out for yourself as usual, Horikita-san."

"You won't help someone whose motives are selfish?"

"You're free to think whatever you like. I just didn't want you to try to lie to me. I'm glad you were honest. Okay, I'll help. We're classmates, after all. Right, Ayanokouji-kun?"

"Y-yeah. You're really helping us," I muttered.

"There's something I want to ask you though, Horikita-san. You're not doing this for your friends or to get points. It's so you can get to Class A, right?"

"Yes."

"I can't believe that, though. I mean, isn't it impossible? Oh, I'm not saying you're stupid, Horikita-san. How do I put this, though? More than half of the class has given up, you see."

"Because the gulf between us and Class A is so vast?"

"Yes. To be perfectly honest, I can't imagine how we'd catch up. I'm not sure we can even get any points next month. It's disheartening."

Horikita smacked the table. "I'm going to do it. Definitely," she said.

"Ayanokouji-kun, are you aiming for Class A, too?" Kushida asked.

"Yes. He's working as my assistant."

Horikita had given me a title without asking me.

"Hmm. I understand. I want in, Horikita-san."

"To help us with the study group."

"No, not for that. I want to work on getting into Class A with you. I want to help with everything else you'll be doing."

"Huh? But..."

"So, you don't want me to join?" Kushida asked.

She looked at Horikita with wide eyes, prompting her to answer.

"Fine. If everything goes well with the study group, I'll accept your help moving forward," answered Horikita.

Kushida probably had some ulterior motive. Even so, Horikita understood that she had no choice but to acknowledge Kushida's value. Having coaxed a victory from the usually stubborn Horikita, Kushida excitedly sat up.

"Really?! Yay!" Kushida cheered, a look of genuine delight on her face. She looked really cute this way. "I look forward to working with you again, Horikita-san! Ayanokouji-kun!"

She extended her left and right arms toward us. A bit perplexed, Horikita and I shook Kushida's hands.

"Getting Sudou-kun and the others on board again will be a problem, though," Horikita said.

"Yeah. Considering the current state of things, it will probably be difficult," I agreed.

"Well, can you leave that to me? It's the least I can do after you've let me join you," Kushida said.

I felt a little overwhelmed by how quickly Horikita and Kushida were moving.

Kushida took out her cell phone, ready to leap into action immediately. Soon after, Ike and Yamauchi arrived, looking like they were on cloud nine after receiving Kushida's invitation. As soon as they saw Horikita and me, though, they looked me square in the eye. They seemed to silently ask, *Did you tell her about the chat?!* I thought it'd be better to keep quiet. Their guilt might help in getting them to fall in line.

"I'm sorry for calling you two over. I have something to ask you, or rather, Horikita-san does."

"Wh-what is it? What do you want from us?!"

What an overreaction. They backed away in fright.

"Are you two joining Hirata-kun's study group?" Horikita asked.

"Huh? S-study group? No. I mean, studying's so boring, and Hirata is annoyingly popular. Besides, we planned to cram the day before. Things should work out. We've gotten by since junior high doing exactly that."

Yamauchi nodded at Ike's words. They were counting on an all-nighter to save them.

"That certainly sounds like an idea you two would have. But if you do, it's highly likely you'll be expelled."

"You're acting the same as usual," Sudou said, showing up. He glared at Horikita. Apparently Kushida had caught Sudou in her honey trap as well.

"You're the one who should be worried, Sudou-kun. You don't seem to have any fear of being expelled."

"I know that. Drop it, or I'll beat the crap out of you. I'm busy with basketball now, anyway. I'll be just fine if I cram before the test."

"C-calm down, Sudou. Okay?" Ike was acting like he didn't know what they'd said in the chat.

"Sudou-kun, won't you try studying with me one more time? You might manage to squeak by if you pull an all-nighter, but if that fails, you won't be able to play basketball here anymore. Right?" Horikita asked.

"Well, I...I don't want any of your stupid charity. I haven't forgotten the bullshit way you spoke to me the other day. If you want me to join, I want an apology first. A completely honest one," said Sudou, displaying open hostility toward Horikita.

Although Sudou probably realized the danger he was in, he couldn't dismiss Horikita's insults. Of course,

Horikita would never give him an apology. No one could ever take pride in saying something that untrue.

"I hate you, Sudou-kun."

"What?!"

Instead of apologizing, she spat harsh words at Sudou, throwing fuel on the fire.

"However, our mutual abhorrence is trivial right now. I will teach you for my own sake. You will do your best for your own sake. Am I wrong?"

"You really want to get up to Class A, then? Even if that means inviting someone you hate, like me?" he muttered.

"Yes, exactly. Otherwise, why would anyone willingly involve you?"

Sudou grew more openly annoyed in response to Horikita's incredible bluntness.

"I'm busy with basketball. The others on the team never take study breaks, not even before a big test. I can't fall behind everyone else by doing something as boring as studying."

As if she'd predicted Sudou's remarks, Horikita opened her notebook and showed it to him. On the page, there was a detailed schedule leading up to the test.

"During the last session, I noticed that style of studying didn't work for you. None of you understand the fundamental basics. For example, it would be like tossing a frog into the ocean. The frog wouldn't have any idea where to go or how to swim. Also, I understand that taking time away from your hobbies will only add to your stress. Therefore, I've come up with a plan."

"What kind of sorcery did you use to come up with that? All right, tell me the plan."

He could make time for studying *and* club activities. Sudou, believing such a thing to be impossible, snorted in amusement.

"The test's two weeks from today. You'll all study every day during class like your life depends on it."

I couldn't believe what Horikita had said. No one else could, either.

"You three don't usually work seriously during class, do you?" she asked.

"You can't know that about us," Ike objected.

"So, you work seriously?"

"Well... No, we don't. We just sit around 'til class is over."

"So, in other words, you waste six hours a day doing nothing. Rather than struggling to study for the one or two hours available after class, we're wasting a far larger and more precious period of time. We must use this time better."

"Well, certainly... Theoretically that would work, but... isn't that unreasonable?"

Kushida was right to be worried. They wasted time precisely because they couldn't study normally. If they couldn't manage to discipline themselves during class, I doubted they'd be able to understand the problems by themselves.

"I can't even keep up with class at all."

"I know. So we'll hold a short study session during our free time."

With that, Horikita turned to the next page, spelling out the details of her plan. After first period, we'd all meet up and discuss what we hadn't understood in the lecture. During the ten-minute break, Horikita would explain the answers to those questions. We'd repeat the process over the next several periods. Of course, this wasn't as simple as it seemed. Since Sudou and the others couldn't keep up naturally, they might not be able to learn the material in such a short time.

"W-wait a minute. I'm kind of confused here. Is this really going to work?" Ike could tell this would be difficult.

"Yeah. I mean, won't it be impossible to understand that stuff in just ten minutes of break time?"

"Don't worry. I'll compile answers to every question and make them easy to understand. After that, Ayanokouji-kun, Kushida-san, and I will each teach you individually, one-on-one."

If we used this system, we might just be able to make them understand in short blocks of time.

"It's just a matter of explaining the answers. You two can handle it, right?" Horikita asked.

"But I still don't think we can do it in that little time. Studying's so hard."

"One class period covers surprisingly little content. Typically, there'll be one page of notes, two at the most. If you narrow it down to only the things that will be on the test, you can probably whittle it down to a half a page of information. If we somehow end up not having enough time, we can always use our lunch period. I'm not saying that you have to understand the material. I just want you to memorize it. During class, you must focus on the teacher's voice and what's written on the blackboard. Forget about taking notes for right now."

"So, you're telling us *not* to take notes?"

"Trying to memorize things is surprisingly difficult when you're writing down notes."

She was probably right about that. A focus on note-taking would simply waste precious time. At any rate, Horikita had laid out a plan that didn't use up any time after school.

"Just try. Give it a go before you say no."

"I don't want to. I'd rather spend my time differently than a bookworm like you. Besides, I don't even think

I *could* learn to study with such a simple, cheap trick."
Horikita had carefully come up with a plan tailored to
the three of them, and yet Sudou still wouldn't agree.

"It seems you've misunderstood. There are no shortcuts or cheap tricks when it comes to studying. You just
have to spend your time carefully. That applies not only
to studying, but to everything else as well. Or are you telling me there are shortcuts and cheap tricks in something
like basketball?"

"Of course there aren't. You only improve by practic-
ing, all the time." Sudou inhaled sharply, surprised by his
own words.

"For people who can't focus or work seriously, it's impossible. However, you put all of your effort into basketball. I want you to apply some of that effort to studying,
even if it's just a fraction of what you have. Put in the
effort so that you can continue to play basketball at this
school. Don't throw away your own potential."

Horikita's compromise was small, but real. Sudou hesitated. However, his pride still got in the way. He seemed
incapable of agreeing to the plan.

"Yeah, I'm still not doing it. I get what you're saying,
but I'm not convinced."

Sudou made to turn around and leave, and Horikita
couldn't stop him. If he left now, the study group was

probably dead. Normally I'd stay out of it, but this called for drastic action.

"Hey, Kushida. Do you have a boyfriend?" I asked.

"Huh? What? I don't. Why would you suddenly ask me something like that?!" she cried.

"If I can get fifty points on the test, will you go out with me?" I extended my hand to her.

"Huh?! Wh-what are you saying, Ayanokouji! No, date *me*, Kushida! I'll get fifty-one points!" Ike cried.

"No, no, me! Go on a date with me! I'll show you! I'll get fifty-two points!" Yamauchi said.

Kushida immediately understood my plan.

"H-how embarrassing... I don't just judge people based on something like test scores, you know?" she said.

"But they need a prize for trying. Look at how eager Ike and Yamauchi are. They'd probably be motivated by a reward."

"W-well then, how about this? I'll go on a date with whoever scores highest on the test. I like people who work really hard, even when they don't like doing it."

"Whoa! Yes! I'll do it! I'll do it!" Ike and Yamauchi breathed heavily in their excitement. I called out to Sudou.

"Hey, Sudou. What about you? This might be your chance."

That was a bit subtler than yelling, *Do you want to date Kushida?*

I generally understood Sudou's personality, but it was still difficult to predict whether he'd agree. So I had to find some common ground.

"A date, huh? That doesn't sound too bad. Jeez, guess I don't have a choice. All right, I'll join," Sudou said, his voice small. He didn't turn around.

Kushida sighed deeply in relief.

"Remember, boys are the simplest creatures on earth."

Horikita probably agreed with me. We welcomed Sudou to our group.

● ●

THE STUDY GROUP seemed to have gotten off to a good start. Of course, no one suddenly loved studying or found great joy in it. However, they all did their part to avoid expulsion so they could continue to spend time with their friends. The Idiot Trio started changing their behavior. They frantically repeated everything written on the blackboard, wracking their brains to understand the problems.

Sudou occasionally came close to passing out during class. His head would bob up and down as he started to doze, but he managed to stay awake, likely because of his professional basketball dreams. Most people would laugh at such high aspirations, but he chased them earnestly. Many of the first-year students, fresh from junior high, didn't have a "dream" yet. Many had only the vaguest notion of what they wanted their future to be. At least Sudou was already working hard in pursuit of his dream. That was worthy of praise.

How exactly did this school define an exemplary student? At the very least, people didn't pass or fail based solely on academics. Considering the fact that Ike and Sudou had been accepted into the school, that much was obvious. If the school enrolled students talented in other areas, though, it was odd that they'd have a system in place to expel students for just one failing grade. At least, that was how I saw it.

Unless the system itself was a lie, there wasn't much I could conclude. Could they be creating such problems for students like Ike and Sudou solely so they could overcome them? It likely wasn't that simple. Both the small test we'd taken and the classes, so difficult for those like Sudou, posed problems.

Once the afternoon class had ended, a satisfied-looking Horikita gave a small nod and glanced at her notes. Apparently, she'd compiled everything together. Even though Horikita was teaching the Idiot Trio, she wanted the best possible results. That was her nature. Our class's evaluation would improve, as would the individual students' abilities. However, trying to get perfect scores was absurd. We didn't intend to reach that far. Helping Ike and the others avoid failing was the best we could do.

When the lunch bell rang, everyone made a mad dash for the cafeteria. Our break was forty-five minutes long. After lunch, everyone had agreed to meet in the library for a twenty-minute study session. At first, we'd planned to study in the classroom. However, for better concentration, we decided to avoid noise and use the library.

However, the main reason was that Horikita wanted to avoid Hirata. His study group also met during lunch, and if we were reviewing materials nearby, they'd likely try to talk to us. Horikita absolutely did not want that.

"Horikita, what are you doing for lunch?" I asked.

"Well—"

"Ayanokouji-kun! Do you want to eat lunch together? I don't have any plans today!" Kushida unexpectedly hopped out in front of me.

"Ah, okay. Well then, do you want to eat together with Kushida—" I began.

"I already have plans. Please excuse me." Horikita stood and stalked out of the classroom by herself.

"I'm sorry, Ayanokouji-kun. Was I possibly...being a bother?" Kushida asked.

"Oh, no. Not at all."

Kushida waved to Horikita's retreating form, as if saying, *Bye bye!*

Had she planned that, by chance? After I'd discovered Kushida's secret, she'd been rather blatant about keeping tabs on me. Though she said that she believed me, she might still suspect I'd tell someone. Kushida and I went to the café to get lunch together. When we arrived, the absolute flood of women overwhelmed me.

"What's going on? There're an insane number of girls here," I said.

I'd say 80 percent of the customers were girls.

"This isn't really a place where boys come to eat."

The menu included items like pasta and pancakes, food that only girls would like. Athletic people like Sudou would probably complain about the small portions. There were a few guys, but you could say that they were either coupled up or playboys. Every guy here was either alone with one girl or surrounded by multiple ladies.

"How about we go to the cafeteria after all? I feel kind of uncomfortable here," I said.

"You'll be fine once you get used to it. It seems like Kouenji-kun comes here every day. See?" Kushida pointed to a table in the back, where Kouenji sat surrounded by girls. He looked just as grand and imposing as ever. I'd never seen him around during lunchtime. Was this where he went?

"He seems really popular. Those girls around him are all third years."

Kushida was surprised, too. I overheard some of the conversation between Kouenji and the older girls.

"Here, Kouenji-kun, say 'Ahh!'" one of them said.

"Ha ha! Just as I thought, more mature girls are the best."

He certainly didn't act shy at all around the third-year ladies. Rather, he ate his food while they practically pressed up against him.

"That guy is really something else," I muttered.

"His name seems to be going around lately. People are talking about him."

I see. So, were those girls after his money?

"What a sad world."

"Those girls are just being realists. You can't afford to eat on dreams alone," she said.

"Are you a realist, Kushida?"

"I'd say I'm a bit of a dreamer. Something like a knight in shining armor would be nice."

"A knight in shining armor, hmm?"

We sat as far away from Kouenji as possible.

"What about you, Ayanokouji-kun? Do you like girls like Horikita-san?" she asked.

"Why'd you bring up Horikita?"

"Well, you're always with her. Isn't she cute?"

Well, *I* certainly thought she was cute. On the outside, though.

"Know something, Ayanokouji-kun? You've caught the girls' eyes for a little while now. You're on a first-year students' ranking chart."

"Caught their eye? Me? Also, what the hell kind of ranking?"

Apparently, we men had been rated without even noticing. Was it like the ranking we'd made for the girls' breast sizes?

"Well, there are lots of different rankings, you know? The hot guy rankings. The rich guy rankings. The creeper rankings. And—"

"Okay, that's enough. I don't think I want to hear any more."

"Don't worry. You're ranked a respectable fifth place in the hot guy rankings. Congratulations! By the way, Satonaka-kun in Class A is in first place. Hirata-kun's in second. The third and fourth place boys are in Class A. I feel like Hirata-kun gets lots of points because of his looks and personality."

I'd expect nothing less from the Class D star. Even girls in Class C and above noticed him.

"Is it okay for me to be happy about that?" I asked.

"Of course. Oh, but you also ranked pretty high in gloominess."

"Let's see..." I looked at Kushida's cell phone. There really were a lot of different ranking charts. I saw a rather disturbing ranking titled, "Boys Who Should Die." Better not look at that one.

"Are you not really happy about it? You're ranked fifth."

"I guess if I cared about popularity it'd be different, but I don't really feel anything." Besides, no girl had ever placed a letter with a heart sticker on it in my bag. "So, does everyone participate in this?"

"Well, not everyone, but lots of people do. I don't know the exact number of votes, though. The comments are also anonymous."

In other words, many unknown variables made it difficult.

"I think you're probably at a disadvantage, Ayanokouji-kun. From my point of view, you're definitely attractive enough to be considered a hot guy, but I don't think people would say you're as beautiful or stand out as much as Hirata-kun. You're not exceptionally smart, you don't have exceptional athletic ability, and you're not a great conversationalist. There's something missing, some element of attractiveness, you know?"

In other words, there was nothing appealing about me at all. "Ouch. I feel like I just got stabbed in the heart."

"S-sorry. I probably should have held back a bit." Kushida appeared sheepish. "Hey, Ayanokouji-kun. Did you have a girlfriend in junior high school?"

"Would it be bad if I didn't?"

"So, you didn't have one? Ha ha, no. No, it's not bad."

"Rankings, huh? What would the girls think if the boys did something like that?"

"They'd probably consider them the lowest of the low."

Her smile didn't reach her eyes. Well, that was to be expected. If the boys ranked girls by cuteness, the girls would vehemently object. There was a definite double standard at play. At any rate, Kushida didn't seem to be treating me any differently than she had before. I'd thought things might have changed since discovering her secret side.

"Hey. You don't have to force yourself to talk to me if you don't want to," I said.

"No, it's not that I don't want to. Talking to you is fun, Ayanokouji-kun."

"Didn't you say that you hated me, though?"

"Ha ha ha, yes, I did. Sorry, but that's how I really feel."

Well, that hurt. Even though she was smiling, she hated me. This was the worst.

"To tell you the truth, I invited you out to lunch today because I wanted to check with you. Hypothetically, if you had to choose either Horikita-san or me as your ally, whom would you choose, Ayanokouji-kun? Would you choose me?"

"I'm no one's ally or enemy. I'm neutral."

"There are some situations where you can't avoid trouble by staying neutral. It's wonderful to oppose war, for example, but you may find yourself in the middle of turmoil at some point, you know? If Horikita and I happen to clash, I hope that you'll cooperate with me, Ayanokouji-kun."

"When you say that..."

"Anyway, try to remember that I'm expecting your help."

"Expecting, huh? If you were to ask for my help, your first priority should probably be to explain the situation."

Kushida, still smiling, emphatically shook her head. "First, we'd need to build a relationship of mutual trust."

"I suppose."

Neither Kushida nor I understood each other yet. Perhaps in the future, I'd come to have deeper knowledge of her.

9.2

. . . .

WE GATHERED IN THE LIBRARY one minute later than we'd agreed. Everyone had their notebooks open, ready and waiting. The library was a popular study spot, it seemed. First through third years fought to move up in the rankings. I understood it with a glance.

"You're late," Horikita said.

"Sorry, the crowds were tough."

"You two didn't eat lunch together, did you?"

Ike turned to us, his eyes suspicious. Kushida and I had actually eaten together, but perhaps it was better to keep that information private.

"Yes, we did. We ate lunch together," Kushida said.

It would have been better if she'd said nothing. Sure enough, Ike and the others glared at me, their discontent plain to see. Ike looked at me like I was his ancestral enemy. Horikita spoke without glancing up.

"Hurry," she said.

"Okay."

At Horikita's cold command, I sat down and took out my notebook.

"I thought I might need more help on this, but geography is actually pretty easy."

"Chemistry wasn't as hard as I thought it'd be, either."

Ike and Yamauchi sounded pleased.

"Most of the problems boil down to memorization, right? You can't solve many problems in English or mathematics if you don't understand the foundation, though."

"Don't let your guard down. I think there might be current events questions on the test, too."

"Current...events?"

"Events of the recent past related to politics or the economy. That means that the questions may not be limited by what's written in the textbook."

"Ugh, isn't that against the rules? That means we have no idea what's going to be on the test, doesn't it?!"

"So that's why you should study everything."

"I suddenly hate geography..."

While the test might cover current events, I thought it'd be fine to ignore them for now. If you worried too much, you'd likely miss out on something important and suffer for it.

"Shouldn't we hurry it up?" I asked. We were wasting precious time talking about this or that.

"Yes. We've been wasting time because *someone* was late."

"Are you still harping on me for that?"

"Here's a question for everyone. Who came up with inductive reasoning?"

"Um. It was that guy we learned about in class before, right? That was..." Ike wracked his brain and spun his mechanical pencil.

"Oh, that's it. That one guy. His name made me super hungry."

"Francisco Xavier! Or something like that, right?" Sudou asked.

Close, but no cigar.

"I remember! Francis Bacon!" Ike cried.

"That's correct."

"Yes! I'm definitely going to get a perfect score!"

"No, not really..."

If we all managed to keep up this pace for another week, everyone might just avoid failing.

"Please be mindful of your health, everyone. If you get sick, you'll have less time to study!" Kushida understood that we had no wiggle room left.

"Don't worry. Not about those three, anyway," Horikita grumbled.

"Just as I'd expect from you, Horikita-chan! I feel like you're starting to have some faith in us!"

Actually, she probably meant something more like, "Idiots don't catch colds."

"Hey, quiet down. Your yammering is getting annoying." A nearby student turned to look at us.

"Sorry, sorry. Guess I got a little carried away. I'm just so happy I got something right. Did *you* know that Francis Bacon was the guy who came up with inductive reasoning? I won't lose points on that question!" said Ike, laughing foolishly.

"Huh? Hey, could you guys be Class D students, by chance?"

A group of boys all looked over at us at once. Sudou, seemingly irritated by this, sounded mildly angry as he said, "So what? What's the big deal if we're in Class D? Do you have a problem with that?"

"No, no, there's no problem. I'm Yamawaki, from Class C. Nice to meet you." Yamawaki chuckled. "I have to say, I'm glad that they separate the classes in this school by ability. That way I don't have to study with losers like you."

"What'd you say?!" Sudou's anger flared.

"Don't get mad. I've only spoken the truth. I wonder...

If we happened to fight, how many points would you lose? Oh wait, you guys don't even *have* any points to lose, do you? In that case, you'd probably be expelled, right?"

"Fine with me. Bring it!"

Sudou's shouting attracted attention and looks of disgust. If things got much worse, then the teacher would probably hear about it.

"He's exactly right. We're not sure what'll happen if you create a ruckus. You should remember that you might be expelled as a worst-case scenario. I don't particularly mind that you're bad-mouthing us, but you're in Class C, right? Honestly, you shouldn't really brag about that," Horikita said.

"Clearly there were errors of calculation in placing Class C and A. But you guys in D are on a completely different level."

"That's quite an inconsistent standard of measurement. The way I see it, everyone outside of Class A is lumped together."

Yamawaki stopped laughing and now glared at Horikita.

"Wow. For a defective product that can't make a single point, you're pretty sassy, aren't you? Did you think you could say whatever you like just because you have a cute face?"

"Thank you for your wholly incoherent and irrelevant statement. I was never very concerned about my appearance until now, but after being praised by you, I must say I feel rather uncomfortable."

"Tch!" Yamawaki slammed the table and stood up.

"Hey. Relax. If we're the ones who start fighting, then word will get around and we'll be in trouble." The other Class C students tugged at Yamawaki's sleeves, holding him back.

"You do know that you'll be expelled if you fail the next test, right? I'm looking forward to seeing how many of you get kicked out."

"Unfortunately for you, no one from Class D will be expelled. Before you worry about *us,* though, perhaps you should worry about your own class. Pride cometh before the fall."

"Ha ha ha! Us, fail? Don't joke around."

"We're not studying just to avoid failing. We're studying so we can improve our test scores. Don't lump us together with you," Yamawaki said. "Also, being happy because you know who Francis Bacon is? Are you nuts? Why are you studying things that aren't even on the test?"

"Huh?" Horikita looked stumped.

"Wait, do you guys not know what's on the test? No wonder you're called defective products."

"That's enough out of you." Sudou, on the verge of really losing his temper, grabbed Yamawaki by the collar.

"Hey, hey! You're really going to get violent even though it'll lose you points? You're okay with that?"

"We don't have any points to lose!"

Sudou pulled his arm back. Uh oh. Was he really going to beat the crap out of this guy? I knew I should stop him. I got up, then—

"Okay, stop. Stop!"

A female student shouted at us. Sudou stopped in response.

"What? This doesn't involve you. Stay out of it," he said.

"Doesn't involve me? I'm trying to use the library, so it *does* involve me. If you want to get violent, might I suggest that you do so outside?"

In response to the blonde beauty's disinterested yet logical argument, Sudou let go of Yamawaki.

"Besides, don't you think you're provoking him? If things continue like this, I'd have to report it to the school. Do you want that?"

"S-sorry. We don't want that, Ichinose," Yamawaki said.

Ichinose. I'd heard that name once before. Wait... That was the Class B student who'd been talking with Hoshinomiya-sensei.

"Come on, let's go. If we try studying here, we'll catch the stupid going around."

"Yeah."

With those last words, Yamawaki and his group left.

"If you're going to study here, please act like adults. Thank you," Ichinose said.

Watching her gallant departure, I had to nod in admiration.

"Unlike Horikita, she managed to keep everyone in line."

"I didn't intend to create chaos. I only spoke the truth."

The truth had led to chaos, though...

"Hey. He said that this question wasn't on the test, didn't he?"

"What do you mean?"

We exchanged looks. Chabashira-sensei had told us that material about the Age of Discovery would be on the test. Horikita and I had written that down.

"Does this mean that each class gets a different test?"

"That seems unlikely. The test should be the same for everyone in the same grade."

Horikita was right. The same fundamental problems from the five main topics should be featured on everyone's midterm. Otherwise, it'd be unclear how to judge our aptitude. Had Class C learned that the test would change before anyone else?

Or was Class D the only group being left out of the loop? We were mystified in the light of this new information. What if every class's test had different social studies questions? No... What if it wasn't just social studies? What if all the test questions were completely different? If that were the case, then we'd wasted a whole week's worth of studying.

9.3

WE DISMISSED THE GROUP ten minutes before our lunch break was over. We packed up and headed toward the faculty room. We needed to confirm exactly what the test would cover.

"Chabashira-sensei, we have an urgent question."

"Quite the theatrical entrance. You surprised the other teachers," she said.

"I sincerely apologize for the sudden intrusion."

"It's fine. We're in the middle of something, so please keep it brief." Chabashira-sensei continued to write in her notebook.

"Chabashira-sensei, last week when you told us what material the test would cover, did you make a mistake? A little earlier today, some Class C students told us that the test's material would be different than what we were expecting."

Chabashira-sensei listened in complete silence and didn't even bat an eyelash as Horikita spoke. Then, she put down her pen.

"That's right. The test's topics changed last Friday. Sorry, I must've forgotten to inform you."

"What?!"

She scribbled something down on a page in her notebook, tore it out, and handed it to Horikita. She'd written down textbook page numbers that referred to material we'd already covered in class. Most of the new material was from before we'd started the group, stuff that Sudou and the others hadn't learned.

"Thanks to you, Horikita-san, I was able to correct my mistake. I'm grateful to all of you. That's all. Thank you."

"Wait a minute, Sae-chan-sensei! Isn't it way too late for this?"

"I don't think so. You still have one week. If you use that study time wisely, it should be easy. Right?"

Chabashira-sensei tried to shoo us out of the faculty room without the slightest hesitation. However, none of us moved.

"Even if you stay, nothing will change. You understand that, don't you?" she asked.

"Let's go."

"B-but, Horikita-chan! We can't just accept this!"

"As Chabashira-sensei said, staying would be a waste of time. Instead, we should begin studying the revised test materials."

"But!"

Horikita turned on her heel and left the faculty room, Sudou and the others reluctantly following after her. Chabashira-sensei didn't even glance at us as we left. I'd thought she would apologize for making such a mistake, but she didn't. If anything, I'd thought that some of the other teachers might react to this incident.

Despite the fact that this was a pretty serious mistake for a homeroom teacher to make, none of the other teachers seemed to care. Hoshinomiya-sensei was seated nearby. Our eyes met. She gave a small smile and waved hello. Well, that was *something*, at least. However, I didn't think that our teacher had simply forgotten to tell us what would be covered on the test.

When I stepped into the hallway, the afternoon class bell rang.

"Kushida-san. I have a small favor I want to ask you," I said.

"Hmm? What is it?"

"I want you to tell the rest of Class D about the changes to the test."

With that, I handed her Chabashira-sensei's paper with the textbook numbers.

"That's fine, but...is it okay for me to do it?"

"You're the best candidate we have. There's no doubt in my mind. Besides, we can't take the test when we don't know what's going to be on it."

"Okay, I understand. Leave it to me. I'll tell Hirata-kun and everyone else."

"I'll get ready for tomorrow. By then, I should have narrowed down everything we'll need."

Horikita tried hard to appear calm, but I could sense her anxiety. That time we'd spent studying had been squandered, and we were back to square one. Plus, we now only had one week left.

However, our greatest concern was keeping the Idiot Trio motivated.

"Horikita. I know I've been difficult, but I'm counting on you." Sudou bowed to Horikita as he spoke those words. "Starting tomorrow...I'll take a break from club activities. Will that work?"

"That..."

Considering that we had only one week left and time was of the essence, it was a rational decision. However, the offer so surprised Horikita that she couldn't immediately accept.

"Will that really be okay with you? It'll be a lot of work."

"Studying is a lot of work, isn't it?" Grinning, Sudou patted Horikita's shoulder.

"Sudou, are you serious?" she asked.

"Yeah. I mean, I'm pissed at our homeroom teacher and those jerks in Class C now, too."

You could call this a blessing in disguise. After being backed into a corner, Sudou had finally developed a positive attitude about studying. He probably realized if he didn't do his best, he couldn't pass the test. His declaration inspired Ike and Yamauchi.

"Guess we don't have any choice. We'll try harder, too," Ike said.

"I understand. If you're prepared, then we can work together. However, Sudou-kun..." Horikita coldly removed Sudou's hand from her shoulder. "Please do not touch me. If you do so again, I won't show you any mercy."

"You're not cute at all, lady..."

"We're definitely gonna do this!"

"Yeah! Me, too!"

Kushida, who also seemed motivated, stuck out her fist. "Come on, Ayanokouji-kun. You do your best, too!" she cried.

"Huh? No, I—"

THE FAILURES MOBILIZE ONCE AGAIN

"Don't tell me. Did you already give up on studying?"

"I've thought about it a little."

"You promised you'd work with me. Did you forget?" asked Horikita while glaring at me.

"I'm not a good teacher. People have different strengths and weaknesses, right?"

To be honest, Horikita and Kushida were better teachers than I was. I didn't consider myself really capable of tutoring others.

"Your test scores weren't that bad, were they?"

"There isn't much time left, so it might be more effective if Horikita and Kushida work together to teach those three rather than tutoring one-on-one. Also, something else is kind of bothering me."

"Something bothering you?"

What had happened in the faculty room was far too serious for me to overlook.

9.4

WHEN LUNCHTIME CAME, I jumped to my feet and headed toward the cafeteria with purposeful strides.

"Where are you going?"

Kushida had noticed me rushing out of class and followed. She popped up before me, stopping me in my tracks.

"It's lunch. I thought I'd go to the cafeteria."

"Hmm. Mind if I go with you?"

"I don't really mind. But there are a lot of other people you could ask, you know."

"It's true, I do have a lot of friends to eat lunch with, but you don't have anyone, Ayanokouji-kun. Even though you'd usually reach out to Horikita-san, you haven't talked to her today. The other day, didn't you say something was bothering you about what happened in the faculty room? What was it?"

Kushida, as usual, was quite observant. To be honest, I hadn't wanted to do this with anyone, but I decided that Kushida was probably fine. I'd come to learn her secret by sheer coincidence. She wouldn't do anything stupid.

"I can tell you if you promise that you won't tell anyone else."

"I'm good at keeping secrets."

Kushida and I headed to the cafeteria together. We navigated our way through the crowd and finally reached the meal ticket machine. I bought tickets for two portions but didn't line up at the counter. Instead, I went to the side of the vending machine and looked at students perusing the menu.

"What is it?" Kushida tilted her head and looked puzzled when I began studying the machine.

"This might answer what was bothering me."

I continued observing students as they bought lunch sets from the ticket machine. After I'd observed about twenty students, my target appeared. He purchased his meal ticket and walked to the counter with heavy, plodding footsteps.

"Okay, let's go," I said.

"Hmm? Okay."

We quickly exchanged our tickets for our meals and sat down in front of the heavy-footed student.

"Um, excuse me. Are you an upperclassman?" I asked.

"Hmm? Who are you?" The student regarded us calmly, a look of complete disinterest on his face.

"Are you a second-year student? Third-year?"

"Third-year. Let me guess, you're a first year?"

"I'm Ayanokouji, from Class D. You're also in Class D, aren't you?"

"What's that got to do with you?"

Kushida looked at me with surprise, as if asking, "How did you know?"

"Because he's limited to eating the free meals. It's not very tasty, is it?" I asked. He was eating the free vegetable meal set.

"What do you want? You're really irritating." He took his tray and made to stand, but I stopped him.

"I want to ask you something. If you listen, I'll show you my gratitude."

"Gratitude?"

The cafeteria's hustle and bustle drowned out my voice. The students were all engrossed in chatting pleasantly with their friends.

"Do you still have the problems from the midterm test from the first semester of your first year? Or, if not, do you happen to know someone from your class who does?"

"Do you even understand what you're asking?" he said.

"It's not particularly strange, is it? I didn't think it was against school rules to study using old test problems."

"Why are you asking me?"

"That's simple. I believed I'd have the highest chance of success if I worked with someone who doesn't have any points. Honestly, that free vegetable meal doesn't look good. Of course, things would be quite different if you actually *liked* eating the vegetable set. What do you think?"

"How much are you going to pay?"

"Ten thousand points. That's as high as I'll go."

"I don't have the old test problems, but...I know someone who does. If you want him to help you, though, you're going to need to offer at least 30,000 points. If you've got that, you're fine."

"I'm afraid that 30,000 is a no-go for me. I don't have that much."

"How much do you have?"

"Twenty thousand."

"Then 20,000... no, 15,000 should do. Nothing under that."

"15,000, huh?"

"If you'd go so far as to ask for old test problems from a stranger, then you must be pretty desperate, huh? Well, the school will mercilessly expel any student who gets a failing grade. None of my classmates are even here anymore."

"I see. I understand. I'll pay the 15,000 points."

"Then we have a deal. Of course, I'll have to ask you to transfer the points in advance."

"Fine, but if you do anything to stab us in the back, I won't forgive you. Even if you're an upperclassman, I'll do anything and everything I can to make sure you're expelled."

"You're a freak. Fine, I get it. Besides, when you transfer points, there's always a record of it. If rumor spreads that some first-year students ripped me off, it'd look bad."

"All right then. Since I'm paying you 15,000 points, can you toss in a little bonus? I want to see the answers to the surprise test that we took after being admitted."

"All right. I'll toss that in, too. I think that your concerns are pointless, though." It seemed he understood what I was after.

"Thank you very much."

After we made our deal, he quickly left. He probably didn't want to be noticed.

"Hey, Ayanokouji-kun? What you did just now. Was that really okay?" Kushida asked.

"It's no problem. School rules allow point transfers, so there was no violation."

"You might be right, but isn't getting the old test problems cheating?"

"Cheating? I don't think so. If the school didn't allow it, they would have outlined it in the school rules to begin with. Also, I felt more confident after seeing that third-year student. That is to say, it's not unusual for students to barter points like this."

"Huh?"

"My request didn't particularly surprise him, and he accepted quickly. This probably isn't the first time he's negotiated like this. Not only did he have the answer sheet for the first-year midterm exam, but he also had the answer sheet for the mock test we took after being admitted. If he saved those, it's clear why."

Kushida's eyes widened in shock.

"Ayanokouji-kun, what you did was unexpectedly daring."

"It's just a bit of insurance to prevent Sudou and the others from getting expelled."

"But, if the old test answers are useless, then it will have been for nothing. I mean, the past test questions are old, aren't they? They might be completely unrelated to what's featured on this year's test."

"The problems may not be exactly the same, but there will definitely be similarities. I noticed a hint on that last mock exam we took."

"A hint?"

"You noticed the really difficult problems alongside the simple ones, right?"

"Yeah, I did. The final questions, right? I didn't understand them at all."

"I did some investigating, and I found that those questions were on the second- and third-year students' tests. In other words, a first-year student generally wouldn't understand how to solve them. Wouldn't it be pointless for the school to purposefully throw us problems we can't solve? Those questions aren't there simply to measure our academic ability. Now, suppose that the problems on the mock test *we* took were exactly the same as the problems on the old mock test. What would happen?"

"If I'd seen the old test, I would have been able to answer every question," she said.

The same thing would likely apply to the midterm exam as well. Shortly thereafter, that third-year student sent me a message with an image file attached. It was the old test questions.

First, I checked the mock test. The key was whether or not the last three problems were the same. Kushida must have been curious as well, because she drew closer and tried to peek at my phone.

"Well? Well?" she asked.

"They're the same. Every single word is identical. The

test from that year and this year are exactly the same, in every way."

"That's amazing! So, if we show this to everyone in class, that would mean an easy victory! We should show this to all of our other friends, not just Sudou-kun!"

"No, we'll hold off. We won't show it to Sudou and the guys yet."

"Wh-why? You went to all of the trouble of using up so many of your points for this!"

"If they learn that the old test questions would be effective, their motivation to study would go up in smoke. We need to be wary of overconfidence. After all, even though the mock tests were identical, it's possible that the questions featured on the midterm this year might not be the same as last year's."

These old test papers were insurance.

"Okay, then how will you use them?"

"I'm going to release them on the internet the day before the test. We tell everyone that the problems from the old test are generally the same as the ones on the new. Then what do you think will happen?"

"That night, everyone will be hunched over their desks, frantically trying to memorize all of the problems!"

"Exactly."

The students with a poor grasp of the basics probably

wouldn't be able to memorize everything in a single day. However, we weren't shooting for perfect scores this time around. The crucial thing was to avoid failing. If we got greedy, we might end up digging our own graves.

With this plan, we could probably get everyone in Class D to pass.

"When did you come up with the idea to get the old tests?" she asked.

"I considered it when we learned that the test material was going to be different. However, I had a hunch back when they first told us about the midterm exam."

"Huh?! Way back then?"

"There was something very peculiar about the way Chabashira-sensei told us about the test. As our homeroom teacher, she had a clear understanding of everyone's grades and academic performance. Despite that, she seemed absolutely certain when she told us that there was a way for us to pass this test. In other words, she indicated that there was a surefire way for us to save everyone."

"And that's...the old test papers?"

"This might be related to why Sudou, Ike, and Yamauchi were admitted to this school despite being academically poor. Even if they couldn't get good grades by studying ahead, perhaps there were other means of addressing the problem, a backup plan they could use to avoid expulsion. This meant that it was possible for anyone to get a near-perfect score if they could get the old test papers. That's what I took from the situation, anyway."

"Ayanokouji-kun, you really are an incredibly observant person, aren't you?"

"I'm just cunning. Besides, I didn't believe that I could pass the midterm without some help. I was just looking to make things easier for myself."

"Hmm." Kushida grinned like some gears were turning in her mind.

"I have one more favor to ask. Could you please tell everyone that *you* got the old test papers, Kushida? I want you to say that you got them from a third-year student you're close to."

"That's fine, but...are you okay with that, Ayanokouji-kun?"

"I like to avoid trouble. I don't want to stand out. Besides, our classmates trust you, Kushida. I think it would be better if you told them."

"I understand. If you say so, Ayanokouji-kun."

"Thanks. Don't say anything else, though. We need to avoid drawing too much attention."

"Okay, we can keep this secret between us."

"Yeah, that's what I was thinking."

"Don't you feel that a strange bond of mutual trust forms between people who share a secret?"

"I don't know about that. I sure hope so."

"Thank you," replied Kushida.

I didn't really know what she meant by that.

10

MIDTERM EXAM

IT WAS THURSDAY. Tomorrow, the midterm would be upon us. Class had ended for the day. After Chabashira-sensei ended the homeroom period and left the classroom, Kushida immediately leapt into action. She took out printed copies of the old test that I'd made at the convenience store and brought them up to the podium.

"Everyone, before you return to the dorm, would you mind listening to me for a moment?"

Everyone, including Sudou, stopped and listened to Kushida. This was a role that neither Horikita nor I could play. Only Kushida could do it.

"I know that you've all been studying a lot in preparation for the test tomorrow. I have something to help you. I'm going to hand out some papers."

Kushida distributed the question and answer sheets to the students in the first row.

"Test...questions? Did you make these, Kushida-san?" Horikita was visibly surprised by this sudden turn of events.

"Actually, these are the old test problems. I got them from a third-year student last night."

"Old test problems? Huh? Wait, will these questions be on the test tomorrow?"

"Yes. To tell you the truth, I heard that the midterm test from the year before last had almost exactly the same problems as this one. So, if we study what's on this test, it'll surely come in handy."

"Whoa! Seriously? Thank you, Kushida-chan!" Overjoyed, Ike hugged his test paper. None of the other students could suppress their elation, either.

"What the hell? If we had *these*, then wasn't it pointless to study so hard?" Yamauchi complained, even as he laughed.

It looked like I'd been right.

"Sudou-kun, do your best when you study today!"

"Yeah. Thanks, you really helped me out." Sudou also happily accepted the test papers.

"Let's keep this a secret from the other classes! Don't be scared, everyone! Do your best and aim for a high score!" Ike shouted with joy and determination. I was inclined to agree with him. We didn't need to send supplies to the enemy. Everyone returned to the dorms with high spirits.

"Kushida-san. Excellent work." Horikita gave Kushida genuine praise, which was unusual.

"Eh, really?" Kushida said.

"I'd never even considered trying to use the old tests. I'm also grateful that you verified that the questions were still useful."

True. The always-solitary Horikita hadn't come up with that idea.

"I just did it for my friends. It was nothing special," Kushida said.

"Also, I think that you were correct to announce that you had it today after class. If you'd carelessly let word get out about this test, it's possible that everyone would have lost their motivation to study."

"That was only because I received the test papers so late. If many of the same problems are featured on the test tomorrow, then everyone will probably manage to get pretty high test scores."

"Yes. It also means that the last two weeks we spent studying weren't for nothing."

The past two weeks had probably been tremendously long for Sudou and the other failing students. Hopefully they'd gotten more into the habit of studying now.

"It was hard but fun."

"I don't think the Idiot Trio found it the least bit fun."

Well, we'd done as much as we could. The next step for those three simply came down to effort.

"I just pray that I don't draw a complete blank during the actual test."

Well, I couldn't really do anything about that part. No matter how much they were taught and what they demonstrated during the study group, everything came down to their performance on the actual test. At least the previous questions were one crucial bit of help.

"Well, should we head back?"

Horikita quietly looked over at Kushida as she put her textbook into her bag. "Kushida-san."

"Hmm?"

"Really, thank you for everything you've done. If you weren't here, the study group would not have succeeded."

"Don't worry about it. I just want to get into the higher-ranked classes together with everyone else. That's why I did it, and why I agreed to help with the study group. I'll help you again any time." Smiling, Kushida grabbed her bag and stood.

"Wait. There's just one thing I want to confirm," Horikita said.

"Confirm?"

"If you say that you'll continue working with me for the sake of our class, then I need to be sure of something."

Horikita looked straight at Kushida, who was still wearing that dazzling smile.

"You hate me, don't you?"

"Hey, hey..." I'd wondered what she wanted to ask, but that was ridiculously unexpected.

"Why do you think that?" Kushida asked.

"You're not answering my question because it's true. Right?"

"Ha ha, you got me." She shouldered her bag and lowered her hands. Kushida faced Horikita without losing her smile. "That's right. I really hate you."

She answered clearly, making no attempt to hide it. She was direct.

"Do you want me to tell you the reason?"

"No. That's unnecessary. Knowing that is good enough. I can continue working with you without hesitation."

Despite what she'd just been told, Horikita spoke calmly.

• •

"**T**HERE ARE NO ABSENCES today. It appears everyone is present."

Chabashira-sensei strode through the classroom with a bold smile on her face.

"That's the first hurdle for you leftovers. Are there any questions?"

"We've studied diligently these past few weeks. I don't think that anyone will fail."

"Oh my. You sound quite confident, Hirata."

Everyone wore a confident look. The teacher promptly took up the test papers and passed them out. Our first period test was for social studies. Out of everything we'd studied, it was probably the easiest subject.

"If anyone stumbles here, the other tests will be an uphill battle, quite frankly. You'll take this midterm and the final exam in July. If no one fails either test, you'll be rewarded with a vacation during your summer break."

"A vacation?"

"That's right. A dream vacation on an island surrounded by the brilliant blue sea."

Of course, the beach in summer meant we'd be able to see the girls in their swimsuits...

"Wh-what is this strange pressure..." one of the boys muttered.

Chabashira-sensei stepped back from the obvious tension the students exuded... mostly the boys.

"Everyone. Let's do our best!"

"Yeah!" Ike howled along with our classmates. I shouted too, my voice getting lost in the cacophony.

"Pervert." Horikita glanced at me. I immediately fell silent.

Before long, everyone had their test papers. On the teacher's signal, everyone began. I held off on starting for a moment and looked around at the others. With everything they'd learned, could the Idiot Trio avoid failing? First off, how many of this test's questions were the same as the ones from the old exam? I needed to check that first.

All right.

I discreetly clenched my fist in triumph. Despite my fears, the questions here were the same as the old ones. I hadn't looked them over in any detail, but I saw no great difference. If I'd memorized what was on the old test, it was clear that I could get a near-perfect score.

Glancing around the classroom for assurance, I didn't notice any students looking flustered or confused. I assumed that many of them had engaged in some last-minute studying. Slowly, I went through and answered all of the problems.

The second and third period exams were for Japanese and chemistry, respectively. While I worked, I discovered something else that intrigued me. Looking over the problems again, I realized that what Horikita had drilled into the study group was consistent with what was on the test. She'd been able to accurately predict what problems would appear just from the lessons. The silent girl beside me was even more impressive than I'd imagined.

Then came fourth period. Mathematics. All of the abnormally difficult questions that had been featured on the mock test also appeared here, but the content was the same as the old exams. Even if Sudou and the other guys couldn't understand the problems, they could still apply the answers if they'd memorized them.

Then came the break.

Some members of our study group, including Ike, Yamauchi, Kushida, Horikita, and myself, gathered together.

"An easy victory! We've got this test on lock!"

"I feel like I might get 120 points." Ike sounded pretty sure of himself. Yamauchi must have felt the same, judging from the smile on his face. Confident, they looked over the old test papers for a final review.

"Sudou-kun, how about you?" Kushida spoke to Sudou, who sat alone at his desk and stared fixedly at the old test material. However, Sudou looked sullen.

"Sudou-kun?"

"Huh? Oh, sorry. I'm kind of busy."

He didn't look up from the questions as he spoke. He was reviewing the English test material, his forehead covered in a thin layer of sweat.

"Sudou, did you...not study the old test material, by chance?"

"Everything but English. I fell asleep partway through." Sudou sounded irritated. In other words, this was his first time reviewing the material.

"Eh?!"

That also meant that Sudou only had ten minutes to review.

"Damn, I can't get any of these answers to stick in my head," he muttered.

Unlike the other tests, the English problems weren't easy to memorize. Trying to cram all of the answers in just ten minutes would be impossible.

"Sudou-kun, memorize the problems that are worth a lot of points and those with the shortest answers." Horikita leapt up from her seat and moved next to Sudou.

"O-okay." He stopped focusing on the low-point questions and instead zeroed in on what would net him the most points.

"A-are you going to be okay?" While trying to avoid getting in the way, Kushida appeared anxious.

"Unlike Japanese, I don't know the basics of English. These letters look like some kind of magic spell or something. Memorizing it'll take time."

"Y-yeah. I struggle with English, too..."

The break passed in the blink of an eye, and the heartless class bell rang.

"I did all I could. I'll try to answer the questions I remember first, before I forget them."

"Yeah..."

And thus began our English test. While the other students calmly made their way through, Sudou clearly had trouble. Occasionally, he'd stop writing and whack his pen against his head. However, no one could help him now. Whether Sudou sank or swam was entirely up to him.

. . . .

AFTER THE LAST TEST, we gathered around Sudou's desk again.

"Hey, did you do okay?" asked Ike, anxiously.

Sudou was on the verge of losing his cool.

"I don't know... I did everything I could, but I have no idea how well I did..."

"Don't worry. You studied as hard as you could. I'm sure you did well."

"Damn it, why did I fall asleep?" Sudou fidgeted, clearly frustrated with himself. Horikita then stepped in front of him.

"Sudou-kun."

"What is it? Are you going to lecture me again?" he grumbled.

"It was certainly your fault for not reviewing the old

test's final section. However, as you said, you did everything that you could with the time that you had. You didn't cut any corners or give up. Considering how much effort you put in, I think you should hold your head high and feel proud."

"What is this? Are you trying to comfort me?"

"Comfort? I'm speaking the truth. When I look at how far you've come, I understand how hard studying is for you, Sudou."

Horikita was genuinely praising him. None of us could believe what we were seeing.

"Let's wait for the results."

"Yeah... Okay."

"There's...one more thing. Something I need to amend."

"Amend?"

"Earlier, I said that your dreams of becoming a professional basketball player were foolish."

"Why are you reminding me of that?"

"I researched how someone could become a professional basketball player, and I learned that the road to success is an incredibly rocky one."

"So, you're telling me to give up because it's a reckless dream?"

"Not at all. I know that you're passionate about

basketball. I also realize that you probably understand how difficult it is to play professionally." Horikita still acted in her normal, aloof manner, but this was clearly an apology, albeit an awkward one. "There are many Japanese people who fight to enter that profession. There are some among those who wish to become internationally renowned. You're one of those people, right?"

"Yeah. I'm incredibly stupid, but I want to play ball. Even if I have to live a pathetic, miserable life as a part-time worker or worse, I'm going to achieve my dream."

"I never thought I needed to understand anyone except for myself. So when you first told me that you wanted to play basketball, I insulted you. However, I now regret that. Someone who doesn't understand how difficult, how arduous basketball is has no right to dismiss that dream as foolish. Sudou-kun, don't forget the hard work and effort that you poured into studying. Apply that diligence to basketball. If you do, you might be able to go pro. At least, that's how I feel."

Horikita's expression was the same as always, but she bowed her head to Sudou.

"I'm sorry for what I said back then. Well. Now that I've said my piece, I'll be going."

Horikita left the room, her apology still hanging in the air.

"Hey, did you just see that? Horikita apologized! And so nicely!"

"I can't believe it!"

Ike and Yamauchi were both completely stunned. I was pretty surprised, too. Kushida was as well. Horikita had acknowledged that Sudou had done his best. A dumbfounded Sudou, still seated at his desk, looked after Horikita as she walked through the classroom door. Soon after, Sudou, put his right hand over his heart and looked at us.

"O-oh, no... I... I think I might be in love with Horikita..." he said.

THE BEGINNING

CHABASHIRA-SENSEI strode into the classroom, looking around at the students in surprise. Everyone was clearly anxious, holding their breath in anticipation of the test results.

"Sensei. We were told that the results would be announced today, but when?"

"There's no need for you to get so worked up, Hirata. You should have passed quite easily."

"So, when will the results be released?"

"Well, if you'd like, now is as good a time as any. If we waited to do it after class, we wouldn't have enough time for other procedures."

Some of the students visibly reacted to the words "other procedures."

"What...do you mean by that?"

"Don't get flustered. I'll tell you now."

As usual, she revealed the details simultaneously and collectively. She stuck a large, white sheet of paper with everyone's names and test scores onto the blackboard.

"Honestly, I'm impressed. I didn't think that you'd score so well. Many students tied with perfect scores in mathematics, Japanese, and social studies. More than ten of you, actually."

Some of the students shouted in joy and delight when they saw the 100s lined up on the results sheet. However, some weren't smiling. The only grade that truly mattered was Sudou's score in English.

Then—

We saw Sudou's test scores. He had scored sixty points in four of the five main subjects, which was considerably high. He'd scored thirty-nine points in English.

"Yes!" Sudou leapt up and shouted with joy. Ike and Yamauchi stood and cheered, too. There was no red line to be found on the results sheet. Kushida and I shared a glance and sighed in relief. Horikita didn't smile or cheer, but she did appear relieved.

"We showed you, sensei! When we really try our best, we can do anything!" Ike wore a smug, confident look.

"Yes, I recognize that. You all did very well. However—"

Chabashira-sensei held a red pen in her hand.

Sudou unintentionally let out a "Huh?"

She drew a red line right above Sudou's name.

"Wh-what is that? What does that mean?"

"You failed, Sudou."

"Huh? You're lying, right? Don't give me that crap! Why did I fail?" he cried.

Of course, Sudou was the first one to protest this. In response to Sudou's failing grade, the entire classroom did a complete one-eighty. We stopped our delighted cheering and erupted in confusion.

"Sudou, you failed the English exam. That's all."

"Don't screw with me! I got thirty-two points! I passed!"

"When did anyone say that thirty-two points was a passing grade?"

"No, no. You said so, sensei! Right, everyone?" shouted Ike.

"Say whatever you want, it won't matter. This is the undeniable truth. You had to score at least a forty to pass the midterm exam. In other words, you were just one point short. You were so close."

"F-forty?! You never told us about this! I won't accept it!"

"Should I tell you how we determine the passing grade?"

Chabashira-sensei wrote a simple formula on the blackboard: 79.6 divided by 2 equals 39.8.

"We set a passing grade for each individual class, just as we did for the last test. We calculated that number by dividing the average score by two. That's how we arrived at our answer."

In other words, anything at 39.8 or lower was considered failing.

"I provided proof that you failed. That is all."

"No way... So... Does that mean I'm going to be expelled?"

"Although your time here was short, you struggled valiantly. You'll be asked to fill out a withdrawal form after class, but you will need to have a legal guardian present when you do so. I'll contact them for you."

As we witnessed the scene unfold, the teacher rattling off the information as if she were casually giving a report, we finally realized that this was actually happening.

"As for the rest of you, good work. You all passed without any issues. Work hard so that you can pass your final exam as well. Well then, next—"

"S-sensei. Is Sudou-kun really being expelled? Is there no way to save him?"

Hirata was the first to show concern, even though Sudou hated him and had lashed out at him verbally.

"He's being expelled. He got a failing grade."

"Could we possibly see Sudou-kun's answer sheet?"

"Even if you look it over, you won't find any grading mistakes. I was expecting that you'd protest."

She took out Sudou's English answer sheet and handed it to Hirata, who immediately looked over every problem. His expression turned dark when he reached the end.

"There...are no mistakes."

"Well, if you're all in agreement, homeroom is over."

Chabashira-sensei had heartlessly announced Sudou's expulsion without offering him a second chance or the faintest bit of sympathy. Ike and Yamauchi, knowing that words of comfort would probably have the opposite effect, stayed silent. Hirata remained quiet, too. Sadly, some of the students appeared relieved by this. Were they happy that a nuisance like Sudou was being removed from the class?

"Sudou, come to the faculty room after class. That is all."

"Chabashira-sensei. May I have a moment of your time?"

Though she'd stayed silent until that moment, Horikita raised her slender arm in the air and spoke. Thus far, Horikita had never voluntarily made any remarks.

CLASSROOM OF THE ELITE

Chabashira-sensei and the rest of the class appeared shocked by this abnormality.

"Well, this is unusual, Horikita. Why?"

"Earlier, you said that the previous test had a passing grade of thirty-two points. You arrived at that number by the same formula you showed us today. Were there no mistakes in calculating the passing grade for the last test?"

"There were no mistakes."

"Then, that raises one more question. I'd calculated the average score for the previous test to be 64.4 points. If I were to divide that by two, I would get 32.2 points. In other words, higher than 32 points. Despite that, the passing grade was set at 32. That means that you left off the decimal. That contradicts what you did this time."

"Th-that's right. If you follow what you did last time, the passing grade for the midterm should be thirty-nine points!"

In other words, Sudou's overall grade should have meant that he just barely passed.

"I see. Did you anticipate that Sudou would just barely pass, then? You only scored exceedingly low in English, after all."

"Horikita, you..."

Sudou had realized something. The other students gasped as they also realized what had happened. Horikita had gotten perfect scores in four of the five main subjects, but she'd gotten an exceedingly low score of fifty-one points in English. Her English stuck out from her other scores.

"You really—"

Sudou noticed what she'd done. In order to lower the average score for the English test, Horikita had purposefully botched her own grade as far as she could.

"If you believe that my thinking is incorrect, could you please tell why the calculation differs between this test and the last test?" she asked.

The last ray of light. Our final hope.

"I see. In that case, I'll explain in more detail. Unfortunately, your calculation is off. We didn't simply omit the decimal when we calculated the passing grade. We rounded the numbers up or down. On the last test, we rounded down to thirty-two points, and on this, we rounded up to forty. There's your answer."

"Tch..."

"You should have noticed that we rounded the numbers, but to hold on to that possibility... Well, too bad. At any rate, first period will be starting soon. I'll be going."

Horikita had nothing left to counter with, so she remained quiet. She couldn't contradict anything Chabashira-sensei had said. Horikita's last resort had been eradicated. The classroom door slammed shut, and silence enveloped the room.

Sudou, still struggling to wrap his head around this new reality, looked over at Horikita. She had purposefully lowered her grades as far as she could, all to stop Sudou's expulsion.

"I'm sorry. I should have tried to lower my score just a little more," she muttered.

Horikita slowly sat back down. However, Horikita's 51-point score on her English test was already considerably low. If she'd scored in the 40-point range, she could have run the risk of expulsion herself.

"Why? You said that you hated me," Sudou said.

"Don't misunderstand. I did this for my own sake. It was all for nothing, though."

I slowly got up from my seat.

"Wh-where are you going, Ayanokouji?"

"Bathroom."

With that, I exited and quickly made my way toward the faculty room. I wondered if Chabashira-sensei had already arrived. As I thought that, I caught her staring out the window into the first-floor hallway, almost as if she were waiting for someone.

"Ayanokouji, hmm? Class will begin any minute, you know," she said.

"Sensei. Would it be all right if I asked you one question?"

"One question? Is that why you went to the trouble of chasing after me?"

"I'm curious about something."

"First it was Horikita, now you. What in the world is it?"

"Do you think that today's Japanese society is fair?"

"What an incredible change in topic. So sudden, too. Is there some special meaning behind this question?"

"It's very important. I would like your opinion."

"If you're asking for my personal opinion, then, no, of course not. The world isn't fair, not even the slightest bit."

"I see. I feel the same way. I think that equality is a fiction."

"So, did you chase after me merely to ask that question? If that's all, then I'll be going."

"One week ago, when you told us that the test's material had changed, you also said something like 'I forgot to inform you.' Because of that forgetfulness, we were notified of the change one week after the other classes had already been informed."

"Yes, I said as much back in the faculty room. What of it?"

"Every class got the same questions, the points were reflected in the same way for everyone, and every class faced the same threat of expulsion. However, Class D was compelled to test under unfair conditions."

"Are you saying that you can't accept what happened? But it's an excellent example of how unfair the world is. In fact, you could call it a microcosm of our unfair society."

"Certainly, society is not equal, no matter how idealistic you try to be. However, we are human beings, living things that can think."

"What are you trying to say?"

"I'm saying that we should strive for equality. At least a little."

"I see."

"Whether or not you truly forgot to tell us, or if it was an intentional slip, isn't really the issue. The fact remains that one person is now being expelled from this school because of those unfair conditions."

"So, what do you want me to do?"

"That's why I'm here. I would like to undertake the appropriate steps to meet with the school, the direct cause of this inequality."

"To tell them you disagree?"

"I just want to confirm with the appropriate people that they believe the school made the correct judgment."

"That's unfortunate. What you've said isn't wrong, but

I can't allow you to do that. Sudou will be expelled. That decision cannot be overturned at this stage. Give up."

She'd ignored my point, but her words remained logical. As I'd anticipated, her words always held some hidden meaning.

"You said it 'cannot be overturned at this stage.' Which means there may be a way to overturn the decision."

"Ayanokouji, I personally hold you in rather high regard. I've thought so since assigning this test. Obtaining the old test problems was certainly one correct solution. Such a notion goes beyond the range of what many would have considered. Furthermore, you distributed the old test problems to everyone in class and raised the average scores. I have to praise such a logical decision. Honestly, you did very well."

"Kushida was the one who obtained the problems and distributed them. I didn't really do anything."

"I understand why you don't want word to get out, but don't forget that there are senior students, too. I already know that you contacted a third-year student."

Apparently, my actions were more conspicuous than I'd thought.

"However, despite your bold move in obtaining those questions, you made a mistake in the end. That's why your plan failed. If Sudou had memorized the material more thoroughly, he wouldn't have failed in any subject, right? Honestly, why don't you just give up and let Sudou get tossed out? Wouldn't things be easier in the future?"

"Honestly, you're probably right. However, I decided to lend a hand. I suppose it's too early for me to give up. I've one thing left to try."

I took my student ID card out of my pocket.

"What are you planning?"

"Please sell me one point that I can apply to Sudou's English test."

"............"

Chabashira-sensei's eyes widened, and then she laughed loudly.

"Ha ha ha ha ha! That's a rather interesting idea. You really are a different kind of student. I never imagined you'd try to buy points."

"You said so the day we were admitted, didn't you, sensei? You said that we can buy anything with our points. The midterm test is just one more 'thing' at this school, after all."

"I see, I see. You certainly could view it that way. However, do you even have enough money on hand to afford it?"

"Well, how much does one test point cost?"

"Now, that's a rather difficult question, isn't it? I've

never been asked to sell test points before. Let's see... Seeing as how this is a special occasion, I'll sell a test point for the exceptional price of 100,000 points."

"You're cruel, sensei."

Everyone at this school had spent at least some of their points. Absolutely no one had 100,000 to spare.

"I'll pay, too," someone said behind me. When I turned, I found Horikita standing there.

"Horikita..." I said.

"Heh. Just as I thought. You two are interesting."

Chabashira-sensei took my student ID card. Then she took Horikita's.

"Fine. I accept your deal. I'll sell you one point to apply to Sudou's test, taking a combined total of 100,000 points from you both. As for the matter of Sudou's expulsion, you can inform the class that's no longer the case."

"Is that okay?"

"You promised to pay me 100,000 points. There's nothing more to be done." Chabashira-sensei seemed simultaneously exasperated and amused. "Horikita, do you understand how talented Ayanokouji is? At least somewhat?"

"I wonder. When I look at him, all I see is a disagreeable student."

"What do you mean, 'disagreeable?'" I asked.

"You get low scores on purpose when you could easily score higher. You were the one who came up with the idea of getting the old test problems, but you gave Kushida-san the credit. You were even crazy enough to buy test points. I don't think that you're special or just deviate from the norm. I think you're disagreeable."

So, she'd heard how I got the old test questions, too.

"Perhaps the pair of you really can reach the higher-level classes," Chabashira-sensei said.

"I don't know about *him*, but I most definitely will."

"No one from Class D has ever been promoted before. The school has already labeled you defective and will coldly toss you aside. How will you accomplish your goal?"

"If I may, sensei?" Horikita unwaveringly returned Chabashira-sensei's gaze. "Honestly, maybe the students in Class D are defective. However, that doesn't mean they're trash."

"What's the difference between a defective product and trash?"

"The difference is paper thin. However, with repairs, a defective product may become a superior article."

"I see. When you say it like that, Horikita, I admit it sounds oddly persuasive."

I shared that opinion, and found Horikita's words to be quite meaningful. Horikita, who had previously looked down upon others and thought of them as bag-gage, was changing. Of course, nothing was that simple. Though you could just barely glimpse the change from the outside, it was actually a major transformation. A faint smile appeared on Chabashira-sensei's lips, as if she also had noticed it.

"Well, I look forward to seeing what you do next. As your homeroom teacher, I'll be sure to watch over you with great attention and care."

With that, Chabashira-sensei headed toward the fac-ulty room, leaving the two of us in the hall.

"Well, let's head back. Class will be starting soon," I said.

"Ayanokouji-kun."

"Hmm? Oof!"

Horikita chopped me in the side.

"What was *that* for?"

"For whatever."

She left me as I clutched my sides in agony. Jeez, what a bothersome classm...bothersome person. With that thought, I decided to chase after her.

CLASSROOM OF
THE ELITE

12 VICTORY CELEBRATION

"**C**HEERS!" Ike shouted joyfully and toasted with a can of juice. That evening, the former association of failures had convened once again. Liberated from our studies, we were all overjoyed that no one had been expelled. Everyone smiled... Well, except for Horikita. We'd shared our burdens, and together, we'd overcome the challenge. Perhaps that was the point of being young. I guess if you ignored the one dark spot, this wasn't terrible.

"What's with the long face, Ayanokouji? Sudou wasn't expelled. Everything's fine now, right?"

"I don't particularly mind that you're holding a celebration party, but why are you holding it in *my room*?"

"Mine's a mess. So are Sudou's and Yamauchi's. And we can't go to a girl's room, right? I mean, yeah, I would've

loved going to Kushida-chan's room. But your spectacu-
larly plain and empty room is the best option."

"It's only been two months since school started. I think
it'd be weird to have a lot of stuff." Aside from daily necessities, I didn't really need anything.

"What do you think, Kushida-chan?"

"I think it's fine here. It's simple, but it feels nice and
clean."

"Right? Man, it must be nice to have Kushida-chan
praise you. Ha ha ha ha!" Ike grudgingly pushed me.

"All things considered, though, that midterm was
dangerous. If we hadn't put the study group together, I
would've been fine, but Ike and Sudou would have definitely gotten kicked out."

"Huh? You were close to getting expelled, too, you
know."

"No, no, I could have gotten a perfect score if I were
serious about it. Really."

"Everything was thanks to Horikita-san's efforts. She
tutored Ike, Yamauchi, and Sudou."

Horikita sat outside the circle, quietly reading a novel.
When we said her name, she bookmarked her page and
looked up.

"I did it for my own sake. If someone had been expelled, Class D's evaluation would've worsened."

"Just say that you didn't want us to get expelled, even if it's a lie. We'd like you better."

"It'd be fine with me if you didn't."

Well, her attitude remained unchanged, but simply participating in this gathering was a sign of her progress. The old Horikita most definitely would not have come.

"Well, I guess, but...you're a surprisingly good person, Horikita," replied Sudou.

Since Horikita had apologized to Sudou, he'd completely stopped antagonizing her. Before, he'd said she was a bad person. But people could change.

"Anyway, why did Chabashira-sensei change her mind about expelling Sudou-kun?"

"I wondered about that, too. What kind of sorcery did you use, Horikita-chan?"

"Hmm, I don't really remember."

"Whoa, it's a secret?!"

Ike tumbled over in an exaggerated fashion.

"Even though we managed to make it through the midterm, we shouldn't lose our heads. Our next challenge is the final exam. We should expect those questions to be even more difficult than the ones today. In addition, we still need to find a way to increase our points."

"Do we really need to start this hellish cramming all

over again? This sucks." Still on the floor, Ike buried his head in his hands.

"Don't you think that if we start right now, it won't be hellish?"

"No!" He sounded sure about that.

"I don't understand this school at all. I don't get the class divisions, the point system, anything."

"Ah, points. I want points! Living in poverty really sucks."

After Ike and Yamauchi had used up all of their points, they'd had to resort to living off the school's free offerings.

"Hey, Horikita-san. Do you think it'll be really difficult to get more points?"

"We tried so hard on the midterm that they'll definitely give us some points, right?!"

"Did you not see Class D's average score? We were the lowest of all of the classes by far. If you think that we'll get points for that, then I think you need to open your eyes." Horikita spoke the truth without mercy, without sugarcoating anything.

"Then we're not getting any points next month, either. Boo."

"I think you should learn to live a more modest life and give up on points."

"Don't worry, Ike-kun. We may not get any points right now, but surely we'll get some soon. Right, Horikita-san?"

"I wonder about that."

"Can I say something? We're all friends here, after all. Horikita-san, Ayanokouji-kun, and I are all working together to get into Class A. If you're okay with it, I want you three to help us," Kushida said.

"Get into...Class A? A-are you serious?" Ike said.

"Yes. I absolutely am. Increasing our points is an inevitable part of getting to the top as well."

"B-but, isn't the idea of reaching Class A kind of ridiculous? They're all smart, right? It'd be impossible for us to win against those guys by studying."

When you considered their average test scores, everyone in that class was probably on Horikita's level.

"Studying isn't the sole factor in deciding who goes into what class, though. Right?"

"Yeah, but if you can't study at *all*, then moving up is out of the question."

The three least-academically gifted people averted their eyes and whistled nonchalantly.

"We're still far from our goal, but we can do it if we all work together. I know it."

"What makes you so sure?"

"What makes me sure, hmm? Well, you know what they say, 'A single arrow is easily broken, but not ten in a bundle,' I suppose."

"I think that even if you bundled these ten together, they'd still break," Horikita said.

"W-well how about this? Three heads are better than one! Or something like that," Kushida said.

"I guess if you combined all three of their test scores, you'd get one normal person's grade." Every time Kushida tried to raise the three up, Horikita would knock them back down. What an amazing pair.

"If we keep going back and forth like this, though, we won't get anywhere. It's definitely better for us to get along."

"I suppose that, logically, you're right."

"Right?"

Horikita didn't try to argue further. At any rate, if we wanted to move up, we'd need to get along with as many of our classmates as possible. We gained nothing by fighting one another.

"So that's why I'd like to ask the three of you to help us."

"Gladly!" replied Ike and Yamauchi in unison.

"Well, if Horikita asked me to help, I would. I guess." Sudou tried to hide his embarrassment when he spoke.

"I never wanted your help, Sudou-kun. Besides, I have a hard time imagining how you'll be useful in the first place."

"Grr. I just thought I'd try to be nice, is all, and—"

"You were trying to be nice? I'm surprised."

Unsurprisingly, Sudou looked angry, but it didn't seem like he was going to raise his fist. Wow, he was making progress, too.

"You're a really annoying girl," he said.

"Thank you. I appreciate your words of praise."

"You are not cute at all, lady."

"You say that, but how do you *really* feel?" teased Ike.

Sudou instantly glared at Ike and put him in a headlock.

"Ow! Ow, ow! S-stop!"

"If you say anything else, I'm going to strangle you!"

"Y-you already *are* strangling me, jeez! I give, I give!"

Horikita sighed deeply. Her eyes seemed to ask, *Is this male bonding?*

"In this school, ability is paramount. I'm positive that our competition will grow even more severe moving forward. If you say you'll work with us, know that you can't do so half-heartedly. Otherwise you'll be a burden."

"Well, if it comes down to physical ability, leave it to me. I have serious basketball and fighting skills."

"I really can't expect anything from you at all."

Ability was paramount, huh? I felt my chest tighten. We'd been isolated from the world and now thrust into this situation. Perhaps we were cursed.

Horikita seriously planned on getting into Class A. Her will was unshakeable. However, our path out of Class D would not be an easy one. Considering our current performance, it was hard to imagine us even reaching Class C. What should we do from here? I imagined that things would turn out as they should. For the time being, I'd do my best. At the very least, though...I wouldn't mind seeing Horikita smile.

CLASSROOM OF
THE ELITE

POSTSCRIPT

I SINCERELY APOLOGIZE for the long silence. This is Syougo Kinugasa. It's a pleasure to meet you. I wrote this story about a year ago. *Classroom of the Elite* came out of my transition from student to adult, and because I wanted to tackle a challenging subject. When I think back to my student days, I recall everyone continuously telling me that I had to study if I wanted to get into a good university, if I wanted to get a job in a good field, if I wanted to have a good life. Recently, I've had my doubts as to whether that advice was actually correct. Unfortunately, I've gone astray, and leapt into a world far different from the one that my family and peers imagined for me...

Of course, studying is important, and there's no doubt that it is useful for a person's future. But I believe that academics aren't everything. For an easy example, sports are often part of an academic curriculum. Many people participate in sports. Everyone's personality is unique, though. A child who has a talent for drawing might become an illustrator, or someone with the comedic gift might become an entertainer. Besides academics and sports, there are a near-infinite variety of callings and professions that suit all different types of people.

When I started thinking about this, I began to consider those regrets that adults face for the first time. I thought, "If only I'd done this," and started to regret my past. Lately, these ideas have been constantly on my mind.

Now, I'd like to list some acknowledgements.

Tomose Shunsaku-sama. Thank you so much for working with me time and time again. The male characters you draw are so wonder—no, I should say I give you my sincerest thanks because you draw both male and female characters that simply overflow with charm.

I will always make sure to show you how appreciative and thankful I am for your help. I sincerely look forward to working with you in the future. We should really go out to get some yakiniku soon. My treat. One of those cheap all-you-can-eat places!

My editor, I-sama. Thank you so much for going over my writing. Though I've placed many burdens upon you with my previous work, I am sincerely grateful for all the effort you've put in, especially when this took a rather long time to complete. Huh? You say to knock it off and cut you a break? Ha ha ha, what a great joke. We have a long, long way to go. A one-way ticket all the way to the depths of hell. At least we're falling together, right?

Finally, there is you, the reader. Because you're holding this book, you could say that in some sense you play a part in its central theme. While I am incredibly grateful to you more than anyone, I think we can conclude this volume here. It's already the spring of 2015, but, as usual, my physical health is hardly perfect. I continue my longstanding battle with insomnia, but I'll keep doing my best not to lose.